Belinda

WITCH'S LAWN

A HOUSE AND HISTORY MYSTERY

NICK CHURTON

Peace and lesser Sorrow

Nick

First published in 2024 by Wrate's Publishing

ISBN 978-1-0686952-7-8

Typeset and Edited by Wrate's Editing Services

www.wrateseditingservices.co.uk

Cover illustration and design by Rachel Middleton

A CIP catalogue record for this book is available from the British Library.

To the memory of my parents,

John Churton (1919 – 2010)

and

Bunty Churton (1917 – 2014)

My father gave me words, my mother gave me books.

CHAPTER ONE

Eliza Arrow studied the familiar man sitting in front of her. Her long-time friend and protégé, Sir Bidian de Butts, was approaching retirement age. He wore one of his usual beautifully tailored, dark blue, two-piece suits paired with a white shirt and striped tie. His black leather shoes were polished to a parade-ground gloss. He was always so tall and straight, Eliza thought, as she took in the now slightly stooped figure. Of course, he was grey now, but as a younger man he'd had sleek, brushed-back dark hair. Eliza mused how he was the last of a breed. They were both from the old school of espionage; he via Balliol College, Oxford, and then the army, and she from the Corinthian wing of intelligence – Cheltenham Ladies' College, family connections and the ability to complete *The Times* crossword with comparative ease. Between them, Eliza and Sir Bidian had spanned the years between the Second World War and the first part of the twenty-first century. Now, mistress and apprentice sat in the comfortable salon of Witch's Lawn, Eliza's spectacular house, which was hidden away in a heavily wooded part of the Chiltern Hills. The salon was filled with a collection of exquisite furniture and artefacts collected by her extraordinary family over five hundred years. Although loved and valued, to Eliza, these pieces were the everyday things she had grown up alongside.

She thought back to the first time she had entertained Bidian at her home. He had just been invalided out of the army after losing his left hand in a grenade explosion deep in a tunnel beneath the Berlin Wall. Bidian had become Eliza's protege in the secret service and had since risen to the position of Head of MI6.

'Comfortable?' Eliza asked, noticing her guest's eyes droop.

From the depths of a huge antique sofa, Bidian opened his eyes, smiled and let out a muffled laugh. 'You know how much I love this house, Eliza. I couldn't be anywhere more comfortable. It's always the same. From the moment I walk through the door, this building seems to possess me. Now, don't chide, but I have a gift for you.' Bidian brought from his leather briefcase a small, slim package.

'What is it?'

'Please do open it and find out.'

With her mildly arthritic hands, Eliza tore away the wrapping paper and found a simply framed picture of a house, her house, rendered in pen and ink with colour wash. 'Why, this is exquisite. Who did it?'

'I know it's against the rules, but I took a sneaky photograph when I was here last. But if I can't bend the rules, who can? Then I asked the Surveyor of the Fabric of Westminster Abbey to copy it – we met at a function. As you can see, he's an extremely accomplished draughtsman and artist. He pleaded with me to tell him about the house, but of course, I didn't. I couldn't resist giving you this, although you have so many pictures here I'm sure you don't need another.'

'There's always room for beauty, and this is most skilfully done.'

'Isn't it? He's a youngish fellow to hold the same position as Sir Christopher Wren – and he beat him by ten years – but when one studies the picture one begins to understand why he's held in such high esteem. I think he's caught the house perfectly. Look how he has captured the oriental looking windows and the gables. He told me he had never seen a house like it. I told him that for me, there *is* no house like it.'

'Well, you shouldn't have, but I love it, Bidian, thank you. I'm going to find a nice place for it on the piano. Now, we had better get down to why I've asked you here.'

Bidian was prevented from answering immediately by the excited yapping of Eliza's dog, a miniature dachshund with a silky coat of chestnut hair.

'Don't take any notice of Cecily, Bidian, she's only looking for attention.'

Bidian laughed and, reaching down, gave the little dog the attention she desired. 'You mentioned you have two pressing personal concerns you need to discuss. So, what may I ask has happened to spoil your idyll here at Witch's Lawn, Eliza?'

'Lately, two things have occurred, Bidian, and not for the first time in my long life, I find myself between a rock and a hard place. On the one hand there's my second cousin, Edward, and on the other is the Church of England.'

'An unlikely pair of bookends, Eliza. I know Edward turns up like a bad penny every now and again, but why is the Church an issue?'

Eliza sighed. ‘Quite out of the blue, and after hundreds of years of silence, the Church claims they own the title to this house and grounds. The rather terse letter I received the other day from the Church’s legal department states they intend to prove they have the superior title to Witch’s Lawn – whatever that means. The problem is I can’t offer definitive proof of my family’s ownership because I have nothing written down – no deed or other document. Nor is Witch’s Lawn conveniently documented with Land Registry. In all these years, the question of the family’s ownership has never been queried, so why should the Church rake this up now?’

‘Things do move slowly in the Church of England; look at women priests and same sex marriage,’ Sir Bidian dryly observed.

‘Well, the Church isn’t moving slowly on this occasion, Bidian. Someone is stoking the fire.’

‘Yes, it certainly seems that might be the case. So, what about Edward? What’s he been up to?’

‘Edward is trying to ensure I don’t pass on this house and its contents to anyone else but him, and the older I get the more unpleasant he becomes. As if I would pass on my legacy to that crooked wastrel. But Edward wouldn’t be above blackmail, and he knows enough about my side of the family to make life extremely unpleasant for me. If he put his mind to it, he could even make it uncomfortable for you and the government. The media would have a field day, not to mention the enemies we have hurt in the past. I can think of one or two who would love retribution if they knew who I was and where to find me.’

Bidian nodded and said, ‘I see your point. Edward doesn’t need to do anything to you himself. He just leaks the information and others do the dirty work for him.’

'Precisely. What with the Church as well, it feels like the vultures are circling, and I'm not even dead yet!'

'I take it you want me to shoo the vultures away?'

'I would see them off myself if I was seventy – or even eighty. But now I'm tired, and I need some help. Otherwise, the ownership of this house and everything in it will slip from the grip of my direct family stewardship. As you know, I am resolved not to let that happen even though I'm last in line. It's just that now I'm nearing my century, I'm not in much of a position to do anything about it. I can still think, but I need younger legs and eyes.'

Eliza's eyes wandered over to the portrait hanging over the fireplace in a heavy gilt frame. The painting was of a man in middle age, dressed in the style of the sixteenth century. In one hand he clasped a dagger, in the other he held a rose. He was a handsome, clever-looking man with the hooded eyes of an owl and the hooked nose of a hawk. Eliza stared at the distinctive man with whom she shared both genes and features. Edmund Arrow: lover, freebooter and spy. Edmund would know what to do with her cousin, and it wouldn't involve a rose, she thought.

The sound of Sir Bidian's voice brought Eliza back to the moment. 'Well, I can certainly speak to the right people about Edward and see if we can't do something to dissuade him.'

'Be careful, Bidian, Edward is a slippery customer – always has been; no doubt he has some powerful people on his payroll. He's like his father but tells everyone who'll listen that he's legit. Somehow, I very much doubt that. He seems to earn far too much money for doing far too little.'

'I'll see what I can do, Eliza. As for the Church, I don't know how much I can do about that. If I'm correct, your issue with the Church of England has nothing to do with dodgy dealers, like your second cousin, and everything to do with common and ecclesiastical law.'

Eliza nodded. 'I hate to say this, but I've a funny feeling there might be a dodgy dealer or two in the church, though I expected you to say something along those lines. I agree, we must first look to the law.'

How times change, Eliza thought. When did she ever let the law get in the way of thwarting her enemies? Once upon a time she had a licence to do practically anything she thought necessary, and not within reason, if it served the state.

As if reading Eliza's mind, Sir Bidian said, 'We live in a different world these days, where we can't move without facing some public enquiry, a splash in the *Sunday Times* or a social media leak. No, you need someone who understands the legal intricacies of these matters and can play the Church at its own game.'

The salon door opened and Eliza's housekeeper, Cairo, entered with a large tea tray. She set down the tray, poured out the delicate blend of Darjeeling and Ceylon that Eliza favoured and exchanged pleasantries with Sir Bidian before withdrawing.

'Mmmm, fresh scones,' said Sir Bidian. Eliza watched her friend and long-time colleague deftly quarter a scone and then add clotted cream and homemade strawberry jam with the natural hand he possessed.

The two friends sat in companionable silence as Bidian ate his scone and Eliza sipped her tea from a delicate china cup decorated with pink rosebuds. She let her gaze wander through the tall leaded window. Outside, the beech trees bordering the neat formal garden were over their autumnal splendour. Eliza loved this time of year, but then she loved every season at Witch's.

After Sir Bidian had finished mopping up the last crumbs of scone, Eliza said, 'I wanted to mention a young cleric that I have become friendly with. Her name is Dimity Fortuna: she's a minor canon at St Eadric's Abbey. Witch's Lawn is in her orbit, and she often drops in for tea and a chat. I haven't asked, but I imagine she's around forty. She seems a bright, bold and resourceful girl, the sort you and I would have willingly recruited. She puts her visits here down to pastoral care, but there is always more laughter than liturgy: I find her refreshing.'

'She reminds you of you, I take it?'

Eliza smiled, 'Perhaps that's it, or it's simply that she makes me feel youthful again.'

'Does this young woman know anything of your past?'

In reply, Eliza raised an eyebrow.

Sir Bidian smiled. 'Quite so, but are you sure she has nothing to do with the Church's interest in Witch's Lawn?'

'Anything's possible, of course, but I'm strongly inclined to think not. And if not, Dimity may be useful on the inside.'

'By that, I imagine you want to recruit a spy?'

'It will be just like the old days.'

'Oh dear, you have that gleam in your eyes. But, you always were a good judge of character.'

'I wasn't infallible – what about Burgess and Maclean? I didn't judge them well.'

'No one did, Eliza.'

'True, plus Guy and Donald were extraordinarily clever men.'

'It sounds as if you admired them.'

'I knew them, Bidian, I didn't admire them. But if you must call it anything, call it a grudging professional respect.'

'So, what about your prospective young recruit?'

'Dimity has packed a great deal into her life so far. Not an easy adolescence as she describes it, went off the rails a bit in her mid-to-late teens and then found mountains followed by God.'

'Would you like me to do some vetting and fill in any gaps?'

'I thought you would never ask. But there is one other thing that might make Dimity important.'

'And what's that?'

'It's a long shot, but there's a young man.'

'Isn't there always a young man?'

'Often there has been,' Eliza chuckled. 'Dimity mentioned an old school friend of hers, one that she hasn't seen for years. He's called Felix Bohlin; it seems he runs an architectural practice with, unusually, a property law division. Bohlin is unusual in that he is both architect and lawyer. He has an office, design studio and even a shop selling textiles and antiques in Pimlico Road, near Sloane Square, and he sounds like a very enterprising chap.

'Bidian, I can see you rolling your eyes. I might be old, but I'm not blind: I'm being serious.'

Eliza noticed Sir Bidian's mouth twitch into a faint smile.

'I know you're being serious, but after so many centuries, don't you think something would have surfaced in this house about legal ownership? God knows how many generations living here must have searched for some evidence of a title.'

'Some things can be deeply hidden, especially by my family. But I need a fresh pair of eyes. I need someone with the knowledge and brain to find what's never been found before.'

'I sense, Eliza, that there is something else deeply hidden.'

'What on earth do you mean?'

'There's another reason you don't want to lose Witch's Lawn that you're not telling me.'

Eliza looked Sir Bidian in the eye. 'Yes, there is another reason, but it is profoundly personal as well as deeply hidden.'

She could see Sir Bidian was intrigued to hear more, but he didn't press her further.

'Look, Bidian, I know this friend of Dimity is probably the last roll of the dice, and besides, there's already one tiny problem with my plan.'

'And what's that?'

'Dimity and Bohlin haven't been in touch since school, before which, I was told, they were very close. I wondered if they might have been childhood sweethearts, until Dimity went AWOL.'

'AWOL?'

'She ran away from school and home when she was in the sixth form.'

'I see. So, this makes Bohlin's involvement in your caper more complicated?'

'Yes, but I'm sure it's something I can manage.'

'Let me guess, you want to reunite them?'

'That's the idea.'

'Eliza, you're such a romantic. But what happens if one or both don't want to be reconciled?'

'Something in the way Dimity spoke about Bohlin suggested she has unfinished business. As for Bohlin, if you ever meet Dimity, Bidian, you will understand why most men wouldn't fight too hard to avoid seeing her again.'

Sir Bidian laughed. 'So, would you like me to add Bohlin to the vetting list?'

'Well, at least you haven't lost your perceptive gift after all these years.'

'I sometimes think you use me as your private intelligence service. But seriously, are you certain you can trust this new young friend of yours – especially with the Church showing such interest in Witch's Lawn? It could put her in a difficult position – conflicting interests and all that.'

'I'm not blind to the risk, but I do think I can trust Dimity, which is more than I can say for the deacon at St Eadric's Abbey who introduced me to Dimity in the first place: in my view, he's shown an interest in Witch's over the past few months that borders on the unhealthy.'

'And how will you approach this?'

'Carefully. The thing is, I don't just want Dimity to make the introduction to Mr Bohlin; I want her to bring him to me here.'

Sir Bidian looked Eliza in the eye and said, 'You never invite strangers to Witch's. This hasn't anything to do with another Felix in your long and distant past, has it?'

'What was I just saying about you being perceptive? That's why I must meet Bohlin: to ensure any deep-rooted emotions aren't clouding my judgement. But the bottom line is I need some particular skills that Mr Bohlin seems to possess. I have to uncover proof that I own Witch's Lawn, and I think Mr Bohlin might be the sort of person to help me find it.'

'What if Bohlin doesn't want to meet you here or anywhere else?'

'I will give Dimity this to show him.' Eliza held up an envelope.

'The sonnet, I take it?'

'Yes, the sonnet.'

'That should do it,' said Sir Bidian with a smile.

The pretty carriage clock, placed on a side table near Eliza, chimed four o'clock.

'Is that the time already? I had better get going,' said Sir Bidian.

Eliza watched her trainee rise a little stiffly from his chair.

He said, 'I'll look into the young woman and Bohlin and have a word with our friends at MI5 and the Serious Crimes and Fraud Offices at the Met and see if they have anything regarding Edward.'

'You have counter blackmail in mind, I imagine?'

'That usually does the trick. If we can find anything on Edward, the strong possibility of a stretch in prison, with no time off for good behaviour, should bring him into line: we could even threaten him with Monster Mansion.'

'What's that?'

'Officially it's Wakefield Prison, but it's nicknamed Monster Mansion due to the large number of murderers and sex offenders held there: nice place to stay for a long stretch.'

Eliza smiled and went to stand up, but Sir Bidian waved her back down. 'Please don't get up on my account; I'll see myself out.'

'Well, it's been lovely to see you as always, thank you for coming.'

'What, and miss one of Cairo's afternoon teas? Delicious as always, please tell her.'

Eliza smiled, and Sir Bidian bent to kiss his old friend goodbye.

Eliza's expression turned serious. 'There is a strong odour of mischief in the air, Bidian. My sixth sense in these matters doesn't often let me down. I don't think these two things are connected, but each greatly threatens my and my family's legacy. I don't want to be the one who brings the whole pack of cards tumbling down after all these years. And, talking about years, I don't have many of those left, so we have no time to lose.'

'I understand. Please don't worry; I'll report back as soon as I have some news, then perhaps you will tell me that other reason behind your concern?'

'Perhaps I will.'

As she watched Sir Bidian depart, Eliza already felt thirty years younger. There was intrigue and danger in the offing, and if there was one thing that excited an Arrow, it was intrigue and danger.

CHAPTER TWO

From: Dimity Fortuna
To: Felix Bohlin
Subject: Hello You

Dear Felix,
Are you sitting down? I'm sure this email will come as a massive surprise after twenty plus years.
For me, I think it is time – beyond time – that I contacted you and explained, if you even want or need me to do that. But I think I owe it to you and, selfishly, to myself.
If that is not reason enough, then I also have another motive in wanting to see you – in a professional capacity and for what I believe is a worthy cause.
I wondered if you would meet me? If not, I will quite understand – but I hope you will.
Mitten

* * *

Felix stared at the screen on his laptop and could feel his heart thumping. That someone could do this to him after twenty years with no contact should have shocked him, but it didn't; it just reminded him of the effect Dimity Fortuna had always had on him.

Memories fought for attention: that first day at school when she had enchanted him with her smile. At nine years old, he had been spellbound. The time she instructed him to call her by her family pet name, Mitten – an honour bestowed on no other school friends, even Santa, her closest girlfriend; the day Mitten's parents told him they named their daughter after a cotton fabric used in covering mattresses. Later, when Felix was older and wiser, he suspected it had been a carnal in-joke between mother and father.

Felix thought back to his youthful rugby days when, from time to time, Dimity would arrive unexpectedly at the clubhouse after a game and stand alongside him laughing and joking with his teammates, making heads turn. It wasn't as though Felix, unlike some other boys, craved or needed street cred or peer envy, but these visits certainly didn't harm his self-confidence and were far from unwelcome.

In those days, Dimity could be unreliable, random and infuriating sometimes, but all was forgotten when she turned up after a game, and Felix felt special in a way no other person than she could make him feel. He might not have fully understood back then, but now he appreciated that Dimity knew precisely what she was doing, and, despite his warring emotions, he had loved her for it.

Felix typed an acceptance, asking for no explanation and telling Dimity that he didn't expect one: his finger hovered over the send button as he questioned if it might not be a great deal more sensible to let that particular sleeping dog lie. Too much regret and anger, and too much love could be exposed through raking up the past.

Felix pressed send.

* * *

Less than a week later, Felix was waiting for Dimity in St Eadric's Abbey. He had no idea why she had suggested the abbey as a meeting place, other than it was near to where they'd both gone to school.

He gazed up at the soaring architecture but, unusually, didn't take it in. Instead, he was thinking what a fool he was to have agreed to this. What a fool he was to ever have become so besotted with the girl in the first place. Well, he was here now, but this time he would deal warily with Dimity and keep a respectful, professional distance.

The abbey bell tolled three o'clock. Despite his resolve, Felix felt nervous as he turned towards the sound of light footsteps on the tiled floor.

Dimity's once long, wavy dark hair was now shoulder length, but the same errant curl still stubbornly escaped the rest to fall over her right eye. Above all, the smile that first bewitched him fought to do so again.

To Felix, Dimity hadn't changed much, except for one thing – a clerical collar. He hadn't been expecting that.

'Felix,' Dimity whispered. She hesitated for a moment before stretching up a little and kissing him, first on one cheek and then the other. It was a gesture that could have been made between two good friends greeting each other after only a few days apart. Disarmed and lost for words, Felix was jolted by the familiar smell of Eau Sauvage, the man's scent that Dimity had started wearing at school, before stepping back and looking into Dimity's dark eyes.

'Tea, coffee?' Dimity suggested brightly, relieving Felix of having to say anything at that moment. 'Come with me' – she led Felix to the cathedral's self-service refectory – 'will you find a table? I'm buying.'

Felix chose a table by a window that overlooked the cloister garden and studied his old friend as she waited at the counter. Her hair was not as natural looking as it once was and her face seemed to reflect as many years behind as might lie ahead. But Felix found his memory airbrushing out the altered contours and time-grown lines.

For a long while, after Dimity went away, she had become his remote obsession: this was painful at first, and although it had become dulled through absence, if he were honest, it had never entirely left him.

Not knowing, all those years ago, how to deal with an object of such strong but young and naïve desire, he had treated Dimity like some delicate and precious artefact. He had hardly been able to touch her for fear of breaking whatever it was between them. That was his error. He understood that now. He should never have treated Dimity with such timidity. He should have been a bolder suitor.

Felix inspected Dimity's uniform – black shirt with sleeves neatly rolled up above the elbows, black jeans and a pair of black ballet pumps. Somehow, she gave the clerically sombre attire a lighter look.

Reaching the table, Dimity placed a tall mug of coffee, a spoon and a sachet of sugar in front of him, sat opposite and said, 'Do you still have a sweet tooth?'

'Yes, I do.' Then looking at Dimity's clerical collar and not knowing quite what else to say, he asked, 'So, how far have you been?'

'Quite a long way.'

'And have you found whatever you were looking for?' Felix had always thought that Dimity was looking for something: it had come as a big blow when he learned it wasn't him.

Dimity looked up from her coffee. 'Maybe I have, for now.'

Felix thought Dimity was going to add something, but she didn't, and he didn't press. Instead, he said, 'So, how come the church?'

'Good question.' Dimity gave her coffee a long stir. Then, looking up, she said, 'Story short, cold Scottish Presbyterianism, from my mother's side, fought hot Spanish Catholicism from my father's—'

'And you compromised with the temperate Church of England?'

Dimity smiled. 'Yes, with a bit of Eastern mysticism from Nepal to spice it up a bit. For a while I worked at a boatyard in the Med. Quite by accident, I became involved in the local Anglican church. One thing just seemed to lead to another. There was an inspirational priest who became my mentor. Anglicanism just felt more comfortable – more me, somehow.'

'It must have been all those school assemblies and services here,' Felix said.

Dimity laughed. 'You might be right. But goodness knows how or why they took me on for ordination after all my doings.'

'Perhaps they saw the pilgrim soul in you.'

Dimity smiled. 'You remember your Yeats from school?'

'Of course.'

'I'm sorry,' Dimity said.

'Sorry for what?'

'Oh, for being me, I suppose.' She paused, then smiled. 'I think I trod on your dreams.'

'Oh, touché. But you didn't tread on my dreams, I was fine,' Felix said with more bravado than honesty; he wasn't ready to analyse his relationship with Dimity yet – if ever. He was feeling off-balance by her behaviour towards him. She was acting as though her disappearance, abandonment and, frankly, her betrayal were all forgotten. Well, they weren't. But remembering his promise to himself to remain professional, Felix said, 'So, why get in touch after all this time? You mentioned that you would like some help in a professional capacity.'

'Does this mean it's time to get down to business?'

'Isn't that why I'm here?'

Dimity looked slightly affronted before replying, 'I have a parishioner who is at risk of losing her house.'

'Is this a financial problem or a structural one? They are usually one or the other, but sometimes both.'

'On this occasion, neither. This problem seems to be legal and historical.'

'Then you had better explain and I'll tell you if I can help your friend.'

'Thank you, I do appreciate this. The thing is, I regularly visit an elderly lady called Eliza Arrow. She must be about a hundred. Not that she thinks she is that old. She still thinks she is a young woman.'

'Has she dementia?'

Dimity laughed. 'No, nothing of the sort, she's just incredibly young at heart. It's inspiring to be with her. She lives in this amazing house where her parents and grandparents lived before that. In fact, there's been an unbroken line of single-family occupation at the house for over five hundred years. Goodness knows how many generations that is.

'Eliza isn't short of money, that's for certain, but she lives without fuss or fanfare. There's a lake and tower in the garden and the house is crammed with art and antiques. I assume they're all genuine, and if so, they must be worth a packet. I suppose the family has lived in the house, in much the same way, for centuries. It's quite extraordinary.'

'It doesn't sound much like an unlavish lifestyle to me, but what's your friend's problem exactly?'

'She's worried that the wrong people will take over the house; she desperately wants the choice of successor to be hers, and hers alone.'

'Why shouldn't she have the choice of successor?'

'That's the point. Now there's a dispute over who actually owns the house. It's not something Eliza needs at her age, and she wants it resolved before she dies. I have to say, it does all seem a little strange to me. Eliza tells me there are plenty of records, accounts, wills and that sort of thing that confirm the family's ownership.'

'But nothing that definitively proves original ownership, I take it?' Felix said.

'That's exactly it. Eliza has evidence that the family has lived there under the assumption of ownership all these years, but there are no deeds. She believes there is some sort of proof or provenance somewhere, but none has ever been discovered.'

Felix shrugged. 'Sounds like hard luck that the family hasn't found any proof. Or maybe there's none to discover.'

'Eliza is confident there was some sort of gift or payment to the family made centuries ago, and each generation has passed that understanding onto the next.'

'Word of mouth; it all sounds a bit airy-fairy to me,' Felix said, 'if it was down to word of mouth, anyone could claim anything. That's why we have deeds, leases and contracts.'

Dimity looked hard at Felix. 'How do you think the story of Christ survives, if not by word of mouth?'

'Considering your calling, you might say that, Mitten. But Christians, like those following any of the world's other religions, don't seem to need any physical proof to support their beliefs. I'm afraid that in cases like this, government departments and legal entities won't be so pious. Anyway, what makes your friend think that she can prove anything?'

'I'm not sure she thinks she can, other than a family legend.'

'Well, she'll have to do better than that to persuade institutions like the Land Registry.'

'It's the Church of England she'll need to convince.'

'What on earth has the Church of England got to do with it?'

Dimity laughed. 'See, you're interested already.'

'Well, I don't know about that, but go on.'

'Some people think the house and land have been owned by the Church all along. Unfortunately, records show that, before the Reformation, the house did belong to this Abbey, St Eadric's. Ludovic thinks—'

'Hold on, who's Ludovic?'

'Oh, he's a deacon in the Diocese. He was a lawyer before he was ordained, and he is also a bit of a history buff.'

'So, what did Ludovic say?'

'He said that now the Church has claimed title, Eliza could just leave the house to them anyway. Even if there is no legal duty, he reckons there may be a moral one. I'm sure he suggested that in Eliza's best interests.'

'If that's not what your friend wants, it doesn't sound much like her best interests to me. And if this house is so wonderful, what's wrong with leaving it to a suitable organisation like the National Trust?'

'I delicately suggested to Eliza the same thing.'

'And what did she say?'

'She said the Church seemed so intent on claiming ownership that it wouldn't matter who she left it to, as they would contest it anyway. Besides, she told me she had a deeply personal reason for wanting to choose who the house goes to, but she didn't elaborate.'

'I suppose she has a point about the Church, but what's any of this got to do with the deacon?'

Dimity gave Felix a frosty look. 'I'm sure Ludovic's heart is in the right place.'

'But the right place for whom? It all sounds a bit Trollopian to me.'

'Trollopian?'

'Yes, Obadiah Slope is alive and well, and living in the twenty-first century at St Eadric's. Anyway, why are you getting involved if you think Ludovic's idea would be best for your friend?'

'Ludovic might well be right, but something is nagging me, I suppose. Eliza seems so certain that her family has legal ownership of the house, and she is no demented ancient, Felix. She's a brilliant lady with all her faculties. I want to help her resolve this before it's too late. Would you at least meet and talk to her? Actually, if it helps, the request isn't from me.'

'Then who is it from?'

'Eliza herself.'

'How come?'

Dimity shook her head. 'I'm still not entirely sure. But when she told me about all this, I mentioned your name, about our friendship at school, and told her that you do property law – I'd googled you. After that, she said she would like to meet you. Anyway, be warned, if you do ever meet her, you will only get what she wants to tell you; she gives very little away. But then she has this funny knack of extracting whatever she wants to know without your realising. The more I've got to know her, the more I have learnt how clever she is. At her age, I'm not sure what she has left to think about, other than her house, but she has an extraordinary life behind her and still acts as if she has a long life ahead.'

'How did you meet?'

'The Bishop asked Ludovic to introduce Eliza to me while on his rounds of elderly communicants. After that, I visited for the sheer pleasure of spending time with her. I think it's reciprocated: she enjoys hearing about all my mountaineering exploits – I was a climber – and I keep on receiving invitations to visit.'

Felix remembered Dimity as an intrepid young girl who, on school hill-walking trips, was always at the front finding the way, often by the most challenging routes.

'Eliza's a bit of a mystery woman to me,' Dimity

continued. 'She's walked all over the Pyrenees and the Alps, but the odd thing is, she seems to have done so in her late teens and early twenties.'

'Why's that odd?'

'Because her late teens and early twenties coincide with the Second World War.'

'I suppose that is odd. But where do I come in?'

'When I told her what you do, she suggested she would like to meet you. She said you seemed to have the right credentials to help. It put me in a difficult position. But, of course, Eliza knew that only too well. I suggested that it might be awkward for both of us and that you may not want to meet up again, which I would have fully understood. But after some cajoling, she managed to get me to agree to contact you. So, will you meet her, Felix? It might be an adventure.'

Felix saw Dimity's eyes light up at the mention of adventure. He remembered that look with a sense of mild foreboding. Dimity's sense of adventure was the only reason he was ever in trouble.

Dimity looked at her watch, the Omega that Felix remembered her parents giving her for her sixteenth birthday.

'They'll be closing here soon,' she said. 'We can pop next door to my flat, if you like, and catch up for as much time as you have.'

Felix hadn't imagined the possibility of their meeting ending up in Dimity's home. The suggestion confused him and made him feel uncomfortable. This wasn't the professional distance he had planned. 'I'm not sure,' he said lamely, before quickly adding he wanted to avoid the evening traffic.

'Oh, come on, Felix, I'm not going to bite, I just want to tell you more about Eliza and her problem.'

Felix felt awkward. It had always been difficult to say no to Dimity, and it was no different now. In the end, he agreed, though he reassured himself he was just being polite. Was there no end to Dimity's gravitational pull?

CHAPTER THREE

Felix walked with Dimity in silence across the Abbey yard to a sizeable, Gothic-styled house that had once been home to the Cathedral's deans. The building had more recently been converted into offices and accommodation for some minor clergy. Felix fretted over his decision to accept Dimity's invitation, but there was no polite way of going back now.

She opened the front door and led the way upstairs. After two flights, she unlocked another door on the small, top-floor landing. 'I'll put the kettle on, or would you like wine?'

'Tea's fine; I'm driving.'

'Take a look round if you want – it won't take long.'

Felix did as instructed. The small flat was simply but comfortably furnished and decorated. Off the sitting room was a tiny galley kitchen that didn't suggest an active cook. Across the narrow hall containing a coat stand and mirror were a small bathroom and bedroom. Felix peeked but didn't enter either; they were too personal. Don't get involved, he told himself again. What on earth was he doing here?

In the living room was a collection of mementoes – a

worn ice axe with prayer flags wrapped around the shaft, a fingertip-to-elbow length of climbing rope, a small Tibetan monastery bell, a Swiss cowbell and a teak campaign table covered with small pieces of rock, glass paperweights and fossils. In the hearth, a large dinner gong acted as a fire screen. Felix recognised some of the furniture and pictures from Dimity's childhood home. But there were some things that he had never seen before, and he couldn't help himself inspecting photographs of Dimity high up on mountains and hardly recognisable in brightly coloured, hooded jackets, and ones of her on yachts in rough seas, grinning from within foul weather gear. There were also photos of her surrounded by dozens of smiling, shabbily dressed, Nepalese-looking children and widely grinning but largely toothless adults. Juxtaposed with these were snaps of her in the company of smiling, dentally perfect and skimpily clad young adults holding drinks in the sunshine. Like Dimity herself, Felix thought, the images were contradictions.

But there, propped up behind a small ebony elephant, Felix noticed a creased photo of Dimity and him with their arms around each other outside a hotel in Glencoe. The picture looked well-travelled. Their school friend, Santa, had taken it on a long, warm June day when they were all fifteen. They had just walked along the exposed north ridge of the glen and looked hot and tired but happy. Felix thought back fondly to that day. He had the same photo.

'Sugar?' Dimity asked from the kitchen.

'Sweetie,' Felix replied without thinking; it was the way each of them had always answered that question. Felix heard Dimity laugh.

'I've missed that,' Dimity said, arriving with two mugs of tea. 'I've missed *you.*'

Felix didn't respond. He had no idea what Dimity was doing or trying to do, but he didn't feel inclined to make things comfortable for her.

They sat on either side of a large, round, Moroccan brass tray, balanced on three spindly legs, which acted as a coffee table. Felix sank into a mahogany and cane library chair with cushions made from an old and well-worn tribal rug: he remembered it fondly from Dimity's parents' home.

'I've always loved this chair. And this is nice.' Felix held up a teaspoon, a delicate, silver piece.

'It was Mummy's – Scottish provincial – she left me some lovely things from her side of the family. I like to use them rather than store them.'

'Including Uncle Cyrus, I see,' said Felix.

Over the mantelpiece hung a dirty, early nineteenth-century oil portrait of a severe-looking clergyman. White preaching bands hung from his round collar. The man was a forebear on Dimity's maternal side. Whatever Felix and Dimity had been doing – good or not so good – Felix imagined Uncle Cyrus looking down on them with the same stern and disapproving gaze as he displayed now. This was the first time Felix had appreciated the man's look of disquiet.

Dimity nodded. 'Perhaps I'm following in a line of clerics in the family, although I don't know of any others.'

'Well, I hope you don't end up looking like this dour relative.'

'Thanks for that vote of confidence. Anyway, if you don't mind me saying, Felix, you're cataloguing my possessions like some antiques dealer.'

Letting his guard down briefly, Felix laughed. 'Some of

your possessions are like old friends. It's nice meeting them again.'

'Old friends are important,' Dimity said, 'that's one thing I have found out over the years.'

'Talking of old friends, you never contacted Santa after you left, did you?'

'No, I didn't.'

'She was exceptionally hurt, as though your friendship meant nothing to you.'

'Is that how you felt?'

'To be honest, yes, it was.'

'Do you think I can ever make amends – with Santa?'

'You must ask her that question.'

'I know I hurt a lot of people I loved. But you stayed close to Santa?'

'Yes, I did – I do. Since Santa's divorce, I see more of her. I'm also godfather to her daughter, Rosie.'

'Oh, that must be wonderful.'

'It is. Rosie is a lovely little girl – she's six now. She's a handful but Santa looks after her beautifully while running her translation business from home. I handled the conversion of her attic into a home office suite. I'm always made to feel part of the family. In fact, I'll be with them on Christmas Day: I can't believe that's only five weeks away.'

Felix fell silent. He wasn't prepared to explain how Santa and he had struggled with such a life-interrupting loss after Dimity's disappearance. Eventually, they had accepted it as best they could and moved on. Felix was sure Santa would think long and hard before readmitting Dimity into her life.

'It was a family I deserted,' she said.

'Your choice.'

The late afternoon sun was setting, its last rays reaching

into the small, top-floor sitting room and cloaking it with a golden glow. Felix and Dimity sipped their tea from well-used mugs acquired from a popular climbers' café in Llanberis, fell into silence again and stared into an old, two-bar electric fire that threw out some welcome warmth against the early evening chill.

'It looks as though you've done well, Felix.' Dimity eventually said.

'So far, my career has worked out OK; I feel what I do suits me best.'

'I'm pleased. You used to tell me that you often felt out of place, even in your home sometimes. Maybe that was why you and I got on so well. But you seem to have found the ideal job. What got you started?'

'I hadn't a clue what to do after school. First, I thought about archaeology, but I discovered that aside from digging up interesting things, there wasn't much money in it. And while I wasn't necessarily anxious to be rich, I didn't fancy being strapped for cash every month either. Plan B was something to do with old houses. I took the architectural route.'

'I remember how you always used to visit those grand National Trust houses on holidays and weekends.'

'Grand and not so grand houses. There can't have been many boys like me, who were reading *Country Life* and *House & Garden* at the age of twelve,' Felix said with a laugh.

'You were a strange boy; perhaps that's why I was intrigued by you.'

'I intrigued you?'

'Yes, I was interested in a girlish way, but I'm interrupting your story.'

'To help with university course fees and living expenses,

I became a gofer in a law firm. Then I figured out I could offer a complete property package if I also specialised in property law. So, after too many years as a student and trainee, I set up Provenance Architecture and Law – PAL for short, and the rest, as they say, is history.'

'So, you've become a bit of a house detective?'

'That's a very romantic way of putting it, but yes, part of my work involves investigating the history of buildings and sometimes looking into past and present ownership.'

'And you're based near Sloane Square?'

'Or Victoria Coach Station: it depends which way you look at it. Not that I seem to be there much at the moment. I'm too busy crawling about old buildings and ferreting around dusty libraries.'

'Which you love, I suppose?'

'Correct.'

Dimity laughed.

'What's so funny?'

'I'm imagining you as Indiana Jones.'

'Without the hat and whip, I hope.'

'No, with those.'

'Well, I occasionally dig up lost documents, so perhaps I am a little like Indiana Jones.'

'And where do you live?'

The question caught Felix off guard; their conversation had suddenly lurched from the polite to the personal. But then he supposed it wouldn't take much detective work on Dimity's part to find out where he lived if she really wanted to know. Instead of evading the question, Felix said, 'PAL's premises occupy the ground and first floors in Pimlico Road, and I have a small flat on the top floor.'

Silence followed, which Felix eventually broke by asking, 'Why haven't you got in touch with me before, Mitten?'

'Is that the question you have been waiting to ask me?'

'Yes, it is, for twenty or so years.'

Dimity sighed. 'Damage limitation, I suppose.'

'For whom – you, me, or the two of us?'

'The latter.'

'What happened to you?'

'I became lost. First, it was the truancy, then I ran away to Scotland. Initially, I went to stay with my grandmother, whom I adored, but I still ended up running away from her. For me, it was always about the hills. I was happiest there. After several years, I got into some serious mountaineering. But then my marriage ended abruptly. There was booze and weed involved, and periods of depression. I was anorexic for a while and as neurotic as hell.'

'How could you have become so lost, Mitten? You had your mum and dad and a secure home – and you had me and Santa. One way or another, we were your family, too. At any rate, you were family to me. Then overnight you vanished from my life – all our lives.'

'I know. At the time, I felt I had to disappear to find myself. Looking back, I didn't know what I was running from or where I was running to. For a long time, I lived a nomadic life, and I ended up climbing all over the world.'

'While I've stuck to a bit of mild hillwalking closer to home,' Felix said, suddenly feeling wanting by comparison.

'There's nothing wrong with closer to home or mild hillwalking: they are hard to beat. I've missed them. Have you been back to Skye?'

'Once every year or so, although not so much recently. I haven't had the time.'

Dimity nodded. 'It was perfect on Skye, wasn't it?'

'Apart from the midges. But it's still there and wonderful; only it's a bit more crowded these days. But it's a great place to go and think.'

'I tend to use the Abbey for my thinking.'

'It is more convenient,' Felix pointed out.

'But far less dramatic.'

'No, just dramatic in another way.'

Felix changed the subject. 'So, how did you get on all those climbing trips?'

'I suppose I came to know the right people, and then, between trips, I worked my passage waiting tables in Ibiza, where Dad was from – remember, I spoke Spanish before English. Mum and Dad retired to the island: then, later, I cleaned and crewed yachts around the Med. For the serious climbing expeditions, I managed to get some sponsorship for clothing, boots and other gear.'

'But you've stopped climbing now?'

'Yes.'

'Because you joined the Church?'

'That, and seeing too many people I knew perish in the mountains. Slowly, I became more interested in doing things that helped people live. That alone saved me. I was extremely fortunate not to die at a high altitude or cause the death of anyone else.

'In Nepal, I became involved in some humanitarian projects. I helped to build schools and taught English to children. I think it was that that opened the door to my vocation.'

'But you were such a party girl at school.'

'And your point is?'

'Over the years, I have often wondered which side of

your nature would win – the good-time girl or the quiet, serious one. Now I suppose I have the answer.'

'That question was partly why I was so lost, Felix. Now I've managed to reconcile the two.

'So, now you're a spiritual partygoer?'

Dimity smiled. 'Something like that. But look at you. You've found your path. If you don't mind me saying, when you were younger, you always looked a bit on the serious side.'

'By serious, you mean nerdy, I take it?'

Dimity laughed. 'Don't get me wrong, I liked that about you; you never followed the crowd, but you did have an air of young fogey back then. Though I must say your clothes look very snappy now. I love the round glasses, and the haircut looks very West End. It's a bookish but... trendy look.'

'Well, I am bookish, and I try to make my style comfortable and age-appropriate whilst also looking good for business.'

'Well, it works,' Dimity said. After appraising Felix further, she added, 'Designer jeans; blue shirt, light tweed jacket and loafers – a good look for you. So, what's in the handbag?'

'It's a messenger bag!' Felix said indignantly.

'Oh, I do apologise, what's in the messenger bag?'

'All the tools of my trade: small laptop, sketchbook, magnifying glass – that sort of thing.'

'A magnifying glass? Now I think of you as Sherlock Holmes – with the hat and pipe.'

'Don't you think it's too early in our reacquaintance for mockery?'

'I wasn't mocking you, Felix. But tell me, I would love to know what surprised you more, my email to you or my job?'

'It's difficult to say, but if you must know, I think it was the collar. By the way, now I'm getting used to it, I think it suits you – and you it. But don't you miss your old life with all the high adventure, the danger and the parties?'

'Part of me does. I left the other part behind on K2.'

'Was that your last expedition?'

'Yes, the ill-fated one.'

'What happened?'

'I'd prefer not to go into that.'

Felix nodded his acceptance. 'I was never like you, was I, Mitten? My physical discomfort red line was set several notches below yours.'

'Maybe I had a greater appetite for adventure, but you clearly have a commercial and professional nerve that I could never match. Can I tell you something?'

'If you want.'

'To be honest, I was nervous about seeing you. I was so pleased you answered my email, but I wasn't sure what to expect.'

'Why not?'

'I didn't know how you felt about me.'

'To be clear, I'm not sure I knew how I felt – or know how I feel now. But we survivors of Hurricane Dimity had to pick up the pieces after she swept through.'

'Was I a hurricane?'

'It seemed like it at the time. But like after most storms, the survivors sweep up and rebuild.'

'And you rebuilt?'

'Santa and I tried desperately to find you when you left. For a while, we kept in touch with your parents, but they didn't know where you were and were frantic. Then, later, we suspected they knew but weren't saying. Why, we didn't know. After they retired to Spain, we lost touch, and I suppose life filled the vacuum.'

'I think it was best you and Santa didn't know. I didn't want you to know. I was a mess, Felix, with a whole cocktail of teenage angst and anger that came out in some pretty self-destructive behaviour.

'But I don't want to go into all that. I told you I was married. Can I ask about you?'

'There's not much to tell you. No entertaining list of one-night stands and hysterical affairs. A couple of longer-term relationships. Victoria and I split up almost two years ago. She was lovely and we lived together for about five years. But honestly, it was a comfortable arrangement that wasn't going anywhere. In the end, she was offered a job in Singapore, and there was a semi-reluctant but dry-eyed parting of the ways. Before that, there was Marta, who was wacky, unpredictable and, in my view, downright unhinged at times. The ending wasn't pretty and finally involved a restraining order. After that, she moved back to Bulgaria, where she's no doubt terrorising some other poor soul, or the whole country for all I know.'

Dimity laughed. 'I know I shouldn't laugh, but you and wacky girls. Was Marta as awful as me?'

'I can assure you, Mitten, Marta gave wacky a whole new meaning. Friendship with you gave me no preparation at all. Marta could teach generals a thing or two about command and control.'

'So, there's hope for me yet.'

Felix wasn't sure what that meant and decided not to pursue it. Instead, he asked, 'Are your parents still alive?'

'No, they are both gone; Dad about eight years ago and Mum last March. At least Mum lived to see me ordained.

That pleased her, and she could stop worrying about me for a few months. How about you?'

'They went about five years ago – within four months of each other; my dad first.'

'I always think that says a lot, couples dying within a short time.'

'I think you are right. They were devoted. We were all devoted in an old-fashioned way. I miss them very much. To tell you the truth, I'm not sure I am over it yet. I still go to call them if I have any news. Mum would have been agog about us meeting again. Dad would have pretended not to bother much but would have been just as interested.'

'Your mum and I got on very well.'

'I know, and Dad secretly admired you.'

'Not after I disappeared?'

'No, he was seriously put out about that.'

Dimity and Felix talked long into the evening. They shared much about each other's intervening years, but slowly, for Felix, at least, they seemed to drift back through time to another period – the spent one of their youth. Felix seemed helpless to fight the creeping enjoyment he felt from this retrospection.

Finally, looking at his watch, he said, 'It's late, Mitten. It's a work night, and I have a busy day tomorrow.'

'More sleuthing and ferreting?'

'Something like that.'

'Look, before you go, there's something I haven't shown you yet.'

Dimity stretched over to the coffee table, picked up an unsealed envelope and handed it to Felix.

'What's this?'

'Open it. It's a copy of a poem, a sonnet actually. It was

found recently in Eliza's old family bible. Its hundreds of years old. Go ahead, read it.'

Felix took from the envelope a single sheet of paper and began to read.

I

To findest that thou seek look to Heaven.
Harken not to a preachers pulpit prose
Or heretic, lest thy purpose leaven,
But chaseth thine eyes and pursue thy nose.
Trust not the lizard nor believe the snake,
And judges words may'st not some verdicts fit.
Care not a king doth roar and people quake,
Read beyond the scribe for some deeper wit.
Let nought persuade thee from thy noble cause,
Nor tempt or throw thee from thy chosen way,
Nor weaken thy dread of Gods holy laws.
Resolute and strong for the answer stay.
In darkness blind the inching midnight thief,
Marks as worthless the lone unbladed sheath.

After he'd finished reading, Felix turned to Dimity. 'What does it mean?'

'That's what my friend, Eliza, wants to know.'

'I suppose by showing me this, you hoped I would be persuaded to join your friend's quest?'

'Eliza did. And, yes, I hoped you would too. Please can I tell her that you'll at least meet her?'

Felix wondered what he might be getting into, but there

was no doubt the story and sonnet had intrigued him. Not wanting to appear too eager, he remained quiet for a while longer, as though weighing up the decision. 'Oh, I suppose it won't do any harm meeting your friend,' he eventually said. 'I may be able to help her one way or another. So, if you like, tell her I'll meet her, if she still wants that.'

As Felix stood up to leave, he added, 'Actually, I'm over this way quite a lot – to see Santa and Rosie, and I have some work nearby too. In fact, I'll be around here next Thursday.'

'Oh, we could have met again; that would have been nice. But I'm busy all day and then going to a concert in the evening – on a date.'

'Who's the lucky chap?'

'Actually, it's Ludovic, the deacon I mentioned earlier.'

'Oh.'

'We've been going out for a while now.'

'Serious?'

'Perhaps, we'll see.'

CHAPTER FOUR

For two weeks, Felix had no word from Dimity other than a text expressing what a nice reunion it had been. Then came an email suggesting a date to go and visit her friend, Eliza. Felix confirmed and offered to pick Dimity up on the way.

On the allotted day, he drove to St Eadric's. As he entered the Abbey yard, he spotted Dimity already waiting for him. She was wearing a sizeable, old, navy duffle coat and a chunky woollen hat that engulfed her head.

'So, where are we headed?' Felix asked once Dimity had climbed into the car and unwound the thick scarf from around her neck. So far, she had remained stubbornly mute on their destination.

'It's about fifteen miles,' she said. After issuing directions, she added, 'I've been ruminating on lots of things since we last met.'

'Such as?'

'I didn't behave very well to you all those years ago, did I? And not just when I left.'

'Sometimes you did.'

'I was awful. Were you deeply hurt?'

Felix didn't reply immediately. Then he said, 'It makes me sound rather pathetic, but looking back, I managed the rejection well. After all, I suppose we both got what we wanted from the relationship – or I did, at least sometimes.'

'I'm ashamed.'

'And you should be. In those days, some people thought you were crackers. Of course, you weren't – well, not to me anyway, but for inexperienced boys or men with fragile hearts and the wrong ideas, you were dangerous.'

'Did you have a fragile heart and the wrong idea?'

'You must have known how I felt, Mitten. You were young, but you weren't stupid. Over time, I figured our friendship was worth the risk of hurt feelings.'

'Was that all it was, a risky friendship?'

'To me it was a wonderful friendship, but not without its risks.'

Dimity nodded. 'I told Santa when we were thirteen that I supposed you and I would marry each other one day.'

Felix laughed. 'Santa mentioned that to me once. But perhaps somewhere along the way, you and I must have decided that our friendship was better frozen in adolescence. Perhaps that was better than testing it in adulthood.'

'That's a kind way of putting it. Talking about friendships, do you think I should contact Santa?'

'Do you mean, will Santa slam the door in your face?'

'I suppose I do.'

'Well, it's not for me to say, but there's only one way to find out.'

'You wouldn't pave the way?'

'No.'

'I deserved that.'

'Yes, you did. Do you know the last time I saw you, Mitten?'

'Wasn't it at school?'

'No, that was the last time you saw me.'

Dimity frowned, 'When, then?'

'On your wedding day. It seems so long ago now.'

'But nobody was at my wedding.'

'I saw you leave the registry office in Marylebone.'

Felix told Dimity how he had been walking back to his old office from a meeting in the Landmark Hotel when, through a flash of kismet, he had caught sight of the newlyweds.

'Oh, Felix, why didn't you say something?'

'I wasn't invited.'

Felix glanced at his passenger and noticed a tear glistening on her cheek. She quickly wiped it away.

'I didn't invite my best friends,' Dimity said softly. 'You say I wasn't crazy, but I was crazy; crazy and insensitive and self-centred and shallow and stupid.'

Felix remembered watching Dimity clinging onto her new husband with one hand while clutching a bouquet of what looked like garage-bought cut flowers in the other as they sped off on a motorbike.

At the time, he was both shocked and upset. But then he recalled feeling oddly relieved that it wasn't him to whom Dimity was clinging. He already knew that knowing Dimity Fortuna was to flirt with rejection. On her wedding day to someone else, he learned that loving Dimity Fortuna was to *accept* rejection. It was a surprising emotion and he'd thought at the time it was a sign of reaching maturity. He had also wondered that day for how long Dimity would hold onto her husband – or rather, how long would Dimity's new husband hold onto her?

'How can you ever forgive me, Felix?'

'I don't know. To be honest, I was doubly disappointed – in you and for me. And perhaps I was also a little jealous. I don't know. It was an impossible cocktail of emotions. Let's put it this way, it was not one of my better days.'

'Nor mine, as it turned out.'

'Well, that was then. We've both moved on. Let's not talk about it anymore. It was a long time ago.'

Felix accepted this was a different Dimity. She was chastened, humble and thoughtful. Seemingly, she had finally met something with gravity stronger than hers: God.

He had reached a wooded Chiltern area that he knew reasonably well. He had even ridden out that way on his bike from school.

'You'd better slow down a bit now,' Dimity warned, 'the entrance is on the right, just after the next bend.'

They arrived at a tubular metal gate with peeling red paint, weathered to pink and succumbing to rust. It was so unprepossessing that Felix understood why he had never noticed it; it looked like thousands of other poorly maintained and little-used field gates. Felix pulled up beside it, and Dimity jumped out of the car to swing it open. There was no padlock, but a rustic sign announced in faded letters, Witch's Lawn and, beneath that, Private Property.

'Eliza told me the house was once known as Witch's Laund,' Dimity said once she had climbed back into the car. 'She explained, laund is a French word meaning an open, grassy area among trees, but the word fell out of use in England hundreds of years ago, when it became lawn.'

'You learn something every day. So how old is the house?'

'You'll see.'

Felix drove the car slowly up an unmade but serviceable road that gently gained height as it curved around a wooded hill. Either side of them were giant rhododendrons that, in spring, he imagined would be a riot of vivid pink, yellow and white blooms. Beyond them, the tall beech trees were just over their autumnal display and had carpeted the ground in russet and gold leaves.

Finally, the shrubs and trees petered out, and Felix stopped the car towards the end of the drive and turned to Dimity in wonder. 'This is truly extraordinary,' he whispered.

Ahead of them was a red brick house – Tudor by the look of the brickwork. The design of the building was an exuberant mix of distinctive styles that, to Felix's mind, should have clashed. Instead, they stood in harmony. The front elevation was dominated by three gables, the centre one taller than its companions, and each topped by a stone pinnacle. The latticed windows looked as if they were from an oriental palace, and they gave the front a decidedly mystical look. If Felix had asked Rosie to draw a house it could well have looked like this; a child's naive imagination running riot. But this was no young fancy: it was a mature expression of originality and joy, and it brought together elegance, grandeur, and even humour. It was the most charming building Felix had ever seen.

'Have you heard of cottage orné style?' Felix asked.

'No, what's that?'

'It dates to the 18th and 19th centuries, when landowners built rustic, picturesque houses to get away from more formal designs. Well, this is cottage orné but, I should say, it was built about three hundred years before that movement ever existed. This is one-of-a-kind. A truly weird and wonderful masterpiece.'

Felix and Dimity left the car and walked quickly up a long, stone-paved path, through a pair of wooden gates that filled a gap in a tall yew hedge and on towards the house. To the side of them, across a close-cropped lawn, Felix watched fallen leaves seemingly race each other, urged on by a cold, unseen force. He thrust his hands deep into the pockets of his coat.

Linking her arm in his, Dimity drew closer. It was an intimate gesture and, Felix thought, an uninvited act of trespass as it made him feel uncomfortable in a way he couldn't quite grasp.

'Chilly,' Dimity said by way of explanation or excuse. She would offer a confounding look or touch when you least expected it, Felix recalled. You could become drunk on the most innocuous of her favours, but it would be wrong to mistake an act of benevolent caprice for serious intent.

They reached a prefabricated, detached garage. To Felix, it was out of place, as though it had been put up hurriedly in the 1930s and then forgotten about or ignored.

'Take a peek in the window,' said Dimity.

'Why?'

'Just look.'

He peered through the glass mostly obscured by dust and cobwebs. Inside, under blankets, he could just make out the outline of a large car. But the front of it wasn't fully covered. He could see the familiar lines of a Rolls Royce radiator topped with the famous Spirit of Ecstasy mascot. By the shape of the blankets, Felix thought he recognised the model.

'A Silver Ghost?'

'It is, but this is only the beginning.'

The uneven path led on to the house. The front door had nine clear panes in its upper half. Dimity pulled a handle hanging from a chain. Felix could see into the entrance hall and heard the muffled noise of a bell ringing from within the house. A dog yapped, and in a short while, a prim, slightly bent lady, great in years and walking with the aid of a stick, opened the door. She visibly brightened at the sight of Dimity.

'Oh good, you're here. Quickly, come in out of the cold, my dear.'

Turning her attention to Felix, she stared for a moment longer than might be considered polite before seeming to collect herself, 'And this must be your young man,' she said. It came out as a statement rather than a question.

'Not my young man, Eliza, as I think you know well, but my old friend, Felix. Felix, this is my new friend, Mrs Arrow.'

The old lady said, 'I'm pleased to meet you, Felix – may I call you by your forename.'

'Of course. I'm very pleased to meet you too, Mrs Arrow.'

A dachshund yapped excitedly at their feet. When Felix bent down to stroke her, the little dog turned onto her back and exposed her tummy for tickling.

'But you must call me Eliza. I may have been born when Edward was on the throne, but I left all that formality behind long ago. And please don't take any notice of Cecily.'

'Cecily is a tart,' Dimity added.

But Felix wanted to take notice: he tried to take note of

everything he could see of this astonishing house and its owner.

Spread across the hall floor was an almost room-sized tribal rug in a vibrant red design. A Regency console table against the left wall had a dark, jade-green marble top, while the ebonised table base was inset with gilt dragons and warriors. An intricate, silver-enamelled samovar stood in the centre of the table.

Hanging on the wall above was a large equine painting of a bay horse in a parkland setting with a fine stately home in the distance. On the opposite side of the hall, and taking up most of the wall, was a tapestry that gave warmth and style to the entrance space. All this detail was beautifully lit by pin-point spotlights.

And this is just the hall, thought Felix. Everything he had seen so far excited him. But there was something else. There was an aura that he couldn't remember having felt in any house he'd been inside. The same feeling also went for the elderly lady in front of him. He didn't know why, but a far from unpleasant shiver ran down his spine.

Felix noted that, with the aid of her silver-handled cane, Eliza Arrow was holding herself as straight as she could whilst battling to control a stoop. Her alert face was surprisingly free of lines, but her hands were wrinkled and displayed several liver spots. Her grey hair was short and well-cut. She wore a black pleated skirt over dark stockings, and on her feet were Gucci loafers. Her jacket collar was turned up, and pinned onto one lapel was a brooch in yellow gold with a large citrine at its heart, from which radiated golden rods set with diamonds and five, navy enamel ribbons.

The overall impression she gave was of an elderly but strikingly elegant woman with a zest for life.

Felix and Dimity were ushered through the entrance hall into a double-height drawing room or salon.

'Felix, you're standing with your mouth open,' Dimity laughed.

But by then, Felix was hardly listening; his eyes were absorbing the room. The salon was about 40ft long. Against one wall was a finely carved, white stone fireplace, singed by heat around the hearth, worn by age and brought to life by a blaze of logs lying in a vast iron basket.

On three sides of the room, at first-floor height, ran a gallery reached by a dark oak staircase with a thick handrail positioned between heavy newel posts at the bottom and top. These were finely carved and topped with caps and finials in the shape of pinecones.

The walls in this imposing room were light beige, as if stained by centuries of tobacco smoke, and were covered with portraits, landscapes and still life oil paintings in fine gilt frames. As far as Felix could see, the décor in the first-floor gallery was the same. In front of the fire, two large, green, velvet, high-backed sofas faced each other; between them, and covered with books and magazines, was a long, low ottoman; its chintz fabric faded and, in places, threadbare.

Towards one end of the room was a large oak refectory table topped by several mismatching chenille cloths. A grand piano supporting a number of silver-framed photos occupied the other end of the room. More rugs, randomly laid, almost completely covered the flagstone floor. To Felix, the texture and colour of the space seemed as glorious as the feeling of warmth and history.

But the most eye-catching feature of all was the gilt script on the almost-black panelling that ran around two walls just below ceiling height. Felix craned his neck but could hardly read the faded old English calligraphy that in some places had been lost to time and never reinstated.

By then, he had forgotten his hostess and companion entirely. Finally, he turned to find them watching him with amused expressions.

'Mrs Arrow, I'm completely overwhelmed.'

'Eliza, please.'

'Eliza, your house is astonishing. I can't believe I've never heard of it spoken of or seen it featured in books or magazines. It's wonderful. I don't mean to sound trite, but I feel like Witch's Lawn has cast a spell on me.'

'Thank you, Felix; the house has that effect on certain people. It is described nowadays as a connection, I believe. I've always lived here, so I suppose I'm connected in a different way. But I'm glad that you like it. It is a wonderful house, but we should keep it to ourselves, if you don't mind. It has always been that way.'

By now, the little dog had begun to chew one of Felix's shoelaces.

'Cecily!' exclaimed Eliza, 'come away from Felix. I'm sure that he's had quite enough of you by now; I know I have.' The little dog took no notice whatsoever.

'I think Witch's is the perfect secret house and garden,' said Dimity. 'Eliza explained to me once that there are no public footpaths close by, and the grounds are well-fenced. The building is screened unless you come up the long drive. It isn't even under a scheduled flight path. So, it remains hidden to those who have no business here. And as you have seen from the entrance, it's hardly advertised.'

'Dimity is quite right,' said Eliza, 'of course, you can't completely hide a house like this, but the only people to pass on the other side of the fence are ramblers well off the established footpaths and the National Trust people who maintain the surrounding estate. It's no conspiracy of silence, but there does seem to have been a coincidence of silence that has protected the family and this house for a very long time.'

'Hidden in plain sight, it's just incredible,' Felix mumbled, as much to himself as to anyone else: he was awed by the house. No, he thought, he was floored by it.

'Would you like to look around, Felix?' Eliza asked.

'I would like that very much.'

'I'm afraid it will take far too long if you have me in tow, so why don't you explore on your own while I talk to Dimity?'

It was a generous offer to someone Eliza had just met, especially in this house, Felix thought as he started with the salon, absorbing the belongings accumulated by a family with an extraordinary eye for quality.

'Is it OK if I push on upstairs to the gallery, Eliza? Felix asked when he had exhausted the salon.

'Of course.'

Felix took his time climbing the stairs. The worn Persian runner was kept in place by highly polished brass stair rods. Shards of coloured light from a high, latticed, stained-glass window mingled with the red and green pattern of the carpet. He caressed the ancient oak handrail and breathed in the unmistakable smell of recently applied beeswax polish. There was no lack of loving and careful housekeeping here, he noted.

As he reached the top of the stairs, the voices of the two

women below became a murmur. It was the comforting sound small children might hear from their beds at night as their parents talked downstairs.

The view from the gallery gave the salon another perspective. In his mind's eye, Felix could see a couple walking down the stairs years ago to greet dinner guests. The men would have been wearing black tie, and the women would have been in full-length gowns accessorised with long gloves. Felix could imagine them standing and talking in loud, happy voices while clutching glasses of sherry. The light of the flickering fire and dozens of candles would have reflected off the crystal glass and silver cutlery meticulously laid out on the dining table.

Felix smiled at the picture in his head before the present muscled in to enchant him once again. His eyes drifted along a wall covered in more framed pictures of extraordinary quality. Although he was more of an enthusiast than an expert, he recognised this was a significant collection of celebrated artists, including old masters. Was that a Pissarro? Could that be a Vermeer? It seemed unlikely that a house like this would have reproductions on its walls. But if they were genuine, what did that mean? It meant, Felix thought, that this must be one of the world's best private collections of art and, therefore, priceless.

Everywhere in this house was antique furniture of the finest quality. But where the paintings and carefully placed objets d'art were nearly all from the continent and the kind of pieces that aristocratic travellers might have brought back from their grand tours around Europe several hundred years ago, the furniture was undoubtedly from closer to home. This place was, Felix decided, an accidentally curated collection covering half a millennium of English gentility.

And currently passing the time of day with Dimity was the living embodiment of that gentility – Eliza Arrow.

Still trying to take it all in, he eventually retreated downstairs and sat down next to Dimity – or rather, he collapsed into the surprisingly deep sofa.

Eliza was seated more sensibly on an upright armchair nearer the fire.

Eliza and Dimity turned to Felix with expectant looks.

'Well, what do you want me to say?' he said. 'This house is utterly amazing. I have never been anywhere like it. How wonderful it must be to live here, Eliza. It's a huge privilege just to visit.'

'I said you would be thankful,' Dimity said.

'Oh, believe me, I am. I couldn't be more pleased to visit anywhere. May I ask about the script beneath the ceiling, Eliza? It is hard to make out in places, even from upstairs.'

'It says, "Look to Heaven lest age or time bring memory's sad distress." I've always taken that to mean, "Look to Heaven or Christ before one loses one's mind" or "Look to God to relieve suffering in old age." Take your pick. My mama used to make up stories about it for me. But whoever had the script adorn this room and why are just two of Witch's many mysteries. But where are my manners? You dears must be parched; I'll arrange some tea.'

'Please don't go to any trouble,' Felix said.

Eliza smiled. 'It's no trouble, no trouble at all. I am still quite capable of doing some things for myself.' With that, she leaned to her side and pushed a button mounted on the wall. 'There,' she said with an infectious laugh, 'that wasn't so hard, was it?'

Felix joined in with Eliza's laughter, and soon after, a woman carrying a laden tray arrived. She was elegantly dressed in a tailored, below-the-knee black skirt and a crisp white shirt. Felix thought the woman looked about his age. She was of average height and slim, and she wore her jet-black hair in a neat bob. Her long, dangly earrings in finely tooled metalwork and her dark-chocolate eyes framed with a flourish of mascara gave her, Felix imagined wryly, the look of a Mesopotamian queen or one from the Nile.

With a warm smile, the woman set down the tray of tea things that included a silver teapot and three exquisite porcelain cups and saucers. There was also a delicious-looking chocolate cake with tea plates and forks.

'Felix, this is Cairo,' said Eliza, 'she is my companion, friend and housekeeper. Nothing would ever get done around here without her and her husband, West. Cairo, meet Felix, Dimity's friend; the one I told you about.'

Cairo greeted him warmly and poured the tea before disappearing from the room.

'After busy and difficult careers where they travelled a great deal, Cairo and West married later in life and have no children,' Eliza explained. 'So now Cairo mothers me, and West is my driver and handyman. He also mixes a wonderful whisky sour. They live behind the house in a cottage converted from the stables.'

Felix tried some of the cake, which proved as tasty as it looked, before saying, 'From what Dimity tells me, you have plenty of provenance for this wonderful collection.'

'Oh yes, much of it is documented. There are a few things that are a mystery, but the biggest mystery of all is the need for something proving our ownership of Witch's Lawn.'

'Haven't you had experts look into that in the past?'

'Over the years, several people have been engaged. They

searched the house but didn't find anything. But there wasn't any great urgency then.'

'But now there is?'

'Yes. This family has been in all kinds of danger over the years, but we have never had a threat like this. Never one that endangered the very fabric of the family – this house.'

'But from what Dimity has told me, you don't even know if there is any evidence of ownership, or, if there is, what form that evidence might take.'

'No, I don't.'

'Then it's like looking for a needle in a haystack when one doesn't know what a needle is or if there is one in the first place.

'That is a good way of putting it.'

Eliza looked intently at Felix. 'Will you help me find this needle? Do say yes; I'm only too happy to meet your usual charges and cover any necessary expenses.'

'You don't know what my charges are,' Felix said with a smile.

'Are they fair?'

'I believe so. My clients seem content with them.'

Then please don't refuse. I haven't much time, and neither has this house.'

Felix looked at the old woman, who suddenly seemed as though her spark had left her, and said, 'If I am to help, I will need the run of the place – unfettered access. I will need to put several of my personal projects on hold but still run my business. This examination could take weeks, perhaps months. And then there is no guarantee of finding anything.'

'I know there isn't, but if it would help, you can stay here whenever you need.'

Felix was surprised to find himself drawn to staying at

Witch's. 'Well, that would certainly cut down on the travel and give me much more time and a far greater feel for the place,' he said.

'How soon could you start?' Dimity blurted out.

'Steady on, Mitten. I'll need some days to put things in order at the office. But how about a week on Saturday?'

* * *

'West doesn't drive Eliza to Sainsbury's in that Silver Ghost, does he?' Felix dryly asked as he and Dimity returned to his car.

Dimity laughed. 'Of course not. There's an SUV round the back by the cottage. By the way, did you notice Eliza's lovely brooch?'

'It was hard to miss. Is it significant?'

'It indicates that the wearer has been awarded the French Légion d'honneur.'

'Impressive, I wonder what for?'

'Your guess is as good as mine.'

As Felix set off down the drive, he struggled with his emotions. Against his better judgement, it felt good that Dimity had gate-crashed his existence once again. But he also knew how heavily he could pay for relaxing his guard even for a moment.

Falling at the first hurdle, Felix couldn't help asking, 'Will you be here when I return?'

'I'm out all that day, I'm afraid.'

'Anywhere nice?'

'Ludovic is taking me to the Winter Fair at Waddesdon Manor, with lunch somewhere

along the way no doubt.'

* * *

That night in bed, Felix reflected on all that he had seen. Above all, he had somehow felt more at home at Witch's Lawn than anywhere else he could think of, and he couldn't wait to go back. Then for some reason he imagined Dimity and Ludovic at Waddesdon, and until sleep took him, it was this image that forced out any more thoughts of Eliza's incredible home.

CHAPTER FIVE

It was Saturday morning and Felix was in his flat, having finished packing for his visit to Witch's Lawn. His top-floor apartment was slightly bigger than Dimity's but similar in nature, with rooms squeezed into the roof space. It was spacious for one person and would just about suit a couple not given to clutter. Over the four or five years he had lived in the 'company flat', as he put it, he had transformed the place into a comfortable retreat. He had converted the original collection of boxy attic rooms into a flowing arrangement of larger spaces. A living room with a dining alcove led to the kitchen, main bedroom, single guest bedroom and bathroom. In the living room and bedrooms, in homage to an interior designer idol of his, he had hung on the walls rugs and tapestries interspersed with paintings and mirrors with heavy frames. Triple-lined, embroidered curtains prevented too much daylight invading the sumptuous gloom. Felix preferred the rooms to be candlelit, and he had candles everywhere, the effect of which enchanted his visitors. His home had even been featured in *House & Garden* magazine. Lately, however, he had felt ready for a change of style; it was time to bring some sunlight into his life.

The entry phone buzzed; Felix answered it immediately.

'Is that you?' said his friend and neighbour, Roger Strand, one of the most highly regarded florists in London. Roger acted for celebrities, royals, business tycoons and many other well-to-do people.

'Who else were you expecting?'

'I live in hope of hearing another sleepy voice coming from your little eyrie in the morning.'

'With my workload, you've not much chance of finding anyone else here,' replied Felix. 'Hang on, I'm coming down. I'll meet you in the shop.'

Roger greeted Felix with a big hug. 'Good morning, petal, I've brought coffee.'

After moving into the flat, Felix had quickly come to know and like Roger, who was in his late 50s. From the outside, he came across as a confident and hard-headed businessman who also doubled as a consummate and often outrageous showman. But Felix knew that at heart, Roger was a deeply compassionate man with a great deal of time for his friends, of whom he had many from all walks of life.

Today, Roger was wearing a white silk shirt decorated with huge purple peony blooms and glossy green leaves. An almost-too-tight pair of slim-fit Versace jeans struggled to contain his tummy, and Todd's loafers were worn with no socks despite the time of year. Roger was a big man, over 6ft tall, with a flourish of floppy and still natural blond hair, which a celebrity stylist from a costly Mayfair salon cut when required. Roger paid him in flower arrangements.

'I've also brought you these.' Roger nodded to a vase containing a sensational flower display. 'I saw that lovely but lonely little table you have for sale in the window and thought it would look more valuable with a decent flower arrangement. Oh, and I have a business card to go beside it.'

'Ever the opportune publicist, Roger.'

'But of course. So, what's your news? I haven't seen you for a few weeks. I've been in Finland on a photoshoot for *Brides* magazine, where I nearly started an international incident – again.'

'What did you do this time?'

'I only demanded serviettes on the wedding breakfast table.'

'That doesn't sound too extreme.'

'You'd be surprised. The Finns thought I wanted Soviets on the table.'

Roger roared with laughter.

They sat with their coffees in the private back office. Felix updated his friend on recent events, although he omitted specific details about Eliza and where she lived. Roger was an excellent listener and Felix was pleased to talk to someone outside the narrow arc of acquaintances and business connections. He couldn't resist unburdening himself over his past and renewed acquaintance with Dimity.

'You are looking for my advice, blossom,' Roger stated.

'Actually, I'm not.'

'Nonsense, darling. Now, the first thing, should you be tempted to resurrect your puppy love affair, is to resist the urge. You're no longer a puppy. Take it from one who knows. I always revisit relationships, and they always end in tears. But then, where would be the excitement in not going for les liaisons dangereuses?'

'Well, if I needed advice, which I don't, you seem a fat lot of good as a counsellor. I'm confused already.'

'But I'm always happy to help with these matters, darling – whether I'm asked or not. But I must say I'm itching to meet this girlfriend of yours. I've always had a soft spot for clerics.'

'The mind boggles, Roger, but I don't see you as very churchy.'

'Oh, my dear, you'd be surprised. I adore all those bells and smells. Perhaps I'll create a new candle in your friend's honour. Did I tell you that we now have a fragrant candle range? We could call this new one Vestry. It would smell of dead flowers, stale incense and damp hymn books, with base notes of dry rot. I'm sure it would sell very well – they all do.'

'I'm not sure that Mitten is quite ready for you, Roger.'

'Mitten – a pet name – how sweet. We'll get on famously.'

'Well, sorry to disappoint you, but I doubt you will ever meet her. I will never become involved, even if I had the chance, which I won't. I keep my life simple, and I don't want it made complicated.'

'But of course you do, darling. Romance is so heartbreakingly addictive. How long has it been since you were in a relationship? Don't tell me, it's too long. You need a companion to frustrate your life – someone to share the hideous adventure with. As a matter of interest, Felix, how long has it been since you were even out on a date?'

'Oh, nine or ten months,' Felix replied, although it had been much longer than that.

'You need to get out more, flower. But I sense there might be something more. What else is stopping you from taking the disastrous path along Misery Lane?'

Felix laughed. 'You may be closer to the truth than you think. There is something – or rather someone – else.'

'Ah-ha, could it be a love rival? This gets even better. How fatally intoxicating. My dear, you just have to engage. It will be deliciously heartbreaking for someone. The victor of this love joust will be ecstatically happy, while the loser will be so unquenchably depressed that he will blame himself for years and wallow in self-pity and recrimination forever. What have you got to lose? Don't be selfish. Be miserable like the rest of us. But tell me, who is the other man in this love triangle? I want to know who you are pitted against. Tell me all about him – or her. You never can be certain nowadays, can you?'

'Not that I'm pitted against anyone, Roger, but it's a male. However, I really don't want to go into it. For all the reasons you so graphically describe, I will avoid getting involved.'

'But you are already involved, flower. Just tell Uncle Roger. You'll feel better. A problem shared is a problem complicated.'

Felix gave up. 'OK, the man is a canon at St Eadric's Abbey.'

'Another cleric. How intriguing.'

For the next half an hour, Felix endured Roger having fun at his expense. Finally, Felix announced that he would have to get on and, after a large hug, Roger left, but not before urging Felix to bring Dimity to his shop or at least buy her some expensive flowers.

* * *

As Felix drove to Witch's Lawn, he reflected how its surrounds possessed their own distinctive beauty, but compared to the Cotswolds, there were far fewer sightseers – just small clusters of ramblers and solitary dog walkers. Somehow, the house seemed separate, even from this pretty world. It didn't belong to any particular town or village, and beyond that, it fell between several urban areas in a picturesque no man's land, its seclusion providing its anonymity and protection.

With mounting excitement, Felix reached his destination. On his last visit, he hadn't inspected the coat of arms – a weatherworn and ancient carved stone cartouche over the front door. But now he could make out a simple shield with three splayed arrows. Under the shield was a motto, "Respice ad Caelum".

He pulled the doorbell chain. This time, it was a tall, well-built man with a rugged face and an air of unnerving confidence who answered the door.

'You must be Felix. I'm West,' the man said. 'You've met my wife, Cairo. I'll take you through to Eliza.'

West was not Felix's idea of a domestic servant. He wore black boots, cargo trousers with a webbing belt and a tight-fitting T-shirt. His hair was cut short, and his arms sported several tattoos. Over the past week, Felix had been wondering about all the treasures within Witch's. He imagined how much of a target they would be for steal-to-order professional thieves. It was hard to believe that of all the people who knew about the building and its contents, not one of them had considered separating the priceless objects from their helpless owner. The house was in the middle of nowhere. It would be easy to rob. Or would it?

Felix realised now that West looked like he could be

handy in another way. Indeed, on reflection, Cairo didn't seem like an everyday housekeeper. Perhaps Eliza wasn't so helpless after all.

Once again, Eliza was sitting by the roaring log fire. She beckoned Felix over to the sofa closest to her. When he had taken a seat, she said, 'Once we've had coffee, West or Cairo can show you to your room, and you can make yourself at home. I've been so looking forward to seeing you again. I think you and I are going to get along very nicely. If I do say it myself, I am usually a good judge of character.' Eliza stretched out to push the service button. 'Now, let's have coffee.'

Several minutes later, a smiling Cairo arrived carrying a tray containing a coffee pot, cups, saucers and a plate of what appeared to be homemade shortbread biscuits.

Once she had departed, Felix asked, 'Have Cairo and West been with you long?'

'Oh, for several years. They came to me highly recommended through a specialist agency.'

'Is West a surname or his forename?'

'It doesn't matter, for as long as I have known him, he has only ever been referred to as West. There are three other members of my small team you haven't met. Frankie is my live-in nurse. She's indispensable, not only as a well-trained carer but also as a lovely young friend. She has a room upstairs next to mine. You won't meet her today as she has some time off, but she will be back tomorrow. Then there's Julius, my full-time gardener, and I also have a cleaner, Mrs Webb, who comes in three days a week.'

'I hope it's not too personal a subject, but Dimity introduced you as Mrs Arrow.'

'Hasn't Dimity told you?'

'No.'

'Dimity can keep her counsel. I hope you can too, Felix.'

'I suppose that keeping secrets is important in Dimity's line of work.'

'And mine,' said Eliza.

Felix seized on this opportunity to learn more, 'What is – was – your line of work, if you don't mind me asking?'

'We'll get to that in good time, but, in answer to your other question, I was married – very briefly. We were young. My husband died at Dunkirk – he was a Second Lieutenant. We've been a long time parted, but I will be with him soon. When we married, I never even had the time to get my name changed. So, I kept my family name – to keep it going as much as anything – the Arrow name is precious to me, but, sadly, as far as I know, I'm the last in my particular family line.'

'It sounds as though you still miss your husband after all these years.'

'Oh, yes, I do. He still visits me in my dreams sometimes, and upon waking, I experience a deep chasm of grief at losing him all over again, which isn't very fair of him, is it? It sends me into deep mourning again for days. Perhaps he's just reminding me that he is still there in my heart. Such loss, when permanent, is something many of us just have to come to terms with somehow. There was no counselling or psychotherapy back then. Perhaps it can help, but during the war, we just had to get on with it. So many suffered, but enough of that. Let us talk about less sorrowful things.'

A longcase clock chimed noon. The chime had only reached six when a carriage clock joined in.

'Eliza, I have to ask, who else knows about this house?'

'Besides those of us that live and work here?'

Felix nodded.

'Dimity, some other clergy, a fast-dwindling circle of personal friends and old colleagues, selected tradespeople and now you.'

'There must be more.'

'Oh a few, they're mostly from organisations like the Church of England, the Victoria and Albert Museum, the British Library and the National Gallery. The National Trust people know about it, as does Historic England. Of course, some are desperate to get their hands on the house and its contents, but I wouldn't break up this collection for all the tea in China. Not on my watch, as they say nowadays.'

'But – and I hope you don't mind me asking, Eliza – how do you have all this... the house, all these pictures and furniture?'

In recent days, Felix had been thinking of other noted private collections he knew. But collectors with substantial means had put those together over relatively short periods. Nor were those collections housed in such an extraordinary building as Witch's. It seemed to Felix that this collection must have been grown by successive generations over many hundreds of years. He wondered how the family, which by no means seemed aristocratic, could have had the means to assemble such a hoard.

As if guessing Felix's thoughts, Eliza said, 'Each generation of my family has added a little more. They weren't major collectors or great connoisseurs – well, not at first anyway. And they weren't like some of the collectors from great families, but each generation added more pieces as opportunities presented themselves. Collecting became an Arrow family tradition, and later, I suppose, it may have become a duty as well as a passion. Mostly, my well-travelled forebears just happened to be in the right place at the right time and came across some artists at the beginning of their careers. I like to imagine that some of these pictures were acquired while the paint was still wet. Sometimes my ancestors were just lucky; sometimes they had good local information – after all, as you will find out, information was their business. Sometimes they were given gifts for services rendered by their masters or by those who wanted to curry favour. But after many hundreds of years, it all mounts up to a great deal of art and other valuables.'

Felix let his eyes rest on a small, contemporary picture supported in its frame by a table-top easel. The portrait was a full-length, exquisitely painted young female figure with a look of pert self-confidence. He leaned in to study it more. In the corner was a small but familiar looking signature.

'But this is by Picasso, Eliza.'

Eliza smiled.

'You have a Picasso?'

'Among many other wonderful artists. But this is my favourite and the most personal to me.'

'May I ask why?'

Eliza laughed. 'The sitter is a much younger me.'

Felix was astonished. 'You sat for Picasso! How did that come about?'

'It was during the war, in Paris. The Nazis had just reached the city. I sometimes stayed in Pablo's studio. The sitting was a snatched moment of pleasure during an otherwise horrific period. Paris was crawling with Gestapo. It was a dangerous time.

'I understand that it must sound rather fabulous now and I suppose, looking back, it was, but at the time it was just two people trying to survive.'

'How did you meet him?'

'Some people I had met in Barcelona just before the war made the introduction...'

Judging that was as far as the story was going, Felix asked, 'Is everything you have here, or do you lend pictures to museums and galleries?'

'I don't lend anything out, even anonymously. It might be wrong of me, but I don't want to invite any questions. But there is more – in a London flat, in St. James's.

'St James's?'

'Actually, it's in St. James's Palace.'

For Felix, this was like peeling an onion. Each layer revealing another one beneath.

'I assure you, it's nothing exciting, just a room-and-a-half over the gates. The place is freezing in the winter and none-too-warm in the summer, I might add. There are no mod-cons. It's what they call a grace-and-favour apartment. But I must say, it is far more favour than grace. My family has had the use of it forever.'

'How long is forever?' Felix asked. By now, he was learning to expect the unexpected.

Eliza didn't disappoint. 'Since just after the Great Fire of London.'

'1666!' Felix exclaimed. Are your family some sort of royalty... descendants of a monarch's secret love child?'

Eliza laughed. 'No, we're not – quite the contrary. We are a family from ordinary beginnings, as I understand it. But then I suppose we couldn't be described as very ordinary now. But monarchs do come into our story. We've served the crown or state for over five hundred years.'

'In what way?'

Eliza studied Felix for a moment. Eventually, she said,

'Are you familiar with the names Thomas Cromwell and Sir Francis Walsingham?'

He nodded.

'Then you might know that they acted as spymasters – Cromwell for Henry VIII and Walsingham for Elizabeth I.'

'You are something to do with spying?'

'I prefer to think of us as a family of shadows. But we are pallium et pugio.'

Felix looked blankly at Eliza.

'It's Latin for cloak and dagger, but I have to say, we've been more the pallium side of things. For centuries, each generation of Arrows has served the state in one shadowy way or another. We have been in the espionage business ever since Thomas Cromwell, and perhaps before him for all I know. We are simply one of those families where one generation follows the next into the same occupation or profession. Only our trade was secrets.'

'Seems to me like a precarious way to make a living.'

'I suppose we have been flexible and fortunate enough to survive by adapting to circumstances. Some of us have been royal messengers, some official emissaries; others were attachés with several of our embassies. One was a privateer running guns, people, letters and secrets in the war against Napoleon and the Americans before and during the War of Independence. He was rather dashing, I believe. Another was a double agent at the Vatican in the 1730s. Now, he was a terrifically good spy, and a wonderful musician by all accounts.'

Eliza pointed to the portrait over the fireplace. 'That's Edmund Arrow. Romantic and dangerous, he'd get up to anything if the price was right. He also worked for John Thurloe, who was Oliver Cromwell's spymaster, although

Edmund looks more like a cavalier than a roundhead, don't you think?'

Felix stared in awe at the portrait before saying, 'Then your family has had friends, or at least contacts, in some very high places.'

Eliza smiled. 'More in low places. But, yes, we've always had access to high powered and influential people.'

'I must say, it sounds very exciting. It sounds as if your family were sort of gentlemen – and gentlewomen – spies.'

'It might sound fanciful now, but the idea of a gentleman or lady spy is based on a great deal of truth. To gain access to governments and royal houses several hundred years ago, one had to be highly cultured, have great connections and be able to speak several important languages. That's why there have been so many artists acting as secret agents to one country or another. Artists and composers were especially useful as spies. They travelled frequently and widely, and they were in demand by wealthy and powerful people. So, in truth, they had the best cover stories. Politics, learning and culture were often intertwined. In some ways, they still are. Powerful and wealthy people often seek to connect themselves with creative and artistic genius.'

'So, your family has been sitting at the top table of British history for over five hundred years?'

Eliza laughed. 'Again, more *under* the top table, Felix – catching whatever crumbs of valuable information that fall.'

Felix had a thought. 'I take it that's the Arrow family crest over the front door?'

'Yes, it is.'

'And the motto?'

'Respice ad Caelum, which, translated into English, means Look to heaven,' Eliza said.

'The same words as in the lines around the walls here?'

Eliza nodded.

'Also, in the poem from your family bible that Dimity showed me?'

'Quite so.'

'What does it all mean? Does it mean anything?'

'That's what I would like to know.'

'I've read that sonnet found in your Bible I don't know how many times,' Felix said.

'As have I. What do you think?'

'Well, the writer – the poet – suggests that there is something to find, a truth.'

'Anything else?'

'That, for some reason, one shouldn't trust anything that is told or written – not even from a king, judge, priest or scribe. Maybe it is some sort of Desiderata type poem, a general dictum. But then again, it could be something more specific, a direct instruction. Interestingly, it mentions the word loyal. At least that is interesting to me.'

'And to me.'

'Do you know who wrote the sonnet?'

'Probably. In the front of our family bible there's an inscription, "Loveinge Kinsmen, the truth is the backbone of this good book." Then it is initialled J.A. I don't think anybody ever appreciated what the inscription meant until the British Library discovered the sonnet tucked into the spine of the Bible while they were carrying out some conservation work.'

'Spine as in backbone?'

'As with crossword puzzles, it seems obvious when you have the answer.'

'Is the sonnet considered to be contemporary with the family Bible?' Felix asked.

'That's the feeling. The Bible was printed in 1568. If that's the case then, according to our family tree, J.A stands for James Arrow. That ties in with the experts' view that the poem was written by an amateur. A Shakespeare or John Donne, he was not, or so I've been reliably informed by the intrigued but politely disparaging scholars at the British Library.'

'I should know the answer to this, but where does that put it in monarchy terms?'

'Ten years into the first Elizabeth's reign.'

'So, what do *you* think the sonnet is saying?'

'Like you, I think it's a warning not to take anything at face value. But most of all, I think it is telling us that there is something to find, especially as there's one other important clue. Did you notice it?'

Felix formed a mental picture of the poem before shaking his head. 'No, I don't think so.'

Eliza smiled, 'At the top of the verse, there is a number – one. So, I think we should find verse number two, don't you? Now, how about settling in upstairs?' Eliza pressed the service button, and before long, Cairo arrived. 'Would you mind showing Felix to his room?' she asked her.

The room selected for Felix was spacious, with a double bed, wardrobe, chest of drawers, dressing table and a small bedroom chair, each a fine antique piece. The window overlooked the front garden and drive. Looking at the bed, Felix thought to himself how long it had been since he had slept under sheets, blankets and an eiderdown: it reminded him of his childhood home before his parents finally discovered duvets.

He emptied his holdall, decanting the contents into the chest of drawers and hanging his jacket in the wardrobe. He laid out his toiletries on top of the chest and sat at the dressing table, which was empty but for several silver-framed black and white photographs of various people, including a young girl on a swing. The picture made Felix smile. The girl, who he imagined was about fifteen, looked so happy. There was a great deal more to learn about this house and family, Felix decided.

CHAPTER SIX

Back downstairs, Felix and Eliza exhausted the subject of the sonnet, giving Felix the opportunity to open another line of questioning. 'This might not be the moment, but I'm incredibly curious about what part you played in the family business.'

'I don't often talk about that period of my life,' she replied. 'It was a long time ago. I prefer to look forward, not back. But you should know I spent the war years in a variety of countries, including France and Germany. I speak several languages fluently and a couple of others reasonably well. Everyone in our family seems to have had a gift for linguistics, although I'm very rusty now through lack of use.

'I was in the First Aid Nursing Yeomanry. Early in the War, we were attached to the Special Operations Executive, based in Baker Street, doing signals, cypher work and that sort of thing – anything but first aid. But later, women – girls more like – became valuable in the field.'

'How does one even start in espionage?'

'For me, it was in the Spanish Civil War – The

International Brigade. Nothing that exciting, just keeping my eye on things for our side. Papa had me recruited, although Mama was horrified. She thought I was far too young. It was in Barcelona where I earned my code name, La Bruixa, which is Catalan for The Witch.'

'There's that word witch again. Were you a witch in Spain, Eliza?'

'Well, the fascists seemed to think so. But it was a long time ago, another life. The world was very different then.'

'But you continued in that line of work after the war?'

'Yes, I did.'

Felix had a sudden thought. 'Didn't you say Cairo and West came from a special agency?'

'They did. Frankie, too.'

'Am I right in thinking it wasn't an employment agency?'

'No, it wasn't. And again, you must never speak of these things to anyone. I am sure I could ask somebody to get you to sign the Official Secrets Act or explain, in a most sinister and scary way, why it would be best if you keep all this to yourself.'

Felix nodded meekly and felt alarmed that he could be intimidated and even frightened by such an elderly lady.

'But,' Eliza continued quickly, 'this is a family matter. It is not about state secrets – although sometimes, with our family, I'm not quite sure where one ends and the other begins. People could still get hurt – or worse. Even Dimity doesn't know many of the things I have just told you.'

'I won't breathe a word.'

'I wouldn't have told you unless I felt sure about you. Now, my dear, you must have dozens of questions about the family and this house still to ask. Where do you want to start?'

'Above the front door, I think. Your family name, Arrow... I take it that has something to do with the splayed arrows on the coat of arms?'

'Yes, it does. But not for much longer, I fear.'

'Why so?'

'Well, my age for one thing, of course, but also because I am the final Arrow – the last in the quiver as we sometimes call the family. The direct family line finishes with me. Unless...'

'Unless what?'

'Just unless. I must also find what I'm looking for.'

'And what are you looking for?'

'That's the problem. Within the family, there are all sorts of stories. I am sure there's a lot of nonsense, but it's often the case that there's no smoke without fire. And my family isn't given to flights of fancy. Facts are critical to us, as I think you can imagine. But I'm afraid that as far as Witch's is concerned, I don't know fact from fiction.'

'What sorts of stories are there?'

'Oh dozens, but one – the most important at the moment – is that this house came to the family for services rendered by a person or persons unknown. Over the years, the family has accepted this as fact, but we have never discovered if there is any truth to it.'

'But it's something you now need to establish?'

Eliza nodded and held up a letter. 'Yes. This tells me that the Church of England is claiming ownership of Witch's and within months could pursue their claim through the courts unless I accept the Church's superior title. I don't know anything about these things.'

'Is there nothing at all that ties your family to the property?'

Eliza shook her head. 'Nothing other than our physical possession.'

'So, what do you want to happen now?'

'I want to listen to the stories and the gossip again, but this time through a fresh pair of ears. I aim to establish if we can find anything at all behind these legends. I need to know, and I need to know soon.'

'So, what do you have?'

'The script around this room and, more recently, the sonnet found in the family Bible.'

'That's all?'

'I'm afraid so.'

'It's not much to go on.'

'No. Otherwise, all I have are stories told to me in childhood. My favourites were about knights and ladies. One story Papa used to tell me, which I loved, was about the Black Prince and two great jewels. He explained that his father had told him the story after hearing it from his own.'

Had Felix not come to understand Eliza a little and believed her to be in full control of her faculties, he might have put this recollection down to a senior moment or the ramblings of an old person. But as things stood, although he didn't know where this bedtime story was going, he believed her when she said this was family history, passed down the generations.

'To start the story, we will need an atlas, as this was how my papa told the tale.' Eliza pointed to a large book on a side table. 'So, first find me Asia.'

Felix located the appropriate pages, handed the opened atlas to Eliza and sat close enough to catch the scent of Lily of the Valley.

'Do you know about the Black Prince's ruby?' Eliza asked.

'Only that it's set into the British crown, the one used for state openings of Parliament.'

'Quite right. But originally it was part of an even larger gem, found in the ruby mines of Central Asia.' Eliza stabbed her finger at Tajikistan. 'The giant stone had just one flaw, so it was split in two. Over the centuries, the two halves were won and lost through love, marriage and war many times over. For a time, they were owned by Genghis Khan. The stones then travelled from Samarkand out of Asia and into Europe along the Silk Road.' Eliza slowly traced the long journey on the map. 'Now find a map of Europe.'

Felix went to the appropriate pages. He was enjoying the tale and could imagine a small Eliza sitting enthralled as her father described the route.

'Well now, the story goes that the stones next appeared in Spain in the fourteenth century. A nasty piece of work called Pedro the Cruel seized them and other riches towards the end of the Moorish era. But then Pedro fled for his life from his even more bloodthirsty brother, Henry. Pedro made his way to Bordeaux, where the Black Prince, the son of our Edward III, kept court. Pedro promised the Black Prince untold treasures in return for helping him.'

'Which he did, I take it?'

Eliza nodded. 'When Henry was finally defeated in battle by the Black Prince, the two stones and many other priceless jewels passed as payment to him. Forty-eight years later, at the battle of Agincourt, Henry V wore one of the rubies in his crown. But its fabled companion, which had become known as the Bloody Star, wasn't with it.'

'Why was it called the Bloody Star? Because of all the bloodshed associated with it?'

Eliza laughed. 'That's what I asked Papa once, but he

told me there might been another reason. Some rubies are cut while others are smooth – these ones are the most valuable. Occasionally, you can see a twelve-point star on their surface, which ups their price. Even scarcer is a double-star ruby, when the star is visible from both sides of the gem. The story goes that this second ruby had a double star, possibly making it even more valuable than the Black Prince's one. Imagine that, more precious than the most valuable known gem in the world. Perhaps that's why it wasn't set into Henry V's crown along with its partner; no one wanted to risk losing it.'

'So, what happened to the Bloody Star?'

'Both rubies passed through the hands of successive English monarchs, including Henry VIII, and then to his daughter, Elizabeth, who kept them in her private collection. But there the trail goes cold.'

'What, the ruby disappeared?'

'Yes. It disappeared from view and also from the records. The strange thing is there was also no record of a hue and cry about its whereabouts. This is strange, because by then the legend was established that the two stones should never be separated, or some great misfortune would befall England. Rather like the ravens leaving the Tower of London.'

'So, how does the story end?' Felix asked.

'It doesn't. That's the point. There is no end. You must make up your own. Anyway, that's what Papa told me.'

'So, what ending did the young Eliza come up with?

'One about being the one to reunite the two stones and becoming a heroine.' Eliza laughed. 'I used to go to sleep thinking about it. But Papa always told me the story with an atlas on one knee and a history book on the other. Now I realise he was teaching me as much about geography and history as anything else. But there should be a happy ending to the story because, without one, the lost ruby would be as much in the dark now as it was for all those years before it arrived in Spain, and that's not a good ending, is it?'

'No, it isn't.'

Eliza paused before suddenly saying, 'Now that's enough of all that nonsense, it's not getting us anywhere. You must think I'm batty. What isn't batty is that I need something that proves, without doubt, that my family owns this house.'

'This may seem an indelicate question, but I have to ask it. If you are the last in the family, then why is proving ownership at this late stage so important?'

Eliza looked indignant. 'Because Witch's belongs to my family, and I don't want to be the one responsible for losing it after all these years. And besides—'

'Besides what?'

'Besides... with my family, one can never be certain.'

'Certain about what?'

'About anything,' Eliza said evasively before quickly changing the subject. 'Now, that's enough of my family for a while. I should love to know some more about you.'

Felix was sure there was plenty Eliza was leaving out. But he left it, and told her instead about his early life and student days. Now and then, Eliza would ask a question that launched Felix into another part of his life. Dimity had warned Felix that Eliza's questioning was a friendly but skilled interrogation. And so it was. But Felix didn't mind – so artful and conversational was Eliza's questioning.

It was late afternoon when West came into the room and announced that a visitor had arrived.

'Good, my other dinner guest,' Eliza said.

Felix could only laugh when Dimity entered the room.

Eliza clapped her hands with delight as she saw the look on Felix's face.

'You two have cooked all this up nicely I see. A real witch's brew.'

'Double, double, toil and trouble,' said Dimity.

'Fire burn and cauldron bubble,' continued Eliza.

'I thought you said you weren't coming today,' Felix said to Dimity.

'Not today, but I didn't say anything about the evening or night,' she replied with a warm smile.

Dimity was carrying a battered and well-travelled leather holdall. The more Felix studied it, the more it resembled the one he used to have years ago.

'Is that my bag?' he demanded.

'Oh, now you come to mention it, I do think it might be,' Dimity said in feigned embarrassment. 'I must have borrowed it from you once and never given it back. How forgetful of me.'

'You could have asked,' Felix said indignantly.

'I didn't think you'd mind. Would you like it back now?'

'No, you can keep it. After I lost that one, or rather, had it stolen, I bought a bigger and better one.'

'You two!' Eliza laughed.

'Did you have a nice day with Ludovic?' Felix asked, with a feeling he didn't want to put a name to.

'I did; it was lovely, so festive,' Dimity replied enthusiastically. Then, turning to Eliza, she added, 'Shall I put this booty upstairs?' She gestured towards the bag.

Felix realised then that this wasn't the first time Dimity had stayed at Witch's. Eliza smiled and nodded, and Dimity trotted upstairs.

Eliza turned to Felix with a big smile.

'Fancy never thinking to mention that you had invited another guest for dinner – especially that one. I think you are a little wicked,' Felix said.

'So I've often been told. Remember my name, La Bruixa? But, on this occasion, acceptable witchcraft, I hope?'

'I suppose so.'

Eliza chuckled.

'But what's going on with this Ludovic character?' Felix asked.

'I'm not at all sure, but I know the two of them have been stepping out together for a while.'

Eliza was prevented from saying anything further on the subject by Dimity coming back down the stairs.

'Time for whisky sours,' Eliza announced, reaching for the service button once again.

After cocktails, it was time for dinner. Eliza insisted that West, Cairo and Frankie, who had arrived back from her day off, join them. They were, as Eliza put it, her 'family'. Frankie was a petite young woman with an elfin haircut. Felix judged her to be in her late twenties. She wore blue jeans, a coral sweatshirt and loafers and seemed at home in the company of people much older than her.

After a wonderful lamb tagine prepared by Cairo, several hours of conversation and laughter followed. West had decanted what Eliza referred to as four 'decent' bottles of wine from the cellar.

'I was twelve when this wine was produced,' she commented, gently swirling the contents of her glass. 'If I remember correctly, I was with Mama and Papa in Rome that summer. It was a good year for wine – and for me. I have so few dinner guests these days that it's nice to have the chance to taste such good memories, even if they were watered down when I first drank them.'

For a while, everyone shared personal stories and anecdotes. Felix was fascinated. West had been a troop leader in the Special Boat Service. His last engagement was in Afghanistan, where he was involved in an attack on a cave complex and had been badly injured in the gunfight.

Felix learnt that after university, Frankie had joined Queen Alexandra's Royal Army Nursing Corps. She saw plenty of military action overseas until she disobeyed a direct order from a senior officer. In doing so, she saved a man's life, but she had still ignored a command. To avoid a court martial and embarrassment all round, the affair was hushed up and she quietly transferred to a service that was glad of her talents and more supportive of personnel who thought for themselves. When Frankie eventually returned to the UK, Witch's gave her the rest and change she needed.

'Out of interest, what happened to the man you saved?' Felix asked.

Frankie smiled and looked to the other side of the table.

'His name was West,' said Eliza's handyman.

Felix looked from one to the other in blank amazement.

Cairo's story was even more intriguing. After being abandoned by her parents, she grew up feral, living off her wits on the streets of an Egyptian slum.

'She was as cunning, resourceful and vicious as a sewer rat,' chimed in West proudly.

'I was fortunate to be kidnapped by modern slavers,' said Cairo.

'How was that fortunate?' Felix asked.

'I was brought to London and set to do housework in the home of a large family living in Knightsbridge. I enjoyed the work. It was a big step up from where I had been. Later, no doubt, I would have been old enough for other duties. I bided my time and secretly learned English. Then I escaped. I was twelve and only got as far as Harrods. A nice man in a green uniform stopped me and asked me what I was doing. I thought he was a policeman, so I told him. That was my second piece of good luck. The man, a doorman it turned out, was a retired police officer. Social services became involved, and they found a home and school for me. My foster parents were kind and supportive and I came to love them. I worked hard and finally went to university, where I was recruited by MI6 for my fluency in English, Arabic, Pashto and Farsi. I was trained as a field operative. West and I met in Helmand Province. But all I ever wanted was to live in a nice house and cook. So now I do.'

'Now she's a momma bear,' said West.

'What do you mean?' Felix asked.

West looked at Cairo. 'If anyone were to threaten her family – her Witch's family – it wouldn't be pretty.'

'After all these stories, I feel a bit lame,' Felix said. 'I haven't any such tales of derring-do. But you must have loads, Mitten. What about K2, your last climb?'

Dimity looked sharply at Felix. At first, he felt ashamed he had asked, and was certain that Dimity would refuse to open up. But then she said quietly, 'It was an American-led and sponsored expedition. I wasn't a lead climber or anything... I was just there to support the summit teams. All I wanted was to gain some experience and brownie points for another expedition down the line. That's how it goes. But the weather had been good, and against the odds, the six principal climbers made the summit ahead of schedule. Another support climber and I were at the top camp – Camp

4. We had an unexpected 24-hour window to make the summit. After that, we were under orders to retreat to the base camp at the foot of the mountain.

'Roped together, we were on the Abruzzi Spur. We had climbed up an extremely scary 300-foot chimney of snow and ice just 1,500 feet from the summit. We were traversing the steep ice field above the chimney when it happened. I can't explain. It was so quick. One moment I was on my feet, the next I was being swept away over a cliff edge.'

'Blimey,' West said.

'There was nothing I could do. I thought it was the end. Talk about your life flashing before your eyes. I must have dropped over a hundred feet or so, but then, abruptly, I came to a painful stop when the rope and my harness held me. My partner might have been able to arrest the fall, or the rope caught around something. I didn't know. I will never know. I hung in space for a while, trying to figure out what to do. I shouted up, but there was no reply. I was looking at the rock wall thinking it would be impossible for me to climb up unaided when I suddenly dropped again. But instead of plunging thousands of feet down the mountain to my death, I only fell a short way onto a narrow, snow-covered ledge. A huge length of rope from above fell on top of me. Somehow, it had become detached from my partner.

'I was winded and probably concussed, but at least I was alive. The trouble was, without oxygen and alone at that altitude, I knew I wouldn't survive for long. Over a quarter of climbers attempting K2 without oxygen die. I can tell you that I did a lot of praying that I was not going to become one of them.'

'Did you break anything?' Frankie asked.

'I checked myself over and seemed to be OK. I was lucky

that the snow on the ledge was deep and fresh. So, I began to look about me and take stock. By then, the visibility was poor. But I could see that the ledge continued into the cloud. Then I saw – or, at least, I thought I saw, something or somebody along the ledge.'

Felix felt goose pimples. 'Who or what was it?'

'I wasn't sure. It looked like the outline of a man.'

'Ooh, that's spooky.' Frankie said.

'It was a bit spooky. It's hard to explain. But it seemed OK somehow. I shouted, but there was no reply. At first, whoever it was appeared to be looking my way, before seeming to beckon to me. I was in shock, of course. I didn't know if I had imagined it or not. Perhaps I was hallucinating. I knew there were no Sherpas up at that altitude, and it seemed impossible that my climbing partner could have got down to that position. So, who or what it was I wasn't sure.'

'I've heard of things like that happening before, especially to lost potholers,' said West. 'So, what did you do?'

'Well, I didn't wait around to think about it. I coiled the rope that had fallen on me and hitched it to my rucksack in case I needed it for the descent. Then I began to inch along the narrow ledge towards the figure. It seemed the only rational thing to do. It took me ages. It must have been a few hundred feet. When I finally reached the spot where I thought the figure had been, all that was there was a spur of rock. But whatever I had seen – or thought I'd seen – saved my life because I found myself at the top of the Bottleneck. I caught sight of the fixed rope we had used to ascend the chimney hours earlier. So, that was the rope I used for my descent.'

'From near the top of K2, alone?' West asked with a deep note of respect.

'Yes. I was in survival mode. By the time I reached Camp 4, it was dark and everyone else had moved lower down the mountain. But at least I could radio that I was alive.

'It was only then, wrapped up in a sleeping bag and waiting for daylight, that I thought about my fall. I still had the rope, so I found the end and saw that it was cut.

'Severed by a sharp rock?' Felix asked

'No, the cut was too clean for that. It could only have been cut by a blade.'

'But the last thing you would do on a mountain is cut a rope between climbers,' West said.

'In which case, why?' Felix asked.

Dimity shook her head. 'I don't know. Perhaps to give me a one-in-a-million chance of survival, or to put me out of my misery.'

Felix was appalled. 'What happened when you eventually saw this climbing partner of yours?'

'Bet that was an interesting meeting,' West said dryly.

'But that's the thing, I didn't see him,' said Dimity. 'I never saw him again. A year later, he was found by another expedition frozen to death in the snow. Those who found him thought he had made it down part of the way, but then perhaps he became lost through poor visibility, or he succumbed to fatigue and sat down to die.'

'Or perhaps he knew that he wouldn't be able to live with himself if he ever got off the mountain,' Felix said. 'Either way, it doesn't make his decision to cut the rope sound too good.'

'No, I'm afraid it doesn't.'

'So, who was your climbing partner? Did you know him well?' Cairo asked.

'That's the thing, I did know him well... I knew him very well indeed. It was Michael.'

'Michael who?' Eliza asked.

'Michael, my husband.'

For a moment, Felix was speechless. 'Your husband did that?'

'It seems so,' Dimity said bleakly.

'But I never saw anything in the newspapers or on the news. Wasn't there a big hoo-ha about it when people discovered what had happened?'

'No, there wasn't. Because I have never told anyone – until now.'

'Why on earth not?' Felix pressed.

'What good would it have done?' West scoffed. 'Dimity was alive, and her husband was dead. At 27,000 feet, the choices climbers make are almost lawless and are often the difference between life and death. Perhaps Michael paid for his choice with his life. But you didn't, Dimity.'

'You're right, of course. Nothing I said after would have brought Michael back or improved the situation. It would have only made matters worse and would have hurt his innocent family more.'

'As a matter of interest, what did you do with that rope?' West asked.

'I threw it away. But I kept a few inches of the severed end to remind me about fortune and forgiveness.'

'I understand you didn't want to hurt anyone else, Mitten, but I'm afraid I wouldn't have been so forgiving,' Felix said, remembering the length of rope on Dimity's side table.

'Something for you to work on then,' replied Dimity with a pointedly priestly smile.

‘If it wasn’t Michael or a Sherpa who beckoned you along the ledge, who on earth was it?’ Frankie asked.

‘Or who in Heaven was it? I don’t know. But my prayers were answered. Was I hallucinating? Was it a ghost? Was it the Holy Ghost? I don’t know. And before anyone says it, no I don’t think it was a yeti beckoning me.’

Everyone laughed.

‘I like the yeti theory much more than your alternatives,’ Felix said.

‘So, that was the spiritual moment that triggered your vocation,’ Eliza guessed.

‘Yes, I suppose it was,’ Dimity replied. ‘It was certainly my rebirth. All those flashing images before my eyes as I fell showed me someone that could do better. I decided that I wanted to help people live rather than watch them die.’

‘And on that poignant note, I think I will retire to bed.’ Eliza said, bringing to a close an evening that Felix would never forget.

CHAPTER SEVEN

The following day, driving rain lashed against Felix's bedroom window. Dimity had left early for services at the Abbey; Felix had heard her car drive off well before seven o'clock. After that, he lay for a while thinking about the previous evening before getting up himself, having a wash and heading downstairs. He was keen to start his survey.

He decided to draw a rough plan of Witch's interior before completing a more detailed layout later. He would then put all the data into the office computer to create an accurate 3D rendition that might show up any hidden nooks and crannies. That way, he hoped nothing would be missed.

When he reached the kitchen, he found West, Cairo and Frankie sitting around the table. Cairo said that after such a long evening, she would be taking a breakfast tray up to Eliza a little later. Felix spent some more time getting to know Eliza's support team as Cairo went about clearing up the breakfast things. Her last task was to let down the kitchen airer by its pulley rope. She hung from it two damp tea towels before hoisting the thing back up towards the ceiling. It's just like the one from my childhood home, Felix thought fondly, but receiving a jolt of sadness at the same time.

After fresh coffee and a warm, homemade croissant, Felix started his rough plan. He had just about finished his drawing when Eliza appeared. She was looking bright and ready for the day in an elegant blue dress that suited her slim figure. She had tied a silk scarf around her neck in a neat knot. She looked rather chic, and Felix told her so. She was still tall and, although stooped, held herself as straight as she could – the habit of a lifetime, Felix imagined.

'I thought you might find this useful,' Eliza said, handing Felix a sheaf of typewritten pages on foolscap paper bound by a faded red ribbon. 'My papa wrote this before he died. It's an account of the house in our family's history and some details about the family, especially over the past three or four generations.'

Felix flipped through the pages and soon understood how valuable the document would be to him. 'This is excellent,' he said. 'I will study it before doing anything else.'

He settled down in the salon with the account and learned all about Eliza's father, who was a diplomat. Next, he went back over the lives of several more of Eliza's forebears. All of them had had something to do with the government, especially trading with other nations or colonies, in anything from tea to opium.

There was not so much information – recorded or orally passed down – of the preceding generations.

Eliza emerged from the kitchen. 'How are you getting on?' she asked.

'It's a great account and will be a wonderful reference,'

Felix replied. 'But, sadly, there's not much family detail before the eighteenth century.'

'You should remember that these people's lives often depended on great discretion and secrecy: they grew up and operated in an often-dangerous world. Just one word out of place could mean death. I'm afraid any researcher or biographer would come up pretty empty-handed. There are very few records, other than what's here in the house – and what the government might have. As far as I know, nothing else has ever come to light. My family seems to have operated mainly at arm's length – with a cut out, as we say in the trade, so there could be nothing traced back by the wrong people. We did everything we could to protect our identities and to avoid any political repercussions, but I've always thought there may be some clues in the acquisitions made over the years. At least they indicate where my forebears lived or visited.

'For instance, one of my ancestors was a messenger for Charles I to the court of Philip the Pious. It was he who acquired some of the Spanish paintings you see dotted about. Another ancestor was an English emissary to a later Spanish court. He picked up the Goya during the Napoleonic war. During the Anglo-Dutch Wars, Edward Arrow collected the Dutch pictures, although I've always thought it a pity he missed out on getting his hands on a Rembrandt when he might have had the chance. In fact, I'm curious why he didn't.

'But all these pictures are like fine wines. When they were acquired soon after their creation, they had relatively little value and were sometimes thought to be nothing exceptional. The works of the Impressionists were, early on, often just misunderstood daubs. I don't need to tell you that great value tends to grow over time through the true creativity of the work, scarcity and the gathering appreciation of critics, dealers and collectors. When our pictures were acquired, they were just nice things to hang on the walls here at Witch's. What has made these paintings so valuable, besides the originality and exquisite quality, is time. And if this family has had anything, it is time – plus a growing talent to appreciate lovely things when it sees them and a reluctance to let them go.'

'Is the large painting in the hall of a horse and groom a Stubbs?' Felix asked.

'George Stubbs? Yes, it is. A rare British painting in the collection. But I think that arrived here through our association with Abbotsleigh Park rather than anything else.'

'Abbotsleigh Park is mentioned in your father's account. He says that Stubbs used to go there and use the horses as models.'

'That's right, but I'm not sure how or why we have our Stubbs. That picture is one of my favourites. I have always loved horses. When I was a great deal younger, I used to ride, well, hunt.'

Felix could imagine Eliza as a young hunt thruster, riding side saddle in a long black coat and a top hat with a veil. He pictured her leading the charge over the highest hedges and deepest ditches in the county.

'How many other families are there like yours, do you think, Eliza?'

'I think ours is the only one. I would be surprised if there were another, or I'm sure I would know about it. Of course, a career in spying was not so remarkable several hundred years ago. For instance, there were many Elizabethan spies. It's just that the Arrow family seems, uniquely, to have made spying a family occupation, passing on contacts, know-how and tradecraft to successive generations.'

'Your father mentions in his account that he believes there is evidence somewhere for your ownership of the house, but none has ever been found.'

'That's correct. We have plenty of provenance for the art and other valuable contents; that's not an issue. It is the house that provides the problem. And right now, this has been brought to a head on two fronts.'

'Two?'

'Yes. You know about the Church but there is also my second cousin, Edward, who is the son of my first cousin, Montacute. Montacute was roughly the same age as me but had a chequered history, including some black marketeering during the last war. He avoided active service and lived in a funk hole somewhere in deepest Shropshire. After the war, he bought up army surplus lorries and built a transport business called Arrow Straight – that's a joke, he was as bent as anything.

'Montacute died over twenty years ago. I freely admit that dodgy dealings are in the Arrow blood. Mostly they are state-sponsored dodgy dealings, which seems to make them OK, or at least seem that way to my family, but Montacute's were decidedly not OK.'

'So, where does Edward fit in?'

'Edward took over the haulage business and is every bit as clever and Faustian as his father was. Edward says the business is now legitimate. But I know otherwise.'

'How do you know?'

'How do you think? I'm a spy, Felix,' Eliza answered dryly. 'How Edward has stayed out of jail, or even kept off someone's assassination list, here or elsewhere around the world, I'll never know. But whatever he is doing, I suspect that he works behind a curtain of offshore shell companies. Sadly, nobody has yet been able to link him with anything illegal. And this is the man in line to inherit Witch's. He is desperate to get his hands on it and to bring it into his side of the family. I would say, "not over my dead body". But, of course, it probably will be. Unfortunately, Edward seems so obsessed by owning Witch's that he will do pretty much anything to get it.'

'He wouldn't stoop to...?'

'Eliza laughed. 'Doing me in? No, I don't think so. But then he doesn't have to. All he has to do is leak information on me and the family. That could do untold damage. But, funnily enough, I'm not so worried about Edward at the moment: I have a feeling he is a problem that can be made to go away. It's the Church that most concerns me. It is claiming a superior right to our family over Witch's. Don't ask me how; I don't understand the first thing about these things.'

'But how on earth has the Church become involved at his stage? It's had hundreds of years to address this. Why now?'

'I have an inkling – I won't say what at present. But whoever is behind this, the Church, as a body, is now involved. For whatever reason, they seem determined to show that this estate was not confiscated from them.'

'When did this interest from the Church begin?'

'About a year ago.'

'And now time is of the essence?'

'Time and a bit of luck, I suspect. But I still think there is something we've missed – like the sonnet in our Bible. It took hundreds of years to discover that, when it was right under our noses all along. And then it was only found by accident.'

Felix noticed how Eliza suddenly seemed deflated and not so confident or defiant. He put her thoughts down to wishful thinking – the last roll of the dice by a desperate woman whose time was running out.

'Perhaps there is no answer,' he said quietly.

'There must be, and while there is breath in my body, I will never stop trying to find it.'

Felix was learning to admire Eliza's resolve. 'So, let's dig a little deeper into history,' he said. 'What happened to the family after the Reformation?'

Eliza led Felix through what she knew of the family up to the period of Oliver Cromwell and the Commonwealth and then the reigns of Charles II and James II.

'How do you know all this?'

Eliza smiled. 'The Arrow family and English history are intertwined.'

'I'm beginning to get that. But what I don't understand is that even if you do prove your ownership of Witch's, where does it get you? What happens to the house after you've gone?'

'That is my other problem. I'm stuck between the Devil and the deep blue sea. On one side I have the Church, and on the other I have Edward.'

'But if Edward is such a bad lot, wouldn't letting Witch's go to the Church, or perhaps the National Trust, be a better alternative? At least one can say that each is the lesser of two evils.'

'On the face of it, you're right. But as far as the Church is concerned, I'm not so sure that the motives behind the interest are as pure as they should be. It's nothing I can put my finger on, just a feeling that's nagging me. I wouldn't want to see Witch's go to someone with his or her own private agenda. If I don't give in and bequeath Witch's to the Church, it seems it is prepared to take it from me anyway. That feels like blackmail to me, and I don't succumb to blackmail – as several know, to their own cost.'

'What about Dimity? Does she know any of this – being involved with the Church as she is?'

'Only a little. I don't have any proof. But I sense she feels uncomfortable about it; I know I would. Do you see my dilemma?'

Before Felix could answer, Eliza looked at her watch. 'It will be lunchtime soon. We usually all eat together in the kitchen – normally soup and fresh bread, both made by Cairo.'

'Have we time for a couple of questions while I think of them?' Felix asked.

'We have a few minutes.'

'What can you tell me about Abbotsleigh Park?'

'It was a stately home about twenty miles away from here. Like Witch's, it was Tudor – although there was probably something else there long before that. The Earls of Rounton owned it – the Chasolct family. The first Earl was in the privy council of Elizabeth I, so a significant and powerful man. That family seems to have had links to ours. I'm not sure how, but one thing I do feel confident about is that they were not our enemies. The house in the background of the George Stubbs painting in the hall is said to be Abbotsleigh Park.

'I've often wondered if we Arrows, given our occupational history, worked for or through the Chasolets in some capacity; my father certainly thought so. Anyway, the

Earls of Rounton lost their influence and wealth over time, and finally, in 1927, the house at Abbotsleigh Park was torn down. The remnants of the family emigrated to Australia, where they set up and ran a small hardware shop on the outskirts of Melbourne. They still have it as far as I know. I heard that the current Earl of Rounton keeps his ermine cloak and gold coronet in a cardboard box under his bed.' Eliza laughed before adding, 'How the mighty have fallen.

'Papa told me once that I visited Abbotsleigh Park when I was very young, although I can't remember the occasion, and it's on record that Elizabeth I stayed there, and Queen Victoria. Apparently, in the 1910s, it was a favourite place for the aristocracy to visit socially. It was a substantial house and had some outstanding pictures and pieces of furniture. The contents were sold off at auction, no doubt to pay off large debts. I have an old copy of *Country Life* that features sepia pictures of the old house and interior. After it was demolished, a housing estate was built on some of the grounds. But the park, which Humphry Repton had a hand in laying out, is still there. The local council bought about two hundred acres. It's now a public amenity. I'm afraid it is the story of many big houses after the First World War.

'But listen to me, Felix, prattling on. I'm telling you things you will know only too well in your line of business. Tell me, what do you think we should do now?'

'What I need to do is finish my rough plan and then turn it into a 3D rendering. I'm basically doing what the old priest finders did in the 15th century – looking for discrepancies in their measurements – for areas where there may be a hidden room or space capable of concealing something – or someone. But in the case of the priest finders, if they found something suspicious, they would rip the place apart.'

‘Take everything apart here if you think it will do any good,’ Eliza said.

‘I hope we won’t have to be that drastic. Instead, I’ll need to do that on the office computer. But only when I have entered all the data can I be confident that I haven’t missed anything structural. What I’m looking for are suspect spaces – areas that don’t appear to the eye but show up in a digital structural plan. But I have to say, if no one has ever found anything at Witch’s over all these years of searching, then there is either nothing to find, or it is extremely well hidden. Also, I would like to visit Abbotsleigh Park. I know it won’t shine any direct light on the Witch’s mystery, but it may give me some context and room to think. The same goes for the grace-and-favour apartment in St James’s Palace, if that’s possible?’

‘Of course,’ said Eliza, ‘let me know when you want to visit the Palace and I’ll make the necessary arrangements.’

CHAPTER EIGHT

Felix spent the rest of the day, and well into the next, inputting measurement data onto his laptop and then sitting down to refresh his knowledge of ancient property rights' case law.

After lunch, he sat again with Eliza in the salon. 'I've been considering your position in all this,' he said to her. 'We need to play for time.'

'What do you mean?'

He waved the letter Eliza had received from the Church of England's solicitors. 'These people will need a response before long, or they will start to get testy. You don't want them testy, Eliza. You need them believing you are dancing to their tune. It would be good to respond within a week, two at the most. Your solicitors should send a reply – second-class post, which will suggest their claim is not being ignored. The letter should state the claim seems very sudden after hundreds of years and is, on the face of it, an unusual and complicated matter, which, of course, it is. Your solicitors should tell the Church we need to make lengthy and detailed enquiries and will get back to them in due course. That should win some more time. Nowadays, lawyers have to work to a set of pre-action protocols. I won't bore you with the details, but it's to clarify matters on both sides. If, after that, there is still a dispute, then the matter could move to a hearing in the High Court.'

'And how long will that all take?'

Felix waggled his hand, 'About a year, give or take – if there is a case to be heard. But if there's no evidence to support the counterclaim, it could be over a great deal sooner.'

'What do you think about the case?'

'On the face of it, this is a tricky issue. Some of those Church lawyers are very clever. I have crossed swords with several of them over the years. There are some very sharp minds in their legal department. Plus, they all think they have a strong and natural ally.'

'Who's that?

'Why, God, of course. With Him on their side, they think they are invincible. You know they used to say that the Church of England was the Conservative Party at prayer?' Eliza nodded. 'Well, the Church of England is also a certain part of the legal establishment at prayer.

'But getting back to your question, this is all a matter of title. It is about who can make the most substantial claim to it. In Roman law, it was straightforward: it allowed anyone in possession of the land, but not necessarily with possession of the absolute title, to become the lawful owner if the original owner was absent for several years. This was only if the property hadn't been taken by force or trickery.

'It's said that possession is nine-tenths of the law: well, in English law, possession forms the basis of title. It gives the possessor all the rights – except to someone who can demonstrate a stronger right to that possession. So maybe you do have a right to the title, Eliza, but the Church may feel it has a superior one. This claim alone might not help it, however, as it took no steps to recover the land for so long. That could count against it. But with the law, there is always uncertainty – there is always a question.

'Unfortunately, good title can't easily be proven, however long the period of possession. The original owner might have been under some sort of disability or duress at the time of the dispossession. Or the real owner might have been the Crown, which, at the time this property seems to have changed hands, trumps everything.'

Eliza held up her hand. 'It seems very confusing.'

'Ah, but that is exactly the point. It may not be what the law is about, but confusion and obfuscation are weapons in the practice of law. Lawyers want to make it as difficult as possible so that no one will come and spoil their party. They want to make the law so impenetrable that if an adversary is intellectually weaker, less well trained or is ill-prepared, then the brighter, more thoroughly trained and better prepared lawyer will prevail. The law is such a sharp instrument, but the practice of the law is often a blunt one. It's theatre. It's like two wizards casting spells at each other, each spell more powerful than the last. Until – POW! – the weaker wizard goes up in a puff of smoke. It's not ideal, but it is the system we've had since the Middle Ages, and it's the only one we've got.'

'So, apart from my running up the white flag, what are my other options?'

'We could dispute the Church's claim and try and prove your right to the absolute title.'

'We can fight?'

'We certainly can, but there lie two other huge hurdles, quite beside the law. As you said, this is a complicated matter. You might well win, but it could take years to argue through the courts. Even if you won the initial round in the High Court, it could go to the Court of Appeal, and later, to the highest court in the land, the Supreme Court. With the best will in the world, the appeals process would, given your age, and to put it bluntly, take much longer than you are likely to have.'

'You're saying I wouldn't live long enough to see this grind through the courts and know the outcome?'

'No, you wouldn't, and the Church knows that. Conversely, the Church has got as long as it takes. Witch's Lawn isn't going anywhere. The Church has been sitting on this for six hundred years already. Another six months, six years or even sixty years are neither here nor there to it. Throughout the case, the costs to you would mount up to somewhere between astronomical and impossibly astronomical. But it wouldn't be nearly as expensive for the Church of England, as it has in-house lawyers. I'm afraid to say, Eliza, and before you mention it, if you wanted me to fight this case, it's way beyond my comparatively meagre resources. I would have to bring in some big and costly guns. You see, if the Church's lawyers can't go for a straight knockout punch with the law, they will bring in another powerful law firm to help them win the case on points – and that firm will do it pro bono.'

'What firm is that?'

'It's a very old-established and successful firm called time and money, and they will often get you before the law ever will. They all too often do. Leo Tolstoy once said that the two most powerful warriors are patience and time. Well, in law, those powerful warriors are often money and time.'

'How does the man in the street ever afford to take up a legal case?'

'I'm afraid that often he doesn't because often he can't. It is as simple as that. The law can be a rich person's instrument at times – most times. It's elitist: it shouldn't be, but it is.'

'So, what's your third option?'

'Oh, that's simple. It's to find something beyond a shadow of doubt that proves you have a superior title to the claimant.'

'And how on earth do we do that?'

'I have absolutely no idea, Eliza. No idea at all. We will have to find some documentation sitting in a dusty and long-forgotten archive – if it exists. But without a deed or similar to prove your title then you have a difficult road ahead. The problem is that whoever is pulling these Church strings is probably a bully. That's what lawyers do sometimes, they bully. They will threaten and shout and try to frighten and intimidate you into submission. You will be weak in the face of the law or the Church's superior firepower. In the end, you will give up. You will have to. You should know that. All the Church has to do is apply the right pressure and you will be putty in its hands. But produce some real evidence and then it's a very different story. Then I can help you. Without it, your only course of action, in my view, is to give in gracefully and save some pride and a lot of money.'

'Gosh, that is a bleak outlook. It's not even fair.'

'I know it isn't, and I don't like to sound defeatist, but that's the way of it. You have to be pragmatic.'

'I suppose I do. And even if we did beat off the Church, there is still Edward.'

Felix nodded his understanding and then laughed.

'What's so funny?'

'Just an idle thought. What if there is someone or something else with an even greater claim to the property than the Church?'

'Who could that be?'

'The Crown. Wouldn't it be ironic if the Church were to win the house and land, only to lose it to the Crown, who could show an even greater superior title? It would be like a mackerel eating a sprat, only to be gobbled up by a shark. It would be as if Henry VIII had returned from the grave for one final pop at the Church. That's why I love the law. It's so full of twists and turns, plots and sub-plots, and payback.'

'But isn't a title a title?

'No, Eliza, it isn't. Let me illustrate. A lawyer in New Orleans, Louisiana, was asked by a difficult mortgage company to prove, all the way back to its origin, the title for a piece of land being offered as collateral. So, first, the lawyer proved the title back to 1803 when the United States purchased Louisiana from France. Then he pointed out that the French had acquired the land by Right of Conquest from Spain, who had obtained it by Right of Discovery through a certain sea captain named Christopher Columbus. It seems that Columbus had been granted the privilege of seeking new sea routes by the Spanish monarch, Queen Isabelle. The queen had sensibly secured the blessing of the Pope, the emissary of Jesus Christ, the Son of God. Therefore, the lawyer claimed he had proved the original title holder to be God and hoped this would be enough for the mortgage company.'

Eliza laughed. 'The point being there can sometimes be someone with a stronger claim to a title?'

Felix smiled and nodded in the knowledge that despite the odds, and for a reason he couldn't quite pinpoint, he felt drawn to trying to do all he could to help Eliza before it was too late. Time, however, was not on Eliza's side. It wasn't on the side of anyone closely connected to Witch's Lawn and its current owner.

'Well, it sounds like Hobson's choice,' said Eliza. 'We had better find something at Witch's to help us because, from where I'm sitting, the alternatives aren't sounding very attractive.'

CHAPTER NINE

It was time for Felix to investigate Eliza's London flat. He had invited Dimity to join him, and he met her outside the Criterion Restaurant at Piccadilly Circus. The weather wasn't as cold as it had been, and rays of misty sunshine cheered the day.

The pair headed west along Piccadilly before cutting down the side of Fortnum & Mason to Jermyn Street.

'This is exciting,' Dimity said as they reached St James's Street. 'Have you been to the Palace before?'

'No, I've never had a royal invite.'

Dimity laughed. 'I've been to the Chapel Royal on several occasions. I have a friend who is Priest in Ordinary to the Sovereign.'

Felix rolled his eyes. 'Is there anyone in the Church you don't know?'

Dimity laughed before replying, 'One or two.'

Arriving at the Palace, they passed two sentries wearing bearskins and their winter greatcoats.

Under the guards' gaze, and following Eliza's directions,

they came to a gatehouse with towers to either side of giant wooden double gates. At the bottom of the left-hand tower was a small, low, Tudor, arched oak door with no number or other outward sign of address.

'I think this must be it,' said Felix, reaching into his pocket for the key and pushing it into the lock.

'Hurry up,' said Dimity. 'I keep thinking that those two sentries will challenge us at any moment.'

With a little persuasion, Felix managed to turn the key. When he looked over at his companion, he could see that far from looking worried, she was thoroughly enjoying the moment. 'I think they must know we are coming, he said, 'or they would either be shooting at us or, at the very least, shouting, "Halt, who goes there?"'

He turned a large iron handle and opened the door. 'Just think who must have let themselves in and out of this door over the centuries.'

'Why are you whispering?' asked Dimity.

'I have absolutely no idea,' replied Felix. He couldn't help laughing at the absurdity of it all.

A narrow, steep spiral of well-worn stone steps accompanied by an iron handrail led upwards. At the top of that flight was another arch that opened onto one end of a vaulted corridor that ran above the palace gates. The two small windows barely provided enough light to see clearly. Felix looked out and up the length of a very Christmassy-looking St James's Street. The thoroughfare, Felix could see, gently climbed to its junction with Piccadilly, where he watched taxis and buses jostling with cars and delivery vehicles. Felix noticed several shops that had been established for almost as long as the Arrows had occupied this little piece of the Palace.

The walls of the gallery were decorated with paintings, which Felix and Dimity took their time admiring. Felix imagined that few people had seen them since they'd left their creators' studios. Eliza had told him that the paintings had never been loaned out to the Royal Academy, or any other national or private galleries. He had fun trying to identify the artists, as there were no handy identifying plaques as there would have been if they were displayed publicly.

In the centre of the gallery's left-hand wall were some arched, oak double doors with a heavily carved architrave that opened to another vaulted space. Felix thought how he would like to recreate this timeless room himself. What looked to him like a French, Savonnerie rug anchored the room, at one end of which was a substantial black marble fireplace with a brass club fender covered in worn and cracked red leather.

Bookending the over-mantel was a tall, white marble obelisk and a cork model of the Temple of Mars. Between them were leather-bound books and a small, gilt-framed icon of a saint. Over the fireplace was a circular convex mirror with a heavy gilt frame.

Facing the fire was a Chesterfield sofa, again in red leather, with a Household Cavalry horse blanket thrown over its back. Behind it was a Regency sofa table, on either side of which were two matching sabre-legged dining chairs with cushioned seats covered in a geometric design needlepoint.

Inside the room, on either side of the fire breast, were more paintings.

'I can't begin to think how valuable these must be,' said Dimity, while carefully studying one of the pictures.

'You know Eliza will never sell any of them,' said Felix. 'She told me she will only keep on acquiring – although I suppose she has slowed down a lot in recent years. In many ways, I think it's a shame that others can't see and enjoy these treasures.'

'What do you think Eliza should do?'

'It's not for me to say. She is ultra-protective of her secrecy. But I would anonymously loan some of them to public galleries, I suppose.'

On the opposite wall to the fireplace was a huge four-poster bed draped with tapestry hangings. Two handsome mahogany circular bedside tables or pot cupboards in the form of fluted columns sat on either side of the ornately carved bed head. In front of the window was a circular library table with a well-worn, green leather top: on it was a magnificent marble bust that looked to Felix as if it was Roman in origin. A scratched and slightly dented military drum with painted but fading regimental regalia and a round glass top served as a side table. Felix imagined that drum beating an advance at Waterloo.

Stirring from his daydream, he studied the room further. All the contents seemed perfectly placed. Whether it had been put together by accident or design, to Felix's eye, it was a masterpiece. Maybe it was accidental, but if so, successive generations had displayed an innate talent and natural confidence in the design.

'This must be the ultimate London pied-à-terre,' he said. 'It's discreet and compact but grand at the same time, and it offers a fabulous sanctuary. If ever a spy needed a comfortable and convenient bolthole then where better than the outer limits of a vast Tudor palace?'

Dimity nodded. 'And if anyone wanted a secure location

to hang priceless paintings, where better than one guarded round the clock by armed sentries?'

'Better still, it is not only close to power but also to those who would seek to support or subvert that power,' added Felix.

Secure, secret and safe as it was, Eliza had warned him that it was also somewhat lacking in amenities. Monarchs may have offered valued subjects some basic accommodation, but their largesse, here at least, didn't extend to luxury.

Halfway along the gallery, Felix and Dimity entered a smaller room: in it was a rough wooden worktop abutting one wall into which was set a small, white earthenware sink with a single tap. Above it was a dated electric water heater. Against another wall, and on four stubby legs, sat a green enamelled gas oven with a grill. The appliance probably left the factory not much later than 1930, thought Felix, as he turned on the gas. There was a rewarding hiss from a burner head.

'Gosh, even *my* kitchen is better than this,' said Dimity. 'I know I'm no cook, but all you could do here is toast some bread, heat soup from a tin, make a cup of tea or pour out something stronger.'

'I suppose anything one wanted to eat or drink, even in centuries past, could have been found locally in the coffee shops and chop houses. Imagine the conversations, arguments, rumours and gossip to be heard around here. I think this would have been the perfect hunting ground for a spy.'

'Do you think there's a loo?'

Felix opened another door along the corridor. 'Here,' he said.

Dimity peered into the small, dark closet and then inspected the lavatory. Wrinkling her nose, she said, 'I think I'll wait.'

It was getting dark outside, and Felix and Dimity returned to the main room. Felix put on the ceiling light and two table lamps. Meanwhile, Dimity found some matches and began lighting the candles dotted around the room. Flame by flame, the room was enriched further until it glowed and danced.

'It's magical!' said Dimity.

Felix admired the furniture in the main room, sometimes stroking solid wood or finely veneered surfaces. He felt doing this put him in closer contact with a piece or a place.

Together, Felix and Dimity investigated all the cupboards and drawers. As they did so, Felix had an uneasy feeling he was trespassing on history. However, Eliza had expressly asked them to carry out a complete search for any papers or records there might be.

There was little to find, save for some women's clothing that must have belonged to Eliza but had long since gone out of fashion.

'I wonder if there is anything in this old thing?' said Dimity, pulling at the lid of a rather nondescript long wooden chest. To Felix, the piece didn't share the quality of the other furniture. 'It seems to be locked, and there is no sign of a key,' Dimity added. Felix made a mental note to ask Eliza about it.

With no more to see or find, the pair turned out the lights and, somewhat reluctantly, blew out the candles and made their way out of the gatehouse, carefully locking the door behind them.

'I had better be getting back,' said Dimity.

'I thought it was your day off. Don't you want to have a bite to eat?'

Dimity pulled a sad face. 'I would love to, Felix, but I have a Chapter meeting at the Abbey tonight – day off or not.'

Felix concluded that this must have something to do with the Reverend Ludovic Poniard.

CHAPTER TEN

Felix had been up and out of his flat early. It was Christmas Day, and he had spent the morning chasing or being chased by his goddaughter, Rosie. After a turkey dinner, he sat in a deep armchair in his friend Santa's drawing room. Rosie had disappeared to play with her Christmas presents.

'That was a wonderful meal, Santa. I can't thank you enough. It's been a long time since I shared a family Christmas.'

'Since your mum and dad?'

'Yes.'

'You still miss them?'

'I do. Despite a slightly odd childhood. I guess I was a bit of a cuckoo in the nest. I was creative and a bit academic while my mum and dad weren't. I don't think they knew what to make of me sometimes.'

'But they loved you.'

'Yes, they did, and I loved them.'

'Which made you a contented and much-loved cuckoo.'

Felix laughed. 'That was all that mattered. Can I get you anything? You look bushed.'

'It's been a long day. Rosie woke at five this morning.'

Felix studied Santa, who had curled her 5ft frame fully into an armchair. She had been a pretty girl at school and was still attractive now. Her shoulder-length hair was ash blonde, and she had retained her youthful figure. Today, she wore tight-cropped jeans, a T-shirt and a checked overshirt. The strain of raising Rosie single-handedly whilst juggling a full-time job was revealed in faint dark circles beneath her eyes. Tragically, her husband had died from a stroke when Rosie was only two. These days, she barely wore any jewellery, including her engagement and wedding rings, though she never took off the eternity ring he'd given her to mark their daughter's birth. Felix reflected how Santa had always been rather studious and hated games at school, but she and Dimity, for a reason he could never quite fathom, got on like a house on fire. Opposites attract, he supposed. Perhaps that was why he and Dimity had got on so well. Felix reflected how life would be wonderfully neat if he was more than fond of Santa and Santa more than fond of him. But that was not how things were, nor had ever been. They had been to the cinema together once in their teens, but it hadn't felt like it ought to somehow, and the experiment was never repeated. But they remained good and close friends, supporting each other through good and bad times.

'Dimity called me,' Santa said.

Felix sensed this was an opening Santa had been waiting to make and so he asked, 'Mending fences?'

'She was trying. Anyway, we had quite a long chat.'

'How broken is the fence?'

'Badly – you know my feelings – but I suppose, ultimately, it's repairable; we are talking about Dimity after all, and a lot of water has gone under the bridge since then.'

'And too much love?'

'Yes. You too?'

'Afraid so.'

Felix had told Santa all about how Dimity had got in touch and his introduction to Witch's Lawn.

'And how do you feel about Dimity now, after so long?'

'Confused. It's brought back a lot of the old feelings – good and bad. But then Dimity is different now – or seems to be.'

'What, no gin and fags?'

'No fags and not so much booze.'

'And how do you like this new incarnation?'

It's not just the clothes that have changed: she seems an altogether different person. The party girl has gone. She is far less frivolous and far more selfless. Did she tell you about her marriage?'

'Not in any detail.'

'What about the man in her life now?'

Santa shot Felix a look of surprise. 'What man?'

'Ludovic, he's another cleric – a deacon at St Eadric's.'

'Have you met him?'

'I haven't yet had that pleasure.'

It was early evening, and Felix told Santa that he ought to be going.

'I told Rosie you would see her before you went. I hope that's OK.'

'Of course.'

Felix went up to Rosie's bedroom, where the little girl

demanded that Felix tell her a story. Felix did so, kissed his goddaughter goodnight and bade a fond farewell to Santa.

As he drove away, he felt Christmassy for the first time in years and called a number on his phone.

'Hello, Felix, to what do I owe this call?'

'To wish you happy Christmas, Mitten.'

'Well, ditto. How was your day with Santa and Rosie?'

'Full on and exhausting. Are you alone?'

'Who would I be with today of all days?'

'Oh, I don't know, Ludovic perhaps?'

'Well, I'm not. Ludovic has his mother over. Where are you?'

'Not far.'

'Fancy a nightcap?'

'I was wondering.'

'Well, what are you waiting for?'

'An invitation.'

'Consider yourself invited.'

Felix had just settled, glass of wine in hand, into Dimity's library chair when she said, 'Oh, I like your socks. They are very gay.'

'In what meaning of the word?'

'The original meaning of the word – and the other one, I suppose.'

Felix laughed. 'Roger, a good and gay friend of mine gave them to me. Good thing I'm very comfortable with my socksuality.'

Dimity laughed. 'And the reindeer jumper is very fetching.'

'It's my Christmas present from Rosie – or was it from the other Santa?'

Dimity laughed. 'I bet *our* Santa loved getting that for you.'

'I imagine so – knowing my aversion to novelty clothing. Anyway, what about your novelty clothing?'

'What, the clerical garb?' Dimity laughed. 'Haven't you got used to it yet?'

'I have actually. It suits you. I told Santa so. Besides, I like dog collars. I remember a rugby club tour to Torquay one Easter. All those who weren't playing had to dress up as vicars. It was great fun – a group of very young, fit vicars rampaging around the town looking for tarts. We found one tart who seemed very interested in first-team rugby – all the first team, as it turned out.'

Dimity snorted. 'You were supposed to be playing rugby, not leading young women astray.'

'I'm still undecided which gender did the leading astray on that tour. I think it was a draw.'

Dimity raised her eyebrows and shook her head. 'So, how are you getting on at Witch's?'

'I've been thinking a lot more about the history – the Tudors, Catholics, Protestants, priest holes, that sort of thing.'

'You think there may be a priest hole at Witch's?'

'Not exactly, priest holes were found in houses of Catholic families.'

'And the Arrows weren't Catholics?'

'That's the thing. At one time I suppose they must have been, like everyone else, but I think they may have changed with the wind, or at least with the monarchy. The state seems to have been more important to the family than a religious denomination.'

'They were a fickle lot then, you think?'

Felix nodded. 'Fickle to the point of being mercenary. But it has to be said, the Arrows are alive to tell the tale. Perhaps they were just highly apolitical. I don't think they could have been religious or political radicals. They were about as establishment as it comes, aligning to whichever religious or political leaning prevailed at the time. But they weren't dealing with religious secrets; they were dealing with state ones.'

'Do you think the Arrows found ingenious ways to squirrel away some of their own valuable and possibly questionable possessions?'

'It seems to me they just hung their assets on their walls. But you never know, there might be some hidden secrets, and let's hope for Eliza's sake there are.'

'So, if you are looking for hidey holes, where do you start?'

'I imagine by doing all the things the old priest hunters did, like counting windows on the exterior and again from the interior and looking for discrepancies. Funnily enough, comparing internal and external measurements is one of the things I'm doing, but in a far more technological and precise way.'

'I'm beginning to realise how much of an undertaking this is,' Dimity said, 'after all, you don't know what to look for or if there is anything to find in the first place.'

'I'm glad you understand what you've got me into.'

'Oh, come on, Felix, admit it, you love all this.'

'I have to say, I do enjoy staying at Witch's. I can't put my finger on it but there's something that draws me there. I'm not sure if it's Eliza or the house – or both – but for the first time in my life, I seem to be totally content somewhere. It's a strange and unfamiliar feeling.'

Felix and Dimity talked into the small hours, drinking several more glasses of wine as they did so.

Finally, Dimity announced that it was time for bed. 'You should stay, Felix, you have had too much wine to drive home.'

So, Felix stayed, scrunched up uncomfortably on the small sofa.

CHAPTER ELEVEN

Felix was working in his bedroom at Witch's one afternoon when he heard a car come to a scrunching halt outside. Looking out of the window, he saw a short, portly man, perhaps in his sixties slide from a Range Rover. The tieless and black-suited figure had greying and thinning swept-back hair that was, in Felix's view, an inch or two too long for his age. As he strutted to the front door, Felix had little doubt this was Eliza's cousin, Edward.

Although intrigued, he wasn't eager to get involved in whatever was going on between the relatives. First, it was nothing to do with him and second, he didn't go looking for confrontation if he could avoid it.

But half an hour later, Felix heard a knock on his door and West appeared. 'Sorry to disturb, but Eliza has someone she'd like you to meet; her second cousin. He just turned up uninvited and unannounced, a real charmer.'

Eliza made the introduction. 'Felix, I should like to introduce my second cousin, Edward Arrow. Edward, this is my friend, Felix Bohlin.

Edward didn't bother to offer Felix his hand. Instead, he said to Eliza, 'and who the hell's Felix Bohlin when he's at home?'

'I'll ask you to keep a civil tongue while you are under my roof,' said Eliza.

'Your roof – not for much longer, cousin, dear, then I'll do and say what I damn well like in my own house. I was thinking on my way here today about what I'll do with this old pile once you are gone. Perhaps I'll open it up as a tourist attraction. I could tear down that old wreck of a garage and build a ticket office. I'll auction off the Rolls, make a pretty packet. One thing I won't do is live here. I'll be off to a beach in South America.'

'No doubt somewhere like Venezuela or Suriname, with no extradition treaty with Britain,' replied Eliza dryly. Still, Felix could see the old lady was upset by the thought of what Edward might do.

'I've only come to make sure you aren't going to do some dotty old lady thing and not leave Witch's to me. If you don't, you know what will happen: life will become very uncomfortable for you and lots of other people. But I don't think you would let your precious house go outside the family.'

How this man could share the same lineage as Eliza, Felix couldn't imagine. Besides the rather sharp and shiny suit, he felt Edward also wore an enormous chip on his shoulder. Perhaps it would disappear when, or if, he ever came into possession of the keys to Witch's. But Felix could readily see how Eliza couldn't abide the idea of him becoming the owner and steward of the house. He now understood fully her determination to ensure that should never be the case.

'Anyway, I have better things to do now,' said Edward. 'But I will look in again soon – just to remind you not to do anything stupid.'

He left without acknowledging Felix. Meanwhile, Eliza was shaking with anger. When she had recovered herself enough to talk, she said, 'Now, as you're downstairs, let's have a nice cup of tea.' Felix smiled to himself: like most of her generation, this was Eliza's solution to most things.

'How are you getting on?' she asked once they were settled.

Felix told her about his plan of the house, which was slowly developing.

Eliza's questions never stopped, and she made lots of useful observations. Eliza, Felix had discovered, didn't so much chat as direct the conversation by injecting a titbit in the hope of prising out some nugget. Eliza disseminated and carefully distributed intelligence. But that, as Felix was learning, had been her job.

That afternoon, she casually asked Felix how he and Dimity were getting on. Felix told Eliza that they were rubbing along nicely but mentioned there were parts of Dimity's life that were still a mystery, such as her marriage. In a rare moment of candour, Eliza told Felix that Dimity had mentioned how her marriage seemed like a terrible idea now. Worse, it had been a terrible idea then. Eliza said Dimity thought it was a matter of two people who, for no real good reason, suddenly figured they should tie the knot and then did so, but to the wrong people – each other. Eliza recalled how she had laughed when Dimity reported that her only explanation for marrying Michael was that she must have been abducted by aliens.

'I'm afraid that Dimity's husband seemed to be a very

controlling and coercive man who should never have been in a marriage in the first place. It's a great shame, but Dimity seemed to run into one of those types at precisely the wrong time in her life. I've seen it happen before. Sadly, some never get over it. But I'm sure Dimity will, if she hasn't already.'

'So, what about Ludovic?'

'Are you asking if he's also a controlling and coercive type?'

'I guess so.'

'Possibly. He's an intriguing character from a very interesting family.'

'Oh?'

'His father was Nigel Poniard... Sir Nigel Poniard. He's been dead for years, but back in the day he was famous for marrying wealthy women and then using vicious lawyers to take them to the cleaners. He couldn't get away with it now. He was also notorious for not paying his bills. Rumour has it, he once refused to pay the full amount for a hugely expensive wedding reception at a top London hotel because the marriage only lasted a few months. He blamed the hotel for the breakdown. It took years to settle through the courts.

'Ludovic was Nigel's second son, so Ludovic got very little when Nigel died. The first son, from one of Nigel's earlier marriages, copped the lot. He knocked down the family pile, sold off the land for development and cashed in everything else. He then severed all ties with the rest of the family – lest they were ever tempted to ask him for money – and moved, lock stock and barrel, to Mustique.'

'So, what happened to Ludovic?'

'The poor boy had to get a job. First, he went into the law – a pupillage at some barristers' chambers at the Temple, which his father influenced – but young Ludovic didn't really cut it in London. So, he went to Hong Kong – and you know the acronym about that, don't you?'

'I don't think I do.'

'FILTH – failed in London, try Hong Kong. But then he didn't cut it in Hong Kong either. So, he came back and did what many second or third sons have done down the centuries.'

'He entered the Church?'

'Exactly.'

'What about Ludovic's mother?' Felix asked, remembering Dimity mentioning that he had been with her at Christmas.

'His mother is Daisy... very charming by all accounts, but a fragile woman. Not fragile as in a flower, but fragile as in a heroin injection. I've always thought that there's a look of Audrey Hepburn about her. Have you heard of her?'

'Audrey Hepburn or Ludovic's mother?'

'Ludovic's mother, of course. And please don't be obtuse, Felix.'

Felix smiled and shook his head. 'No, I haven't.'

'She started out as a classical pianist – a very young, beautiful and successful classical pianist. Then, tragically for her, she met Brandon Hope, the singer in a 1970s rock and roll group called Fe26. One of the Sunday tabloids dubbed him, "Abandon Hope", and it stuck.'

'I do remember him,' Felix said. 'Fe26 was a heavy metal band.'

'If you say so, my dear. When Hope died in Berlin from a huge drug overdose, the headline in *The Sun* ran, "Brandonburg Date with Death". Daisy went off the rails: she even lived rough on the streets around Soho for a while. After that, she was in and out of clinics for years. She finally straightened herself out only to meet and marry Nigel Poniard, who was convinced she was wealthy and could make lots more. I'm afraid Daisy went out of the frying pan and into the fire. When Nigel discovered she had no money – as she seemed to have injected it all into her arms or sniffed it up her nose – and wasn't going to make any from her music, he ditched her in double-quick time. He took up with an Argentinian beef heiress, but not before Daisy had become pregnant with Ludovic.'

'Does Dimity know you know this?'

'I certainly haven't told her – but it's all in the public domain.'

'So, what happened to Daisy?'

'Well, she eventually straightened herself out again and devoted herself to her son. She lives for him, although she mostly resides in Paris now with dozens of cats. I read an article once where Nigel was quoted as saying that what Daisy loved most in the world were her cats – and what she loved next in the world were other people's cats.

'I understand she now comes to London only occasionally. Although I also read somewhere that she has just finished a record – her first in decades. It's in collaboration with a popular boogie-woogie musician.

'I have to say, despite all her failings, I hope Ludovic takes more after Daisy.'

'Why do you say that?'

Because if he takes after his father, he may have inherited an unhealthy interest in women with money.'

'But I don't think Dimity has money,' Felix said.

'No, but through Dimity, I suspect he might be showing an unhealthy interest in mine. Look, I hope you don't mind me asking, Felix, but you had feelings for Dimity yourself once, I presume?'

Eliza asked the question matter-of-factly, but for her, Felix suspected, crucially.

'I thought I did – back then. But we were kids.'

'And now?'

Felix sighed. 'There is no now for us. That ended twenty years ago. But if we can remain good friends then I think that would be very nice.'

'I don't think there is much doubt about the friendship between the two of you, my dear,' said Eliza with a smile.

'Perhaps so, but I'm not sure how long that would last if Ludovic were a fixture.'

Eliza nodded. 'We'll have to see. But who am I to know about affairs of the heart these days? I'm just an old lady.'

'Who's seen more of life than the rest of us put together.'

'Perhaps too much life for one person.'

'I'm sure you don't think that for a minute.'

Eliza smiled. 'But what about you, Felix, isn't there someone special in your life now?'

'What, with all my late nights, weekend working and commitment to building the business? I'm afraid they have taken their toll more than once.

'To be honest, there has never been a person in my life quite like Dimity. But I was never strong enough for her, and nothing has changed. Looking back to those years when we were growing up, I remember myself as rather timid, while she was so headstrong and exciting. The truth is she became a bit of a tearaway, and eventually she tore away from me. Even if I were interested, I would soon be back to doing the whole unrequited thing. So, I'm simply never going back there, even in my head. Besides, Dimity would never be interested in me. Not like that.'

Eliza looked stern. 'You can't see why she would be interested?'

'Frankly, no, I can't.'

'Well, and this may come as a surprise to you, my boy, but whether or why Dimity may or may not be interested in you, or anyone else for that matter, is not for you to decide or necessarily to understand.'

* * *

A few days later, Felix had most of the information he needed to complete his survey. He had called Dimity so they could all view the finalised plan at Witch's.

'Are we going to crack the case?' she asked.

'I do hope so,' said Eliza. 'Now, Felix, do we all gather in the drawing room to find out who done it?'

'Whoever it was who done it, I think that may be a bit premature,' Felix replied. 'First, I need to check a few things, and then we can take a look at the complete picture.'

Felix's laser meter gave pinpoint dimension readings. On a previous visit, he had shown the instrument to Eliza, who had been thrilled with the result. Felix noted that Eliza seemed to take on any innovation without a moment's hesitation: she always looked forward and rarely looked back. She never said, 'That wasn't how they did it in my day.' This was Eliza's day, and despite her age, she was a woman of the moment, and woe betide anyone who thought otherwise.

Felix moved upstairs to the gallery: he had already

measured it twice, but something didn't quite make sense. So, he measured it again, and things still didn't add up.

At one end of the landing was Eliza's bedroom. At the other end, the wall was covered to three-quarter height in linenfold oak panelling, which, like the staircase, was blackened through time and wax. Covering this panelling hung a vast, faded tapestry of a biblical scene depicting God and angels. Felix didn't know much about tapestries and the scene wasn't to his taste, but he had no doubt that like everything else in the property, it was of unimpeachable provenance and great value.

The hanging was on the west wall of the house. The gilt script that was so much a feature of the two-storey salon stretched out along the top section of the wall above. Felix checked the measurement yet again and then headed downstairs to enter the latest data on his laptop.

'Have you got everything you need, my dear?' asked Eliza, as Felix tapped away on his keyboard.

'Yes, thank you. I'll just be a moment, then we can look at the results.' Felix entered the last measurements and checked the plan on the screen. But still, there was a discrepancy. He must have looked uncertain, as Dimity asked, 'Is anything the matter?'

'I'm not sure. Something doesn't make sense.'

'What?'

'I'm missing about six feet. That's the difference between the landing's length plus Eliza's room and the length of the wall outside.'

'So, where's the missing space?' asked Dimity.

'Well, it can't be at the end where Eliza's bedroom is as she has an outside window along the east wall of the house, so there is nowhere there to hide six feet. But there isn't a window on the west wall.'

'Well, then, it must be there.'

'Let's not get too hasty. What I can't do is attribute the missing space to a structural element like a chimney, although it could be a roof void I suppose – but that's not logical from a structural or architectural perspective.'

Outwardly Felix was trying to appear calm, inwardly, he had never felt like this before over a building. Before he could suggest taking a look, Dimity and Eliza were already heading for the stairs. He quickly followed.

They stood together looking at the tapestry. The panelling behind it seemed sound and solid when Felix lifted the cloth and tapped the wall, and nothing moved when he pushed and pulled it.

'Remember the sonnet from the family Bible?' Eliza said, looking up at the script overhead. 'It warned us to take nothing at face value. What if the script on the wall is like a cryptic crossword clue?'

'I've never been that good at crossword puzzles,' Dimity said, 'but you are, Eliza. I've often seen a completed *Times* one on your table.'

'It went with my job,' said Eliza. 'I was trained to receive intelligence, analyse it and then make sense of it. It demands a particular way of thinking that goes hand in hand with being good at crossword puzzles.'

'So, how would you look at this potential clue?' Felix asked.

'Well, the words around the walls say, "Now set down this script and look to Heaven." What if it doesn't mean look to Heaven, as in a place, but something more literal? Look again at the tapestry – God surrounded by angels. One could say they are in Heaven. So, what if "look to heaven" in this context just means look up high?'

Eliza studied the tapestry for a while longer. Then she turned her attention to a sturdy-looking, Gothic oak chair in front of it. Pointing to it, she said, 'I've always disliked that chair. It's heavy and uncomfortable. It's regularly dusted but few, as far as I know, have ever sat on it. Yet it's always been in that place.'

She walked over, studied the chair and then removed the loose seat cushion.

'My eyes aren't too good nowadays. Can you two tell me what you see here?'

'I can't see anything, but the seat is a bit scuffed I suppose,' said Dimity eventually.

'How do you think it came to be scuffed?' Eliza asked.

'Someone stood on it, perhaps for dusting,' said Felix.

'Or to reach something,' said Dimity.

'And what is there to reach here?' Eliza asked.

'Nothing that I can see,' Felix replied. 'But hang on, the word heaven in the script is exactly over the tapestry.'

'Ah ha,' said Eliza, 'so what if "look to heaven" doesn't mean look to God or even look up high? What if it means to look at the actual word itself? If the chair is too heavy to move easily, is seldom sat upon and scuffed, then what is it for?'

'To reach up,' Felix replied.

'Then perhaps we should see what we might reach,' said Eliza.

Stepping onto the seat put Felix within touching distance of the script. He studied the word heaven. It was uniform except for the cross stroke of the letter H. Running his fingers along its surface, he found it to be slightly raised.

'There is something here not quite as it seems from below,' he said.

He placed his fingers on the raised stroke and pushed lightly at first and then more firmly. Stepping down from the chair, he began pushing and prodding the panelling, first to the left and then to the right. Finally, he pushed in the centre. With a small creak, a portion of panelling moved half an inch. He pushed harder to be rewarded with more creaking and movement, revealing a small, narrow door about 5ft in height. It was clear that most adults would have to crouch down to get through it.

'Ta-da,' said Felix triumphantly.

Eliza stood, her mouth agape. 'Well, I never,' she said in a whisper. 'Some intelligence officer I am.'

Meanwhile, Dimity looked as if she might explode with excitement.

'We need a torch,' Felix said.

'West will have one,' said Eliza, squinting at the man's watch on her wrist. 'At this time, he's usually in the kitchen with Cairo.'

Felix ran downstairs and found West, who grabbed a large torch. Together with Cairo and Frankie, who had heard the rumpus, they all charged back upstairs to join Dimity and Eliza.

Crouching down, Felix tried to push the door further open. At first, it resisted any pressure before finally opening enough for him to squeeze through. The torch sent its beam across a small room, which was cramped and musty.

The ceiling was high, so Felix could easily stand to his full height, but otherwise, there wasn't much space. The area was about four feet wide by six feet long. Along the wall in front of him and taking up the chamber's width was a large bureau with its lid open to reveal a desk, though the items on it were covered in a thick layer of dust and cobwebs. In the beam of his torch, Felix could just make out two candlestick holders with burned-down candles, a bottle and a glass. In front of the desk was a Windsor chair similar to the ones in the kitchen and on the wall behind it hung a painting. The subject, a man, was indistinct. Felix sneezed and then sneezed again.

'Are you all right? What can you see?' called Dimity.

'It's very dusty – filthy actually – but there is a desk and a chair, and a picture that I can only just make out. We need some more lights in here. West, have you got anything like an inspection lamp?' As an afterthought, he added, 'and some easing oil for these door hinges?

'It's pretty cramped in here,' he continued. 'We will only fit two people in at a time – three at a pinch. Eliza, I'm not so sure if you'll want to try and come in, but I am going to take some photos on my phone and then hand it out so you can see what I'm seeing.'

Felix felt like an Egyptologist discovering a tomb. He took some photos and, each time, the phone's flash momentarily brought the little room to life. He passed it through the small door and heard exclamations of excitement as the images were viewed.

In what seemed like no time at all, West was back with the lights. He plugged them in outside and handed them through to Felix.

'OK, who's first?' Felix asked.

A moment later, West appeared through the door holding an oilcan. He paused to take in the secret space. 'Who'd have guessed?' he said.

'I know, pretty incredible, isn't it?' replied Felix. 'It's so well hidden. It seems to me that the landing was longer at one stage, but someone has put up a wall to create this room and make it look as if nothing was here. But why?'

'Secrets, of course,' said West.

'Well, I'm not so sure it holds that many secrets now. As far as I can see, there doesn't seem to be any papers in the desk drawers. West covered the antique door hinges with oil and worked the small door back and forth until the liquid had done its work. He then left the small room to let in Cairo, who was equally as astounded. Frankie entered next followed by Dimity, who stood there for a minute or two taking it all in.

'Oh, Felix, this is incredible,' she said, 'and isn't Eliza amazing for working all that out with the chair?'

'Formidable,' Felix said, before adding, 'Look, we aren't going to get much further without some careful examination. Right now, we can't see much for the dust. Let's join Eliza and work out what to do next. After all, it's her house.'

Outside on the gallery landing, Felix asked Eliza, 'Should we press on investigating the room tonight or make a fresh start in the morning?'

The others looked horrified.

'What are you talking about?' said Dimity.

'I'm not sure any of us want to stop now. I may not even be here tomorrow,' Eliza added.

'Well, we will have to take this slowly. We don't want to harm anything,' Felix said.

'It's not a crime scene,' argued Dimity. 'We aren't looking for forensic evidence.'

'No, but we are looking for historical clues that may have

important consequences, and I think we should take a great deal of care.'

'In that, I quite agree,' said Eliza, 'but, now we've started, I think we should press on. I would have a sleepless night anyway thinking about it all. Besides, tomorrow is Sunday. Dimity has services, and we can't deny her all the thrill of the chase, can we?'

Felix could see her point.

Together, they agreed a plan. The group would set about getting rid of what looked like several hundred years of accumulated grime, dust and cobwebs.

Cairo prepared some sandwiches and fresh coffee, and the clean-up began after they'd eaten. West had brought up some small aluminium steps and a vacuum cleaner that fitted through the little doorway. With Cairo's help, he started at the top of the room in the corners and worked his way down.

Meanwhile, Felix tackled the desk. His efforts revealed an excellent piece of furniture, the surface of which had never been left to fade in the sunlight. The interior of the desk had pigeonholes and drawers, all of which were empty. Above and at the back of the writing surface were five frieze drawers: a wider one in the middle and two to each side of it.

Finally, the picture revealed itself to be a half-length, indistinct painting of a seated man.

Once the room was as dust free as they could get it, Cairo, West and Frankie went off to have a wash. By then, it was the early hours of Sunday morning. Felix sat at the desk, imagining the last occupant of the chair, while Eliza and Dimity peered in from the landing. He looked at the desk, idly rechecking its drawers and pigeonholes. Still nothing. 'Don't you think it strange that someone sat here without any papers or anything else save for an unopened bottle and a glass?' he called out.

'It's certainly frustrating to have a secret room with no secrets,' Eliza replied.

'Perhaps, at that time, they didn't have any secrets to hide,' said Dimity.

'People always have secrets to hide, and they especially did then,' replied Eliza. 'And remember, my family also dealt in other people's private affairs – people far higher up the pecking order. Perhaps that's why there is nothing here – or nothing seems to be here. Dimity, help me get into the room, would you?'

By the sound of Eliza's voice, Felix sensed this wasn't a question but an order.

'It's a good thing I still do my exercises every morning,' she said, a little breathlessly, as Dimity guided her through the door. When she had finished inspecting the room, she said to Felix, 'Let me look at this desk.'

Felix made way for her to sit down, observing her closely as she removed each drawer for inspection and traced her fingers around the pigeonholes. Next, she asked him to shine the torch inside the niches before peering into each one in turn. Each of the five had a pretty, arched, decorative frieze about one and a half inches deep at the top. Eliza used her fingers to probe the niches. Felix was about to tell her he had already done that when the centre frieze popped forward a little. Eliza gently pulled the frieze towards her, slowly revealing a shallow inner drawer.

'How on earth did you do that?' Felix asked.

Eliza smiled. 'Tricks of the trade, my dear.'

Felix thought how she looked remarkably calm but also extremely pleased with herself.

Inside the drawer was a small book.

'It's a missal,' Eliza said. Felix saw that it was printed in Latin and contained the texts used in the Catholic mass.

'Interesting,' said Eliza.

'Revealing,' said Felix.

'Very,' replied Eliza.

'What's going on?' called Dimity from the landing.

'Squeeze in and see for yourself,' said Eliza.

Felix idly slid his hand to the back of the small drawer. 'Hang on, there's something else in here,' he said. When he withdrew his hand, he saw that he was holding a rosary.

'Well, by the looks of it, that's a mystery solved,' said Eliza, 'it seems we were Catholics, or some of us were, around the time this rosary was last held.'

'When do you think that was?' Dimity asked.

Felix opened the missal and read MDCXXVI on the front page. 'According to this, 1626,' he said after a quick calculation.

'Charles I was on the throne,' Eliza said.

Eliza took the missal from Felix and began to delicately turn the pages. 'Well, what have we here?' he suddenly exclaimed, as a separate sheet slipped from between the pages and fell to the desk.

'It's another verse,' cried Dimity. 'Quick, read it.'

'Steady on, Mit,' Felix said.

'But it's so exciting.'

Dimity looked Felix in the eye for a moment. 'You haven't called me Mit for a long time,' she observed.

'I'm sorry to break into your charming reminiscence,' said Eliza, 'but before we read the verse, I think West, Cairo and Frankie would want to be here, don't you? They wouldn't want to miss anything.'

'Of course, I'll go and get them,' said Dimity. 'Don't do anything without me,' she called as she swiftly headed downstairs.

Felix helped Eliza from the room, and she took a seat on the Gothic chair.

Meanwhile, Dimity and the others arrived back in double-quick time. Cairo's hair was still wet from the shower.

'Now, go ahead and read it, Felix,' said Eliza, 'it looks similar to the verse from our Bible.'

Felix studied the words and started to read them without achieving anything like the rhythm that he felt the writer had intended.

III

Loyal men are humour'd not by toll'd day,
But shaken rudely from a mareless rest,
To serve this realm in hidden ways, and pray
For guilty souls to meet the hangmans test.
Heedest thou well the call that mornings bring,
Whilst others sleep be watchful to the last,
Lest we diverted miss the tocsin ring,
And leavest cloak'd the secrets of our past.
Now look ye not to heavens lofty part,
But bow thy head and leave this poets script,
And minding word from riddle take ye heart,
To look within a masons chisell'd crypt.
Seekest thou not the blackbirds summer hymn,
But delve instead where fowl and serpents swim.

Everyone was quiet for a while, letting what they had just heard sink in.

'Read it again, Felix,' Dimity said.

Felix did so.

'And notice this is verse three,' added Felix. 'So, your question about more verses has been answered, Eliza. We can now safely assume there was a second verse, and possibly more.'

'This shows that at least some of the Arrow family must have been secret Catholics throughout the Protestant reign of Elizabeth I,' said Eliza.

'Well, you did say they were a shady lot,' was all Felix could think of to say in response.

CHAPTER TWELVE

Two days had passed since the great find. Felix almost bumped into Eliza at the kitchen door. Excitedly, he said to her, 'I think there's a Moore in your garden.'

'Ah, yes, dear, one of the Yorkshire Moors.'

'Now who's being obtuse?'

Ignoring the comment, Eliza continued. 'He came in the mid-40s and never left.'

'How did you get hold of a Henry Moore?'

'Oh, I didn't, my dear. It was very heavy and slippery in the wet. As I recall, we had to use a crane and several rather large and dishy men.'

Eliza was having one of her twinkling days, Felix thought.

'Mama and Papa were quite friendly with Kenneth Clarke – you know, the art historian and broadcaster. He came to Witch's on several occasions and suggested that an abstract sculpture would be ideal for the garden. He found quite a few commissions for Henry. At the time, I remember that Mama and Papa were a bit sceptical, and I think they even wondered if it might have been jobs for the boys, but time has proved Kenneth to have been a very skilled and forward-thinking art advisor.'

'Did you ever meet him... Henry Moore, that is?'

'Oh yes, on several occasions. He and his wife even stayed here once or twice after they were bombed out of their home in London during the Blitz. I love that piece, and I'm glad to know you have ventured outside at last.'

'It seemed the day for it.'

In all his time at Witch's, Felix had concentrated on the interior of the property. Now that some warmer weather had arrived, he was taking some time to explore the grounds.

The formal part of the garden was made up of a series of distinctive landscaped areas surrounded by the deep woodland: the trees helped to screen the house and maintain its secrecy.

Followed by Cecily, who was seemingly interested in all that he was doing, Felix walked along a path between two high yew hedges and well-cut narrow strips of lawn. He tried to imagine the garden in summer, when the path's borders would be a profusion of vegetation interspersed with large box plants clipped into balls. The plants were cut back now, but neatly written labels revealed them to be saxifrage, alliums, Welsh poppies, tulips, artemisia and santolina. This was the work of an artist, Felix thought; in the warmer months, they would offer up a palette of pink, silver, yellow and white.

To Felix's left, another path struck out under a pergola with rough brick pillars. Labels indicated that clematis would soon provide a shady roof, while long stems of euphorbia would soften the harsh brick edges of the pillars.

Through a split chestnut-wood gate – on which any

attempt of maintenance had long since been abandoned – Felix came to a lake about half the size of a football pitch. The surface was largely covered in lily pads and its banks were half-hidden by the faded reminders of summer blooms. Felix could see that, in the spring, irises would provide bold splashes of blue or yellow and, after them, white lotus flowers would bejewel the small lake.

He watched the sedate progress of a moorhen across the surface of the water until it vanished into some reeds. Seemingly with great effort, a heron launched itself into the air as though heavy from fishing. The bird gradually gained height and disappeared above the trees. Felix could imagine the darting flash of kingfisher blue on a warm summer's afternoon.

At the far end of the lake stood a tall, octagonal red-brick tower with a circular hole towards the top. Felix assumed that at some time in the past it had housed a clock face. The tower seemed to have no other purpose than an ornamental one. It was an eye-catcher built before garden landscaping in England had become an art form.

The base of the tower disappeared into the lake's reeds and rushes. To Felix, it seemed an odd building to be placed there, but it was no less beautiful for that.

At one point along the woodland walk, flanked by rhododendrons, a swing hung from a high bough of a beech tree. But its wooden seat, held up by long ropes, looked decayed enough to deter testing. Who had swung there over the years? Felix wondered. Eliza? Who else? Suddenly, he remembered the girl in the photograph in his bedroom.

Once again, Felix came to the Henry Moore sculpture and studied it further, brushing away wet, dead leaves from the surface of the plinth. The bronze was a powerful work in three-quarter size of a four-strong, family group – three adults of indeterminate gender but possibly two females and a male. There was also a small child in arms.

'Good morning.'

Felix swung round to see Julius, Witch's gardener. Felix had met him on several occasions in passing. He didn't seem to retreat indoors much, and only then to warm himself with a cup of tea or coffee in the kitchen. Felix had been informed that he preferred the outdoors and, when needing to in time of foul weather, mostly retreated to his office room at the end of a range of greenhouses, which came equipped with a warming stove.

But, like everything and everybody at Witch's, Julius was not all that he seemed. Eliza had revealed how his father had been the head gardener, back when there were also several under-gardeners and an apprentice. The young Julius had shown a prodigious intellect and, with the encouragement and financial support of Eliza's father, had won a scholarship to Oxford. It seemed that a sparkling academic career lay ahead of him. But after graduating and spending a few years in the civil service, he turned his back on that life and returned to Witch's, where he'd always been happiest. When his father retired, he took over the garden. According to Eliza, Julius spent his leisure time reading, writing books on gardening and keeping mostly to himself.

'Good morning,' Felix said to him. 'I've finally come outside to explore your garden.'

'It's not mine, but nevertheless, it's a good day for it,' replied Julius.

'Yes, the weather is lovely, and so is the garden. I suppose you have seen lots of changes here over the years?'

'None at all,' Julius said bluntly. 'Mrs Arrow likes it kept as it's always been. She says she has happy memories of it that way. She doesn't want it changed because if someone were to return after many years away, they wouldn't know their way around. It's the same in the house, least, that's what I'm told.'

Felix wondered who this mysterious returnee could possibly be. 'Well, was the garden much different before you came here?' he asked. 'Or before your father?'

'Can't really say. There's nothing left of the garden that began with the house in Tudor times. It's difficult to tell how that was. The lake is the same, of course, but we have found the foundations of what may have been a knot garden, and there would have been lots of fruit trees.'

Julius, it seemed to Felix, had led a cloistered but perfectly agreeable life mostly in the confines of Witch's garden. Which of them was richer? Each to their own, he supposed, but it was nice to see someone so apparently content with his lot in life.

'I noticed you looking at this,' Julius said, pointing to the statue. 'I remember it coming here – a real fuss.'

Felix idly brushed away more of the dead leaves that covered the base. In doing so, he fully exposed the stone block. Set into the upper surface of the plinth was a layer of bronze. As Felix studied it, he realised that it was shaped to act as a shadow to the sculpture. It was a clever and effective device that Felix had never seen done before. But then he had a second surprise: the base depicted four adults rather than the three on the main sculpture.

'Why do you think the base has one more adult figure?' Felix asked Julius. But the gardener just shrugged and shook his head.

'The tower is interesting,' Julius said, moving to another subject.

'How in particular?'

'It's called the Stone Tower.'

Felix frowned. 'But it's made of brick.'

'Exactly. There are some interesting things here at Witch's... some interesting things indeed.'

Julius was right, Felix thought, it was another question to add to the growing list he had about the house and garden.

'Mrs Arrow told me she played in the tower when she was a child and teenager,' Julius said. 'She even camped there overnight sometimes, especially in the summer when it was hot. The family used to have picnics there back in the day.

'I keep some of my garden things in the tower now. When I was younger and more agile, I used the upstairs room, too. The tower is haunted, you know.'

'Haunted? By whom or what?'

'By the ghost of a recluse called Rachel. Apparently, she lived there in the 18th century. It's said that Rachel couldn't cope well with people – I know how she felt – so, she found her way here, where no one bothered her. The family let her live in the tower. She was there for years until her death. She foraged in the woods, and I think the family left food and clothes out for her. They say she never spoke, but she could be heard singing in the woods. She had a beautiful voice.'

'Have you heard Rachel, Julius?'

'I fancy I have, when the wind is still, and the May is in blossom.'

Felix smiled at the thought. 'What a lovely place for a

recluse to live,' he said. 'By the way, when was the tower built? I suspect it's contemporary with the house.'

'Within a generation of Witch's being built, or that's what the people at Historic England told Mrs Arrow. But no one seems to know the reason why it was built, other than to look nice and tell the time. It's a pity the clock has been removed. In my view, it should be restored. All the parts are still in the tower, along with the bell that used to chime the hour – although I can't remember it ever doing so. I think it became a bit of a nuisance in the end. It must have been loud, and the sound would have carried across the lake to the house. My father told me that it used to wake visitors in the dead of night – especially those who weren't used to it.'

'I agree, it would be nice to have the clock back in its place and working. I'm sure there's now a mechanism for turning off the chime at night or at certain hours.'

'But that's pandering to the townies, like removing tractor mud from the byways. They'll be deodorising pigs next; you mark my words.'

Felix laughed. 'I'm sure they'll try. But tell me, why do you think the tower is called the Stone Tower when it's made of brick?'

Julius shook his head. 'It's just another Witch's mystery. There might have been a good reason, but it's another question where the answer has been lost over the years.

'Now, I'd best be getting along,' he added, 'these paths won't sweep themselves – even here at Witch's, with our brooms.' He smiled at his own joke, and it was the first time Felix had seen the gardener's weather-worn face crack into a grin.

'I'd like to look at the tower,' said Felix.

'Well, you can look at it from here,' Julius observed flatly.

Felix thought he should have known better with Julius than to turn a question into a statement. Julius, it seemed, was fond of taking any spoken ambiguity in the way it wasn't intended, deriving from it some perverse but harmless amusement. He corrected himself. 'I meant that I would like to see inside the tower. Is that possible?'

'Well, why didn't you say so? It isn't locked, but it does have a particular atmosphere – I don't think a bad one if you are susceptible to that sort of thing. And you won't meet Rachel or hear her song. The May won't be in blossom for a few months. Go, help yourself. Don't let me keep you,' he added brightly. Felix took it that he was being dismissed.

Julius wandered off, and Felix was left alone with Cecily. The little dog had found something to dig up and was now caked in mud.

As he walked around the lake, along the rough, earthen path that separated it from the woodland, he wondered about hauntings.

Even from where he walked, the tower certainly had a mysterious quality; it stood defiantly at the end of the lake like some ancient citadel. There was something Arthurian about the scene, as if at any moment a sword-wielding hand would emerge from the surface of the lake. All it needed was a moody blanket of mist lying over the mere for the dream to become a reality. But there was no mist today, just sunlight reflecting off the surface of the water, lightly rippled by the gentle breeze. As Felix walked, he found himself reciting some words he remembered from a Strawbs folk song about a battle. It included lines about an archer that, given the family name, seemed apposite. Although the Arrow family had apparently served powerful masters, they certainly appeared liberated enough to make their choices, to act as they thought best, to come and go as they pleased and to serve and to travel. The Arrows were, Felix mused, a remarkable family. Who knew what great state secrets they had known – still knew, perhaps? Maybe that was why influential people seemed to have left them alone. But with the Church of England looking covetously at Witch's Lawn, that castle and the family's freedom, enjoyed for centuries, was under assault.

Three steep, stone steps rose to a door at the back of the tower. Felix climbed up the short flight and pushed the heavy oak door, which swung open easily on well-oiled hinges. Inside was a room about 15ft across. On the wall, opposite the door, was an arched window overlooking the lake – it provided an excellent view for a reclusive resident or for a family picnic, Felix imagined.

Inside the octagonal room was a rough workbench on which were various gardening tools, pots and watering cans: all were neatly laid out and looked well-maintained.

An iron ladder, fixed to one wall, disappeared into an opening in the ceiling above. Felix closed the door to keep Cecily in, walked across the room, grasped the ladder's side rails and tested that they were secure before climbing up and through the ceiling aperture until he could step, a little awkwardly, backwards off the ladder to the next floor. He could see why Julius's days of using this room were behind him.

The humble space was sparsely furnished with a canvas chair and a folding card table, its dusty and faded green baize top pitted with moth holes. On the table sat a rusty hurricane lamp and a small pile of dog-eared and warped gardening magazines. The top one, Felix noticed, was a decade old. Around the walls were several small windows that were little more than arrow slits.

The iron ladder continued upwards, and Felix continued with it. A trapdoor above opened when he put his shoulder to it, a cascade of dust showering him as he did so. The portal led to what was apparently the clock room and belfry. There were several large boxes that, on inspection, contained the clock's parts that Julius mentioned. In one corner, on the floor, was a large, heavy-looking bronze bell.

This level was as far as Felix could go. While there was a maintenance trapdoor to the roof, somewhat oddly, there was no ladder.

He retraced his steps to the ground floor and looked around once more. It was a simple room with wall plaster that was crumbling in parts and a flagstone floor. Three giant oak beams supported the ceiling. From a hook halfway along the central beam hung a circular and extremely heavy-looking, two-tier iron candleholder, with cups for dozens of candles. Felix could see that, once upon a time, this had been painted, as small areas of peeling black paint stubbornly remained, the rest having given way to rust. To replace spent candles and maintain the chandelier, there was a pulley system with blocks and a chain to raise and lower the fixture. Felix saw that, after nightfall, the chandelier would have provided the only light, as there was no electricity supply.

He spent some time looking through the window and across the lake to the main house. There was a clear line of sight. What a beautiful picture it made, Felix thought – the connected happenstance of history, mystery and architecture. It was a heady cocktail and created a tantalising Arcadian landscape. But, again, Felix reminded himself, at Witch's, just as in the theatre, nothing was quite as it seemed. He wondered if the tower might give him some clues to the Witch's mystery, but on the face of it, he decided, it offered none.

* * *

'I had a look inside the tower,' Felix told Eliza, when he saw her later that day.

'And what did you think?'

'It's an extraordinarily beautiful building, and I can see what Julius meant about it possessing a special atmosphere.'

'You spoke to Julius?'

'Yes, for quite a while. He was most helpful.'

'Well, wonders will never cease. Julius hardly speaks to anyone, including me.'

'He told me about Rachel, the recluse.'

'Did he now? I've often thought how Julius takes after her in many ways – he's both solitary and has a fine singing voice, which he uses when he thinks no one can hear.'

'Having now seen the tower, it looks to me like someone's flight of fancy. I'm not that sure why a tower was needed in the first place. I went up as far as the belfry and saw all the clock parts. And, I have to say, the chandelier and the pulley on the ground floor are quite something, aren't they?'

'They certainly are, and I can tell you, that place is enchanting when all the candles are lit. And I really should get that clock working again.'

Eliza suddenly put her hand to her mouth. 'Oh, silly me, I forgot to let you know earlier, Dimity is coming for tea.'

That explained Eliza's bright mood, thought Felix.

'You might want to wash and change, my dear, your hair and jacket are covered in dust.'

'When's Dimity arriving?'

'Soon. Oh, and she's bringing Ludovic.'

CHAPTER THIRTEEN

This must be a mistake, Felix thought, as he stepped into the drawing room and saw Dimity standing next to a man. Surely this couldn't be the boyfriend.

Eliza turned her twinkling eyes towards Felix. 'May I introduce Ludovic Poniard,' she said. 'Ludovic, I would like you to meet Felix Bohlin.'

Felix tried to hide his surprise. The man in front of him was not what he had been expecting, although he couldn't for a moment think why not. After all, he was lean and tall – over six foot three. He looked to Felix to be in his mid-forties, with matinee idol teeth and well-cut, swept-back blond hair that showed no signs of greying. His clothes-horse physique perfectly modelled a well-cut, grey suit and a stiffly laundered, white cotton shirt with starched double cuffs held by discreet gold links. All this was topped off with a tastefully patterned tie and contrasting pocket square. This was a man who carried himself with brimming confidence and a grace and ease that suggested he was used to having people fawn over him.

Here was someone who, Felix had little doubt, was on a fast and steep trajectory up the greasy ecclesiastical pole. Ludovic seemed to have it all. Felix was horrified to find himself feeling intimidated.

Ludovic stood with Dimity's arm in his, which gave Felix a jolt: partly, Felix had to admit, because the pair looked so good together – they made the perfect Anglican power couple. There was probably nothing, it seemed to Felix, that these two couldn't achieve in their chosen field – Dimity with her drive, personality and beauty, and Ludovic with his height, confidence and handsome looks. Ludovic, Felix thought, could have made an excellent living just modelling. As a pin-up boy for the clergy, he was ideal. The Church could make a fortune with a Ludovic calendar.

Dimity detached herself from her consort and greeted Felix with a kiss before Ludovic stepped forward and gave a firm handshake.

'I am very pleased to meet you, Mr Bohlin,' he beamed. 'Dimity has told me so much about you.'

Ludovic made his introduction with a practised charm. Felix was already prepared to slap him. He had a subtly patronising air, and smug and condescending were some of the words that immediately came to Felix's mind. He also displayed an easy intimacy with Dimity and Eliza. Felix suddenly felt jealous.

'Mitten mentioned you to me, too,' he said. 'I'm delighted to meet you, but please do call me Felix.'

Felix thought he noticed Ludovic wince slightly at his use of Dimity's nickname. He knew that indifference was often harder to bear than dislike, or even hate, and while he didn't *want* to dislike or hate Ludovic, he was more than prepared to be indifferent to him. Except Felix knew he *wasn't* indifferent. In fact, he felt seriously put out. He tried to tell himself that he didn't know why – but who was he trying to kid? He knew only too well.

Felix looked over to Eliza, who seemed, if anything, rather pleased with the unfolding drama.

'Call me Ludo,' said Ludovic.

But Felix didn't want to call him anything, he just wanted him gone, and although he was ashamed of himself, he couldn't help his feelings.

'I understand that you've been having an exciting time measuring up,' Ludovic said, making it sound, Felix felt, as though he was providing carpets or curtains. 'Have you sized up anything interesting?'

Felix knew this was a barely disguised put-down, but was it also a trap? He didn't want to discuss anything about Witch's with Ludovic, so he replied, 'The whole house is so interesting, isn't it? Every measurement is fascinating.'

This seemed to satisfy Ludovic, and the atmosphere relaxed. Eliza gave Felix the slightest of nods.

The small talk continued until Eliza excused herself. As she brushed past Felix, she held his arm and whispered, 'Friends close, enemies closer.'

Felix decided that given Eliza's background in intrigue, if anyone knew about enemies, it was her.

With Eliza out of earshot, Ludovic turned to Felix and said, 'I understand that Eliza has told you about the Church's outrageous claim to the ownership of Witch's?'

'Yes, she did mention it.'

'I have to say, this has come as a surprise to everyone, none more so than me, but the Church seems confident it has some sort of ancient claim on this house and land. I came here today to offer Eliza a solution.'

'Not that it is any of my business, but may I ask what that is?'

'Are you aware of Eliza's cousin, Edward?'

'I've met him.'

'Then you may know that when Eliza is gone, to keep Witch's Lawn in the family, the house and its incredible contents will pass to Edward, as he is her closest surviving relative. Eliza has expressed to me how much she doesn't want this to happen. So, to avoid this and to prevent her from having a protracted and expensive legal case with the Church, I've suggested that she bequeath everything to it now, as time is of the essence. That way, the house and its contents will be protected for posterity. I realise that this is a most sensitive subject, Felix, but I'm concerned that Eliza's extraordinary legacy will fall into not-so-reliable hands once she is gone. As you have met Edward, you will have some idea of what is at stake here. I was hoping you would join Dimity and me in helping Eliza through this difficult time.'

Felix glanced at Dimity, who was, he thought, looking sheepish.

Good, he decided, she should look sheepish. And how dare this man try and recruit him into this land grab? Worse still, Ludovic was clearly using Dimity to help him. With Eliza's words about friends and enemies still ringing in his ears, he merely said, 'Well, Ludo, I think I can honestly say that I'm on the side of what is best for Eliza. Naturally, it's correct that her interests and affairs are in order and that there are no loose ends. So, yes, you can count on me to do the right thing. After all, I'm on the side of the angels.'

Ludovic beamed, seeming to take Felix's words as some sort of agreement to join the cause. The arrogance of the man, Felix thought.

Ludovic smoothly replied, 'Thank you so much, Felix. I hoped that I would be able to rely on you. Now, I think it would be best if we pooled our resources. If you do find anything of interest and importance here, you will let me be the first to know, won't you? Here are my details.' Ludovic handed Felix a beautifully embossed personal card.

Choosing his words carefully once again, Felix said, 'I will certainly let you know the moment I find anything I think you should know about.'

Ludovic seemed more than happy with this assurance.

Dimity gave Felix a quizzical look, which he ignored. But at least, it seemed, Dimity hadn't told Ludovic about the secret room.

Eliza had referred to Ludovic as one-dimensional, but the more Felix saw, the more he disagreed with that assessment. He seemed to him a Janus-like character, with one face looking to the past whilst the other looked towards the future. What was in it for him? Was it career-advancing kudos or, bearing in mind his father's greedy habit, something more basic, like a small Renoir or Matisse that managed to slip off the inventory? But, in the end, Felix didn't care what Ludovic wanted. Whatever it was, he wasn't going to let him have it.

When Eliza returned, Ludovic said to her smoothly, 'I must say, I have been looking at your lovely Broadwood piano. Would you mind very much if I tried it?'

Eliza looked slightly taken aback. 'No, no, not at all, Ludovic, I wish you would; it needs to be played. I am afraid I no longer do – arthritis. But I didn't know you tinkled the ivories.'

'Oh, not very well, I'm afraid. I'm very rusty, but I like to try my hand whenever I get the chance.'

Without any more encouragement, Ludovic strode over to the beautiful instrument, sat down elegantly on the leather-covered stool, opened the piano lid, and began to play. What followed was a master class in Bach. Felix felt routed – it was game, set and match to Ludovic. Whatever Ludovic had inherited from his father, clearly his musical talent came from his mother, Felix thought, as he listened to the slow and flawless strains of a sonata.

* * *

'To follow on from your dictum, Eliza, the enemy does seem alarmingly close,' said Felix, once the two visitors had departed.

'In your view, how much of an enemy?'

'It could be as much as Edward. Who knows, perhaps more so – especially with the Church behind him. I have an uneasy feeling Ludovic could be a self-serving individual, but what I can't work out is what he might be up to and why.'

Looking rueful, Eliza replied, 'Well, I don't know either – and I made a living out of anticipating these things. But you can bet your bottom dollar that it is for money or power, or both. I could add love, but seeing Dimity holding his arm, he's probably feeling confident in that department already.' Brightening a little, she added, 'But as Churchill said, "Never yield to the apparently overwhelming might of the enemy".'

Felix found he didn't much want to think about the love angle, but he replied, 'Well, what about Dimity? Clearly, she hasn't yet told Ludovic about the hidden space upstairs. Why not, do you think?'

'I think that is something you should find out, my dear.'

'Me?'

'Of course. It would set alarm bells ringing if I questioned her.'

'I suppose we should concentrate on the things we do know and the things we can find out.'

'I agree with you there, Felix. With that in mind, what is your next move?'

'I think we need some specialist advice about our hidden picture and see if it will give up any secrets. We need a specialist with the utmost discretion.'

'I can try and put you in touch with someone at the Victoria & Albert Museum – although the director has changed, and I haven't met the new one. Eliza reached for an address book perched on top of the pile of books beside her and gave Felix a name and telephone number.

'Oh, by the way, I'm out of commission tomorrow,' said Felix. 'I've promised my old school friend, Santa, that I'll look after her six-year-old daughter, Rosie – she's my goddaughter. Santa has an outpatient appointment at the hospital and none of her usual sitters are available. It'll take most of the day apparently.'

'Where will you stay with the child?' Eliza asked.

'Santa said to stay at her house.'

'And exactly what do you know about looking after a little girl?' Eliza asked.

'Not a great deal, to be honest. Actually, nothing at all. But how hard can it be?'

Eliza gave a snort. 'Naive boy, you have a lot to learn. Why don't you bring her to Witch's?'

'Here?'

'Why not? It's not as though she's going to tell anyone exactly where she's been and what she's seen. And she can have the run of the house and garden, as long as you keep an eye on her around the lake.'

'That's a wonderful offer,' said Felix. He hadn't thought about Witch's as an option, and if he had he would never have dreamt of suggesting it.

'I don't think you understand what a day with a six-year-old on your own can be like. It's relentless, exhausting. Here, there is all the space in the world for a little girl, and with Cairo and Frankie, there is all the support you and Rosie could ever need. And it may ease your friend's mind still further when she learns that Frankie is a qualified nurse. I can't be much use, but at least you needn't have any worries.'

'Well, if Santa agrees and you can stand an active and precocious little girl who never stops asking questions, it is a wonderful idea. Thank you, Eliza.'

'Of course, I can stand it. It's not as if... it will be fine. Tell your friend we will all look after Rosie as if she were our own.'

* * *

'Where are we going?' Rosie asked, once Felix had collected her the following day.

'We are going to a magical house.'

'Like Elsa and Anna's house?'

'Well, I'm not sure,' Felix said. 'What is their house like exactly?'

'It's a magic castle.'

Felix had no idea who Elsa and Anna were, probably friends from school, but he said, 'In a way, the house we're going to *is* like a magic castle.'

When they arrived, Rosie was introduced to Cairo, Frankie and West, who had all come to greet her. But the big hit was Cecily. The little dog and Rosie immediately took to each other.

Then Felix introduced Rosie to Eliza, who became more animated than he had ever seen her. In turn, Rosie seemed fascinated with Eliza.

'Are you very old?' Rosie asked.

Eliza smiled. 'Yes, I am, my dear, very old indeed.'

'Will I ever be as old as you?'

'If you look after yourself, I very much hope so. Then you will have seen and done a great deal, and hopefully, you will have made the very most of the precious long life you will have been given.'

'I like you, Eliza. You can be my fairy godmother.'

'And I like you, Rosie. I should be honoured to be your fairy godmother.'

Felix was surprised to see a tear form in Eliza's right eye. It was quickly dabbed away with a delicate, lace-trimmed handkerchief that she had pulled from her left jacket sleeve.

'What are we going to do now?' Rosie demanded.

'We can try and find secrets,' Felix suggested.

'What sort of secrets?'

'If we knew, they wouldn't be secrets.'

'I know, you could play hide-and-seek,' Eliza said. 'I loved playing that game when I was a little girl, and there are plenty of places to hide around here.'

'Me first,' Rosie demanded, before bolting upstairs with Cecily following close behind furiously wagging her tail.

'I'll count to one hundred,' Felix shouted after Rosie as she disappeared.

'I like the sound of a child's laughter in the house. It

brings it alive again,' said Eliza. Felix wondered when the last time Witch's was alive to her, but he didn't ask.

'Ready or not, I'm coming,' Felix called.

Felix thought that finding Rosie would be an easy task, but he'd been wrong. He searched every room and then searched them again. There was no sign of Rosie and Cecily anywhere.

Felix had to admit he was baffled. He looked again, and still there was no sign.

'Er, can I have some help here?' Felix called downstairs.

Frankie responded to his plight. 'Has a girl ever given you the slip before?' she cheekily enquired.

'It's the story of my life,' Felix replied, 'but search for yourself. There's no chance that she slipped back downstairs is there?'

'Not that I saw.'

Felix and Frankie looked high and low. They were starting to get concerned.

'Rosie can't have got into the secret room, could she?' Frankie asked.

'I can't see how. The door is shut tight.'

Suddenly, there came the sound of a muffled bark.

'That's Cecily,' Frankic said.

Another yap was followed by a muffled giggle.

'Where's that coming from?' Felix asked.

'It sounds as if it's from the next room.'

But there was still no sign of Rosie when Frankie and Felix searched again.

'We give up, you win,' Frankie called out. 'Where are you?'

'I'm under the window,' came Rosie's muffled voice.

Beneath the window was a panelled seat. Suddenly,

there was a shuffle and then some scraping before the seat arced open. Like a jack-in-the-box, up popped a little girl and a small dog.

'Here we are, we win,' shouted Rosie, while laughing and clapping her hands. Cecily yapped.

'Good hiding place, Rosie. We never thought to look there,' Felix said.

'Wasn't it very dark?' Frankie asked.

'Yes, it was.'

'Weren't you scared?' asked Felix.

'I had Cecily. She wasn't scared, so I wasn't. Anyway, we could hear you outside. Cecily kept moving, so I tried to stop her. Then she barked and gave us away.' Rosie looked sternly at the little dog, wagged her finger and said, 'Naughty Cecily.'

In return, Cecily wagged her tail.

'How did you know to hide in there?' Frankie asked.

'Yes, how did you discover that the seat opened?' Felix added.

'I was exploring,' said Rosie. 'There is a place like that at home. I sometimes hide in there.'

Felix recalled the window seat in Santa's house, then went over and peered into Rosie's hiding place. It was empty except for a green leatherette carry case full of old single records, including 'I Got You Babe' by Sonny and Cher and 'Ticket to Ride' by the Beatles. They were a bit before his time, Felix concluded, but certainly long after Eliza's. He wondered if they had been left there by a previous member of staff.

'Rosie,' Felix said, 'what's that in your hand?'

'I found it. It was sticking into my back,' replied Rosie. She held out her hand to reveal a large key.

'Show me where it was, will you?' Felix asked.

Rosie pointed to where she'd found the key, which had clearly been wedged in the framework of the window seat.

'Have I found a secret?' Rosie asked, wide-eyed.

'I think you might have done,' Felix replied.

'I've found a secret, I've found a secret,' Rosie chanted as she went down the stairs.

Felix held out the key for Eliza to see. 'How come it was in there, do you think?'

'I haven't a clue,' she replied. 'Perhaps it was put there and forgotten about, or dropped or hidden, who knows? But the more intriguing question for me is: where's the lock?'

CHAPTER FOURTEEN

Felix answered a call on his phone. It was Dimity.

'As it's such a nice day, how about a walk, Felix?'

'Where did you have in mind?'

'Abbotsleigh Park.'

'Now, that is a very good idea. It's on the to-do list.'

'I know, so no time like the present. Unexpectedly, I have the afternoon off.'

Reaching the outskirts of Huxley, Felix turned off the attractive, tree-lined main road that acted as the town's main western access route and entry to the Abbotsleigh housing estate.

Rows of detached and semi-detached houses – most with garages – sat comfortably behind generous front gardens.

'Welcome to Pebbledash Paradise,' said Felix.

'It looks very genteel,' added Dimity.

Felix found somewhere to park close to one of the park's entrances.

There was, Felix imagined, a small but telling gap

between him and Dimity as they walked into the park. Felix had felt this way before when he and Dimity had strolled together. It was as though the space between them created a vacuum that ached to be filled by one or both of them moving a little closer towards the other, except, neither Dimity nor Felix did that. So, the gap remained. Felix wondered if Dimity felt the same. Probably not, he decided, as she was chattering away happily as they walked, seemingly oblivious to the vacuum or the question it posed to Felix.

The weather had turned a little milder and less windy than it had been, and there was only a gentle breeze to sway the bare tree branches. The sun had banished the morning mist, and now the day was bright, with a clear blue sky.

On warm and sunny weekends, Felix felt sure the park would be packed. But on this weekday, they almost had the place to themselves.

'I've been reading up on the park,' said Dimity.

'Oh, and what did you find out?'

'After the big house was demolished, the housing estate was built in the 1930s. The local town council kept much of the park as a public amenity and golf course.'

'By the looks of it, the golf course is over there beyond the river,' Felix said, pointing to where the grass was neatly trimmed.

Dotted around the park were tennis courts, a bowling green, a croquet lawn, a children's playground, a paddling pool and a miniature railway. They all looked closed for the winter, but Felix could still admire the well-maintained parkland that was studded with mature oaks, grand cedars and other varieties of fine trees. Felix imagined this landscape hadn't changed much since the second Earl of

Rounton employed Humphry Repton to enhance it centuries before.

'I was just thinking how this park was built for a special purpose,' Felix said.

'Which was?'

'Providing pleasure for one family and showing off to others. Only the rich had large areas of land that didn't earn anything but respect or envy – preferably both.'

'Nothing changes,' sighed Dimity, 'it's a shame the park was only available to the Chasollets.'

'Oh, I don't know, it wasn't all bad. Many estate owners lent out their parks for horticultural shows, cricket matches and that sort of thing: let's hope the Chasollets did the same.'

'I hope so too, then I can imagine Sunday afternoons by the bandstand, the women wearing cloche hats and the men in boaters.'

'And all of them ignorant of the fact that, in a few years, the country would be plunged into a catastrophic world war that would change everything, including this park,' added Felix.

They continued their tour by crossing over the river on a rustic footbridge and walking up through woodland to an impressive avenue of lime trees.

'This is lovely, Felix. In full leaf, these trees must be magnificent. I really can't think why I haven't heard about this place before.'

'Nor I, but as there's no big house to look at or visit anymore, I suppose the park is simply an amenity with little or no revenue generation. Hence, it isn't widely publicised.'

'Well, I think it should be. Had I known about it, I would have loved to come walking here. Just look behind us, the view must have looked down to the big house. I'm sorry so much has gone.'

'Including a most important landscape feature.'

'What was that?'

'Repton was the first to link the house and park with formal gardens.'

'How do you know all this stuff?'

'When it comes to gardens, Google.'

Halfway along the lime avenue, a path led onto the golf course. Felix and Dimity walked down the empty fairways between the trees and greens set within a beautiful, wooded landscape. Their shoes soon became soaked by the dew-laden grass.

'Have you ever played golf, Felix?'

'I tried several years ago, but I was never hooked – or rather, I managed to hook every ball with anything under a nine iron. I think pitch and putt would have been more my game.'

Dimity laughed. 'I think crazy golf would have been mine; I don't like to play unless it involves green windmills and pink castles.'

'At least it's quicker than eighteen holes; I don't think I would have had the time to take the game up seriously. But you would be good, Mitten; you always excelled at hockey and tennis.'

'Probably not. I imagine that if it could test the patience of a saint, a priest would find it infinitely more difficult.'

'Eliza would love all this,' commented Felix.

'I'm sure she would, both the place and the history. You get on well with her, don't you?'

'I enjoy her company and her wisdom.'

'I watch you two together sometimes; in some ways, you're surprisingly similar.'

'Do you think?'

Felix and Dimity continued chatting until they came to a large information board about the flora, fauna and history of the park.

'Look, Felix, there's a Huxley Museum that holds all sorts of artefacts and information about Abbotsleigh. We should go.'

Felix looked at his watch: they would have time if they didn't dawdle. They quickly returned to the car and headed to the town.

* * *

The museum occupied the ground and first floors of an elegant Georgian house that had once been attached to the town's largest brewery. In 1979, the beer house became the casualty of an ugly one-way system that encircled the town and, in Felix's view, had turned it into a glorified traffic island. The museum was free to enter, and they found themselves alone, save for a woman wearing sensible tasselled brogues, a long, tweed, pleated skirt and a thick polo neck to protect her from the constant draught. Her greying hair was piled on top of her head in a bun. Felix was unsure if the woman was a member of staff or the public.

They began their tour of thousands of years of local history. Given their quest, they weren't too interested in the ancient exhibits, so they moved quickly to the section on Abbotsleigh Park, where there were plenty of early photographs and paintings.

Studying one photograph of the original house, Felix

said, 'The old place wasn't a classic, was it? It ended up as a Gothic pile that had lost much of its Tudor and Elizabethan identity. Pretty, it wasn't.'

'But impressive enough to be painted by both Constable and Turner according to these copies,' Dimity said.

'That's a good point. I shouldn't be so sniffy.'

Around the walls of the exhibit room were several portraits of the Chasolets, or the Earls of Rounton, as they became.

'Some of these paintings are very good indeed,' said Felix. 'There was clearly no lack of family funds, as they employed some extremely talented artists.'

Several wall panels gave information on Abbotsleigh Park from the time Henry VIII had granted it to the Chasolet family following the Dissolution of the Monasteries.

'So, most of this was monastic land,' said Dimity, 'after Henry seized as much as he could from the Church, he either sold it off or gave it away for services rendered.'

'I wonder what the Chasolets did to receive such a splendid gift?' asked Felix.

'I don't know, but it says here that, over the generations, the family's income began to dry up. Ill-advised investments into things like the South Sea Company and Dutch tulips, coupled with poor estate management and some high stakes gambling at cards meant that parcels of the estate had to be sold off.'

Felix read that originally, the estate extended to over five and a half thousand acres, with dozens of tenanted farms and smallholdings. But in the end, only Abbotsleigh Park and 800 acres was left. Then the land that remained was sold off to developers and the local council, and what was left of the family emigrated.

The next panel caught Felix's attention. 'Look at this, Mit,' he said. 'The contents of the house were sold off in a huge, ten-day sale. Then, once the house had been demolished, all the fixtures and building materials, including the oak beams and tons of Tudor bricks, were sold too. It says here that most of the materials were shipped to America where they were used in the construction of houses over there.'

'Where did the Abbotsleigh Park material end up, I wonder?' asked Dimity.

'It doesn't say, but I would love to know.'

Just then, the woman Felix had noticed earlier entered the room.

'May I be of any assistance?' she said. 'I'm the museum's curator, Valerie Puddifoot.'

'That's kind of you to ask,' said Dimity. 'We're doing some research for a friend who's interested in Abbotsleigh Park and the family who owned it.'

'Well, you have come to the right place. In fact, you have come to the *only* place. What would you like to know? Perhaps I can help.'

'Are there any maps that show the extent of the earl's original estate?' asked Felix. 'Or even the extent of the monastic holding before and after the Reformation?'

'Map making was in its infancy in those days, or at least accurate cartography. But we have one or two maps that you might like to see.'

The curator took them to a plan chest. After unlocking it, she opened a drawer and pulled out a large sheet. 'Here's a map from the 17th century.' The map was not drawn to any sort of scale, but some of the place names, such as Netilede, were familiar to Felix, even if they were spelt differently. Netilede was now Nettleden.

Felix traced his finger over the map and finally found the area where Witch's should be. A hand-painted line marked the boundaries of the Chasolets' land. Witch's was marked as woodland, and in the correct spot was a rectangular symbol delineating a building within an oval-fenced area of land surrounded by trees. By this illustration was the word Laund.

'That's it, Felix! It must be,' Dimity whispered. 'And look, it is clearly outside the Earl's estate.'

'It might mean that Witch's was given or sold to the Arrows by the earls, or by someone else. In the worst-case scenario, it was still held by the Church,' Felix murmured, 'but it didn't belong to the earls when this map was published, or at least when the boundary line was drawn, and we have no way of knowing when that may have been. I'm afraid this map doesn't help us.'

'Have you found something of interest?' asked the curator.

'We're not sure,' Felix said vaguely. 'Are there any earlier maps?'

'I am afraid not. It's strange, there was a man here a few months ago asking that very same question.'

Ignoring the remark, Dimity asked, 'Do you have many records here about Abbotsleigh?'

'Very few, I am afraid. All the books in the Abbotsleigh Park Library were sold in the big auction sale, and the family papers seem scattered to the four winds. The family have some books in Australia, and we have a few copies, but that's all. We keep an eye on the market for that type of thing, but not much surfaces nowadays.'

'We're also interested if you have any references to a family called Arrow,' said Felix. 'They may have worked with or for the earls.'

'That name doesn't ring a bell with me. Had I heard it, I'm sure I would have remembered. But let's go and look at the index and see if we can find anything.' The curator led the way to a small office, where she tapped away on a computer for some minutes. Finally, she looked up. 'Nothing here at all, I am afraid. What's the link between the two families?'

'That's something we're trying to find out,' said Dimity. 'We think a connection may have been established hundreds of years ago – perhaps as long ago as the Elizabethan or even Tudor periods. The Arrows may have had something to do with the earls, but we are uncertain what. It is just something we are following up.'

'I'll try the old card index,' the curator said. 'We keep finding bits that weren't transferred to the computer database.'

But again, Valerie Puddifoot came up empty handed. 'I am sorry not to have been able to find anything more,' she said. 'Is your name Arrow by any chance?'

'No, it's not,' replied Dimity, as Felix looked at his watch. It was nearly time for the museum to close. They thanked the curator for all her help and made their way out of the museum.

'She mentioned there was someone here asking the same questions,' said Dimity, as they walked down the front steps.

'Sounds like someone is on the same trail,' Felix replied. 'I wonder who that could have been?'

If Dimity had caught Felix's pointed remark, she didn't react and just said, 'What do you think it all means?'

'It means that unless we can find something like an earlier map, which sounds highly unlikely, it looks like the trail has gone cold. It also looks as if, without some documentation to the contrary, the Church may feel they can press its case for ownership – especially if they know about this map.'

'Which they probably now do.'

'Quite.'

'Then what shall we do?'

Felix shrugged. 'I suppose we just have to look harder.'

Dimity squeezed Felix's arm.

Felix had a fleeting feeling that he liked having his arm squeezed but then quickly brushed the notion aside.

CHAPTER FIFTEEN

Usually, Witch's Lawn was quiet save for the loud ticking of the longcase clock at the bottom of the gallery stairs and the murmur of soft voices in the salon, where Eliza held court. However, from his room, where he was spending the afternoon working, Felix could hear a heated argument, and he guessed Edward must be visiting again. Part of him felt he should leave well alone. Family disputes had nothing to do with him and he shouldn't interfere. But Edward's raised voice was concerning, and at the very least, Eliza might need some moral support.

As he descended the stairs, he could see that she was sitting in her usual chair. Edward was looming over her threateningly, but she appeared as calm and collected as ever.

'Look, you old bitch.'

'I'm sorry, Edward, my hearing isn't quite what it was. Did you say bitch or witch? Because a witch is exactly what I am.'

'I said bitch, and you are not going to stop me inheriting this house,' screamed Edward.

'But that is precisely what I am going to do.'

It was then that Edward noticed Felix's presence. 'And you can go back to where you came from,' he shouted.

Ignoring Edward, Felix asked, 'Are you all right, Eliza?'

'It's nothing I can't handle, my dear.'

Edward continued his rant. 'I've told you before that I have friends in high places. I know people and I know things about you.'

'Edward, your friends are only in the foothills of high places.'

'I'm going to make your life a misery.'

'Mate, if you're not careful, I'm going to make *your* life a misery.'

Felix, Eliza and Edward looked around to see West entering the room.

'Everything OK here, Eliza?' he asked.

'I think Edward was just leaving. Perhaps you will show him the door.'

'My pleasure.'

'Your attack dog doesn't frighten me,' said Edward.

'Well, that's your second mistake today, because he should frighten you. Your first mistake was coming here at all, but happily for me, it will be your last visit. If you ever come here or near me again my attack dog, as you so accurately describe him, will become your worst nightmare. West, please do the honours.'

As West went to move towards him, Edward raised his hands and hurried to the door while screaming that he would sort 'it' and Eliza, if need be.

'Handbags,' was all West said as Edward sped away.

'Pah,' said Eliza. 'Edward was comfortable enough threatening an old lady, but not taking you on, West.'

'Do you think that's the end of it?' Felix asked.

'I shouldn't think so,' replied Eliza. 'Edward will try and disrupt things as much as he can.'

'What can you do about it?'

'Ah, well, I have another attack dog, but you haven't met him yet. Now, West, after all this excitement, will you ask Cairo to make a pot of tea.'

To try and take her mind off things, Felix sat down and told Eliza about his visit to Abbotsleigh Park and the museum in Huxley. She insisted on a blow-by-blow account. Felix was getting used to providing these reports and he didn't leave anything out, including the curator's comment about someone else having enquired about the Abbotsleigh estate. Felix knew Eliza wanted to live every moment. She didn't just want to know where he had been but also whom he had met, how he had felt and what he had seen and heard. At times, she even wanted to know what he had smelt and tasted, and he could imagine her building up a detailed picture in her mind.

'To tell you the truth, Eliza, I have been thinking more about the possible connection between Abbotsleigh Park and Witch's. I know it sounds tenuous, but my mind keeps wandering back to this business with the building materials from old houses finding their way to America in the 1920s. I've done a bit of research in the area.'

'Good to see you thinking about the peripherals,' said Eliza. 'We'll make a spook of you yet. So, where has your research taken you?'

'I've discovered that selling salvage wasn't unique to Abbotsleigh. It went on a great deal. Our stately homes were being taken down, while in the US they were being put up.'

'I should imagine it's difficult to know where to start looking.'

'You're right, but it seemed to me the most likely destination for all the materials would have been the East Coast. It was the shortest route and, in those days, where most of the money was.'

'So, you think that's maybe where the Abbotsleigh Park house ended up?'

'It could be – albeit in bits. It's a long shot, but it may be that we're not just investigating two buildings in England but one in America too – four if you include the flat at St James's.'

'I take it there's more?' Eliza asked with a smile.

'Yes, there is.'

'Well, spit it out, my boy.'

'I spent yesterday afternoon trawling Google for references to Abbotsleigh Park. There was page after page of entries, but all of them about the one in Huxley. I was beginning to despair when I found an entry about an Abbotsleigh House in Neugent, New York. I looked up the address online and then found it on Street View. The house certainly looks old enough. I have written to the owners. I might not hear back, but you never know.'

'No stone unturned, dear. That's the spirit.'

'It's luck that the house is still there,' Felix said. 'Americans are all too happy to tear down homes that are past their sell-by-dates and replace them with new, sparkly ones. This house doesn't seem to have met that fate... yet.'

'What will you do if you hear back?'

'Explain as much as I can under the circumstances and see what happens, I suppose.'

'Have you been to America, Felix?'

'Quite a few times. I've got clients there, so I've made several trips for work, and I've had a two-week holiday in Florida and spent a long weekend in New York Christmas shopping. How about you?'

'I spent some time there in the early '60s. I was in a place called Langley in Virginia.'

'Eliza, that's where the CIA is based!'

'So, it is,' replied Eliza with a straight face.

Felix laughed. 'Oh, and I wanted to mention that as the key Rosie found in the window seat doesn't fit any lock at Witch's that I can find, I'm curious to know if it fits one anywhere else... I wondered about St. James's.'

'The old chest you couldn't open?'

'It's worth a try. I thought I would take Dimity again, if that's OK with you?'

'Of course it is, but you might also take West. There's a little job I want him to do for me. He might as well go when you're there.'

* * *

'Eliza told me to bring this,' West said, holding up Rosie's key after meeting Felix and Dimity at St James's Palace.

'Thank you,' Felix replied. 'I'm not holding out much hope of finding anything, but one never knows.'

'You don't want to leave any key unturned, and quite right too,' said West with a smile Felix had last seen when he had ejected Edward from Witch's.

West unlocked the outer door to the apartment with a high degree of familiarity.

'You've been here before?' asked Felix.

'Oh, yes, Eliza lets Cairo and me use the apartment sometimes if we are in London overnight for dinner or the theatre – Cairo likes a musical from time to time, though I'm not so keen.'

The admission alarmed Felix, who asked, 'What happens to Eliza when you are here? Who looks after her and Witch's?'

'We get in some cover,' West said casually. 'Actually, we never have to ask twice. All the guys we use love staying at Witch's. But what they really like is talking with Eliza. She's a legend.'

Together, the three of them headed up the spiral stairway and walked along the gallery.

'What's it like staying here in the Palace?' Dimity asked West.

'Special... that's all I can say really. It's good for a bit of seduction, if you catch my drift. Cairo and I love staying here. It's a bit basic, but better than living in a cave.'

'I do get your drift,' said Dimity with a smile.

Felix decided it was the most animated he had ever seen West.

'Moment of truth,' West said, crouching down and inserting Rosie's key into the lock of the large chest.

It slid in easily enough, but then West grunted and said, 'Either it's the wrong key, or we need my oilcan.' He was straining to turn the key before seeming to exert some extra heft, at which point the key turned grudgingly in the lock. Felix watched with a tingle of excitement as West went to raise the lid.

'Blimey,' he said suddenly, 'that thing is heavier than it looks. West had to use two hands to prise the lid open. The reason soon became clear. It was no ordinary box. Beneath the rather undistinguished wooden exterior was an iron strongbox.

'That's a fantastic disguise,' Felix said, 'you'd hardly give the thing a second look. No wonder we didn't give it too much thought before.'

'Talking of wonder, look at what we have here,' said West.

Felix stared into the chest. While the rest of the room had thrown up little in the way of fascinating objects, this was full of them.

'Not exactly what I was expecting,' said Dimity, sounding less than impressed.

'It's a small armoury,' West explained, as he reached in and lifted out a sword. 'This is a rapier; there must be four or five more here. And here's a tuck.'

'What's a tuck?' Felix asked.

'It's a bit shorter than a rapier.'

'And what's that gruesome-looking, wavy, bladed thing?' said Dimity.

'It's a dagger called a Kris. It comes from Indonesia and is supposed to possess magical powers. I don't know about that, but it looks as if it has the power to do some nasty damage.'

Felix noticed Dimity shudder.

'And look at these other knives,' continued West, 'beautiful handles.'

He caressed the weapons and then returned to rummaging, bringing out a swordstick, a cudgel, several flintlock pistols of various sizes and a box of assorted musket balls and powder flasks.

'The tools of the Arrow trade, perhaps?' wondered Felix.

'Once upon a time, I imagine so,' replied West.

'And I thought it was all rather romantic sounding,' Dimity said. 'This chest brings the story into an altogether more sinister light, doesn't it?'

'It does,' said Felix. 'Eliza once told me the family was more cloak than the dagger. But these weapons seem to suggest otherwise.'

'Oh, I don't know,' said West, 'they would have had to look after themselves if need be. In the right hands, a sharp blade or musket can do some serious looking after.'

West had now reached the bottom of the chest, where he found a small collection of leather items. 'There's some leather belts, baldrics and an empty scabbard,' he said.

'I'm afraid it looks like a wasted journey,' Felix said. 'I'm sorry to have dragged you both here for nothing.'

West replaced all the arms in the chest and locked it back up again. 'That's OK,' he said. 'I have one other thing to do for Eliza while I'm here.'

He lifted a rug in the living room and took up two short floorboards to expose a floor safe, which he unlocked using another key. 'Eliza wanted me to check in here,' he explained, 'just in case she had forgotten anything.' He whistled. 'Just look what's in this one.'

Inside were two large bundles of banknotes of different denominations and currencies, most of them, Felix feared, now out of date. There were also several passports with photos of a much younger looking Eliza, and a handgun.

'More tools of the trade,' said West approvingly. 'This

gun must be Eliza's. I suspect it's been here since the war, or soon after. It's a Berretta... beautiful.'

West checked there was no ammunition in the gun's magazine or chamber before returning it to the safe. 'It needs a good clean. I'll do that next time I'm here.'

'With all the security here, why would Eliza even need a safe?' Dimity asked.

'You can never be too sure,' said West.

Dimity blew out the candles and switched off the light. The three of them then retraced their steps down the spiral staircase.

As they reached the door, Dimity told them to wait.

'Why?' Felix asked.

Dimity turned to West. 'Did you say there was an empty scabbard upstairs?'

'In the chest? Yes, I did, why?'

'"In darkness blind the inching midnight thief/Marks as worthless the lone un-bladed sheath,"' Dimity recited. 'Might not Eliza, in crossword mode, ask if an empty scabbard is the same as an un-bladed sheath?'

'Why, yes, I think she would,' agreed Felix. 'We'd better go back; it's worth checking.'

They returned upstairs and reopened the chest.

West took out the empty scabbard. 'I think we could do with some tweezers,' he said. 'If I remember right, Eliza keeps things like that in one of the bedside cabinets – and we'll need a knife from the kitchen.'

Using both utensils, West fished around the inside of the scabbard until, with a barely audible small scrape, he slowly revealed a tightly folded piece of vellum. 'So, what have we here?'

'Another sonnet, by the looks of it,' said Dimity, taking

hold of the vellum and unfolding the small sheet, which she carried to the window to make use of the light. She began to read.

II

Beloved kin, thy loyal duty sworn,
Fight bold and true for lord and mistress state.
Then service done and deepest passion worn,
May short life's bitter ending longer wait.
Now set ye down this script and look to Heav'n,
Lest time bring on memorys sad distress,
Or words deceit do mask those gages given,
And true reward the rise of deep recess.
The sweet deeds our mistress in her good part,
Ever carv'd in hard oaken majesty,
Are kept within a pierc'd finial heart,
As my lord did tread in fair Abbotsleigh.
For shrouded seal in deepest coven hidd'n,
We look to Heav'n for our riches given.

'I've gone all tingly,' said Dimity.

'Not so sure I haven't,' said West.

Felix reached for his phone. 'Eliza,' he said breathlessly, when she answered after only three rings, 'we've found another verse – verse number two. It was hidden in the casket.'

A barrage of questions from Eliza followed, which Felix did his best to answer.

'She wants to see the verse as soon as possible, and we better take the scabbard,' Felix told Dimity and West after the call had ended.

'Pity,' said West. 'I thought we'd have time for a bevvy.'

Together, they left the quiet, secret world of the Palace for the noisy, public one of St James's Street, before heading back to Witch's Lawn.

CHAPTER SIXTEEN

Felix was pleased to have been invited to a meeting at the Victoria and Albert Museum. His enquiry had bounced relatively quickly up the chain of command to the desk of the cheerfully welcoming director, Dr Timothy Kindred.

Dr Kindred was not what Felix had expected. For some reason, he had imagined an older man in an out-of-shape suit. So, he was surprised to be greeted by someone of average height in his mid-thirties. His shoulder-length, dark hair was parted in the middle and he wore round, metal-framed glasses and an open black frock coat over a billowing white shirt. A thin, red, yellow and green striped scarf was loosely knotted to create a cravat, and he was showing a lot of cuff. But to Felix, the most notable item of all was his purple silk and monogrammed slippers. Of course, this was the newly appointed director of the V&A, so how else should he look, Felix thought, while still regarding him more bohemian aesthete than the director of a national museum.

Over coffee, Felix ran through some background to Witch's Lawn. Several of the director's predecessors had been to the property. Timothy, as he urged Felix to call him, hadn't visited but knew of it through briefing notes. He listened carefully to what Felix had to say and told him how much he would like to see the secret room and its contents for himself.

Then he imparted some advice about art experts who could look at the portrait found in the secret room. At first, Timothy suggested one of his curators at the V&A. But when Felix described the condition of the painting, he had no hesitation in recommending Professor Aria Broughton, the director of the Courtauld Institute of Art. She was, Timothy told Felix, regarded as a world leader in the study and conservation of art.

As an afterthought, Felix asked, 'Have you ever come across the practice of sending salvaged building materials to the US in the early 1900s – bricks, timber and that sort of thing – from stately homes?'

'Now you come to mention it, the Metropolitan Museum of Art has some architectural pieces collected that way, but I know nothing more specific. May I ask why?'

'It's just personal curiosity at this stage, but I came across a story about a house in New York that was possibly built from one demolished in England. I wondered if you might have an expert here who knows something about it. Otherwise, do you know someone in the States – at the Met, perhaps?'

Timothy looked appalled. 'Oh, I don't think we need to involve our American friends, do you? I'm regularly in the US on the lecture circuit and visiting other museums – especially in New York. I should be delighted to look into it myself if you don't object? It sounds an intriguing story.'

The highly competitive worlds of curatorship and

scholarship were alive and well at the V&A, Felix thought, as he told Timothy he would welcome the assistance.

After the meeting, Felix phoned the Courtauld Institute. After dropping Timothy Kindred's name, he was put through to Aria Broughton, who sounded equally intrigued by the story and the description of the portrait. Felix offered to bring the painting to her, but she asked him not to touch it. 'I think, if you can arrange it, I should come and see the picture in situ,' she said.

* * *

With Eliza's agreement, Aria wasted no time and arrived at Witch's several days later along with a petite, ethereal-looking woman in her thirties. Felix was struck by her appearance. A mass of flame-red curls cascaded over her shoulders and made her hair seem alight. She wore an above-the-knee skirt, a blue-grey, cable knit Aran jumper, a Barbour jacket that had already seen good service and suede knee-high boots. Aria introduced this wisp of pre-Raphaelitism, as Felix saw her, as Dr Margaret Petrie, a specialist in spectrometry.

Aria Broughton was about six feet tall and looked a serious woman, but then, Felix reasoned, as head of the Courtauld Institute, she had a serious role. She wore her straight, dark-brown hair in a sharp, asymmetrical bob and was dressed smartly in well-cut dark blue jeans, a plain red jumper under a tweed jacket and high-heeled ankle boots, which emphasised her height to an even greater extent.

The two women spent some time politely talking to Eliza and Felix about the find, but all the while, Felix could see they were itching to look at the painting, so he wasted no time in taking them upstairs and into the hidden room.

'All we have done is get rid of the dust and cobwebs,' Felix told them. 'We were, of course, especially careful with the picture.'

'That's a pity; we would have liked to clean the room ourselves, but never mind, what's done is done,' said Aria.

'Do you think we have done any harm?' Felix asked, suddenly concerned.

'No, of course not, I'm just jealous not to have discovered this under the grime in the first place,' Aria said with a laugh.

Amid murmured conversation, the two experts carefully inspected the painting with magnifying glasses and small, high-powered torches.

'What do you think?' Felix eventually asked.

'It's hard to see in these conditions, especially with the state the picture is in,' Aria replied.

'I couldn't help thinking there was a certain resemblance to the portraits of Sir Thomas Moore and Henry VIII by Holbein,' Felix said.

'I can see why you'd think that,' said Margaret Petrie, still peering at the picture.

'So, this could be by the great artist himself?' Felix asked hopefully.

'I only said that I could see why you might think so,' said Margaret.

'Yes, that is a big stretch,' Aria added. 'It is far too early to even speculate about the artist. But personally, I don't think it is... Holbein was much imitated. It will take more than a quick inspection to even begin to conclude who the artist is or even if this is real or an elaborate fake.'

'Did you make out the small piece of parchment in the foreground?' Felix asked.

'We did notice that,' Margaret replied, 'it would be wonderful to know what it is.'

'Actually, I think I know exactly what it is – or an item very like it. There's something I haven't shown you.'

'There's more?' asked Aria.

Felix smiled. 'Yes, there's more.' He revealed to the two women the secret drawer in the desk along with the missal, rosary and, finally, the sonnet.

'It certainly does look just the same as in the picture or, as you say, Felix, something very similar,' Aria said, almost in a whisper.

'So, does that throw up any further light on the matter?' Felix asked.

'Well, we will have to do some in-depth research,' Margaret replied.

'What date do you think we are we looking at here?' Felix persisted.

Margaret sighed. 'If it is genuine, then judging by what we can see of the figure's clothes and the style of the painting, the early to mid-1500s would be my guess. Wouldn't you agree, Aria?'

'If it's authentic, then all the signs suggest so,' she said. 'But we must not get ahead of ourselves. Without any provenance, we can't be sure, although one thing is certain; unless our friend here in the picture had good contacts at court or a great deal of money, he would never have been able to commission a portrait such as this.'

Felix nodded his understanding. 'The former is not at all out of the question. But whoever this is by, is it real or fake?'

'My gut tells me it's genuine,' Margaret said. 'It's just one of those feelings that, as a scientist, I shouldn't have or, at least, admit to. But from what I can see of the colours and texture, it seems right somehow, don't you think, Aria? Especially in the context of this secret room – I just don't know by whom it was painted.'

Felix suddenly remembered Eliza waiting downstairs and suggested to the two women that they fill her in on their findings.

'Why don't we take the picture to her?' Margaret suggested.

They gently unhooked the painting from where it had hung for hundreds of years and carefully carried it down to Eliza, who stared at it for a long time. She listened keenly as the two experts explained their views.

'I feel as if I am staring into a deep well,' said Eliza. 'It's strange, but somehow it makes me want this man to be proud of me, in the same way that for some reason I feel proud of him. I didn't know him, and I don't know what he did... I'm not even sure of his name, but I feel a bond. I feel that he is part of me, or I part of him.'

Turning to Felix, Eliza added: 'I am so appreciative that you have helped me discover this. Without you, I would have died without knowing. I don't think you will ever understand how much it means to me. For pity's sake, I didn't know what it would mean to me until I saw it just now. Do you know that if this is a Tudor picture then this man could be my great-grandfather fifteen or sixteen times removed? Imagine that?' Turning to the two experts, she asked: 'What else can modern methods tell us about the picture?'

'Well, now it gets scientific,' explained Aria.

'We will have to use some infra-red photography,' Margaret added.

'What will that do?' asked Eliza.

'It can show up any underdrawings that may expose an artist's methods and any changes made in the composition as they worked,' Margaret replied. 'The photography may also reveal something about the painting technique. Sometimes that can be as good as a fingerprint in identifying the artist. As you mentioned Holbein, Felix, infra-red could show up signature ability to capture individual details of the subject such as eyes and eyebrows.' Margaret smiled before adding, 'Holbein was very good with facial hair.'

'You can tell all that with infra-red photography?' asked Eliza.

'That and much more,' said Aria, 'if this is a Tudor period portrait by one of the recognised painters of the day, I have to say it could be worth a great deal.'

Eliza shrugged. 'I have no interest in the value, nor really who painted it. It will never be sold. No, what is important to me is the person in the picture. I need to know more about him.'

'To do that, we must carry out some research at the Institute, where we have all the facilities we could possibly need. We will then marry up our scientific findings with some historical detective work,' Aria said, 'but it might help to have a copy of your family tree, Eliza, if you have one?'

'I can arrange that for you,' replied Eliza.

'I have something else to ask,' Aria said, 'could we take the painting back with us? We took the precaution of bringing one of our special cases for transportation. I hope that you don't feel we were too presumptuous.'

'Not at all, my dear,' said Eliza, with an understanding

nod, 'that was good forward planning; just let me have a receipt,' she added.

Later, Felix phoned Dimity to tell her about the day.

'What were the ladies from the Courtauld like?' Dimity wanted to know.

Felix gave her his impression of Aria Broughton.

'And the other one?'

'Her name is Margaret Petrie; I looked her up online,' Felix said. 'She has a doctorate in the history of art and a degree in spectroscopy. Otherwise, there's little else I can tell you other than that she's a dish.'

CHAPTER SEVENTEEN

'I've heard from New York,' Felix told Eliza excitedly. 'It seems my hunch was right. The owner of the house in Neugent, Maurice Glasgall, has emailed me and confirmed the connection with our Abbotsleigh House. He said he should be pleased to help in any way he can. It seems he and his wife, Mona, know all about the history of the house – that's partly why they bought it in the first place. Maurice mentioned that they visited Abbotsleigh Park on a couple of occasions when they were on holiday in the UK, and there were lots of features in their house that came from the original one. He's invited me to go and see for myself.'

'That was good of him.'

'I have an American client in New York, and I've been thinking how it's about time I went to see him. I could kill two birds with one stone.'

'What are the chances you will find something to help us?'

'Minimal, I would say.'

'But if you don't go, how would you feel if we missed some vital piece of information?'

'Gutted.'

'Do you want to risk feeling gutted?'

'No.'

'Then go, Felix.'

* * *

Felix arranged his flight to New York before spending a few days in the office catching up with paperwork and meeting the firm's accountant as well as several clients. The day before he was due to fly to America, he popped into the ground floor showroom in Pimlico, where he was surrounded by fabrics, rugs, lighting and some lovely furnishings. These were put together by a small team of specialists, who steadily grew this important part of Provenance Architecture & Law. The shop was one of his favourite places, as it kept him in touch with customers and helped him to spot fashion trends. The design studio, which handled building and interior commissions, along with the shop were becoming increasingly well-known, partly due to some excellent marketing and what Felix saw as eye-wateringly expensive advertising in glossy house and interior design magazines. But the results certainly seemed to speak for themselves and were steadily helping to build the PAL brand.

The old-fashioned bell above the shop door rang, alerting staff that someone had entered. Felix looked up, and for a second blankly looked at a familiar figure. It was only when the momentary fog cleared that he recognised an out-of-context Margaret Petrie. It was pouring with rain outside and she had dressed for the weather in a belted trench coat with the collar turned up and a waxed Fedora hat.

'Hello, Margaret, what brings you to my humble establishment?'

Looking around the shop and sliding her dripping umbrella into the brass stand by the door, she replied, 'Hardly humble, by the looks of it, Felix. I have an appointment with the art dealer Peter Stafford nearby, and, as I'm early, I thought I would pop in for a snoop. I'm pleased to see you here. Aren't you at Witch's Lawn a great deal these days?'

'I am, increasingly so, but I like to put in some shop time when I can.'

'I must say, it looks lovely. I can already see plenty of things I should like, though they're all too big for my little flat. But as I'm here and if you have time, I can give you an update on the portrait, even if it won't be long before you can see for yourself what we've unearthed.'

'That sounds most intriguing.' Felix glanced at his watch.

'Oh, I'm sorry, you must be really busy. I shouldn't have barged in like this.'

'No, no, not at all. I was just thinking that as it's past twelve, have you time for an early lunch? I usually go around the corner to the Fig Tree. They make the best roast beef and horseradish sauce sandwiches anywhere on the planet, and they brew their own beer.'

'Actually, I'm a vegetarian, but the beer sounds good.'

Sharing Margaret's umbrella, Felix steered her to the pub, which was already heaving. They were lucky to find two stools at the bar, where they ordered two halves of *SW1* bitter, a cheese selection platter with crackers and a roast beef sandwich made with fresh, doorstep-thick granary bread.

Perched on their stools, Margaret told Felix about her research into the portrait and how far she had got with the cleaning, which was halfway complete. The picture had, Margaret said, held up surprisingly well over the hundreds of years it had hung in the secret room. She put this down to a reasonably consistent temperature and the lack of daylight, which meant the colours hadn't faded.

The pair chatted easily together about a range of other subjects until Margaret said she must get to her appointment and offered to pay for lunch, which Felix declined on the basis it was his suggestion and his treat.

They walked together as far as Felix's showroom and, with a quick hug, bade their farewells.

* * *

The Virgin Atlantic 9.05am flight from Heathrow to JFK Airport, New York, landed on schedule at 11.45am local time.

Felix collected a mid-size SUV from the airport rental car centre. He crawled in heavy traffic until he was over the Whitestone Bridge, with its sweeping view of the Manhattan skyline. After that the road cleared somewhat and he was able to join the Taconic State Parkway.

Felix imagined that, in the autumn, this would be a spectacular drive through a rich palette of colours. But now the scenery was dank and drab.

Running early for his appointment with the Glasgalls, he drove into Neugent and down its pretty Main Street. Amongst the clapboard shops and houses, he found a bar and grill just across from the railway station, where, having not eaten on the plane, he swiftly devoured a lobster omelette and a piece of homemade apple pie, which he washed down with a large mug of hot coffee.

Back in the car, he headed to Abbotsleigh House. Drawing up to some impressive double iron gates set between twin brick, pepperpot gatehouses, he announced himself over the entry phone and was duly told to enter. As he drove onto the forecourt of an elegant and substantial double-storey house with a parapet roof, he reflected on how incredible it was that it had been constructed almost a century earlier from material salvaged from a mansion 4,000 miles away.

A housekeeper met him at the front door and ushered him inside.

Before long, both Glasgalls appeared. Maurice and Mona looked to Felix as though they were both in their early eighties, but they seemed exceptionally spry. Maurice was about 5 feet 6 inches and was dressed in grey slacks, a crisp, white polo shirt and black lattice leather slip-ons. His face was tanned, as was the top of his head, which was mostly bald. Mona was about five feet and was dressed beautifully in neat, navy trousers and a white T-shirt. It seemed to Felix as if the Glasgalls looked after themselves very well, but, he supposed, there was no shortage of money to help in that department. The couple appeared to be enjoying the fruits of their working lives in a comfortable retirement, and they couldn't have been more welcoming.

It wasn't long before Felix and his hosts were talking about the history of the two Abbotsleigh houses, and it soon became apparent to Felix that Maurice and Mona knew as much as him, if not more.

After a cup of tea and cookies, the couple showed him

around the house. Not only was it made from the Tudor bricks and wooden beams salvaged from England, but the wall panelling, interior doors and several fireplaces had also made the transatlantic voyage. Felix knew that in a country of immigrants, it wasn't surprising that settlers used the architectural styles and building methods they were familiar with from their homelands. But it remained both strange and thrilling to be surrounded by the materials that had once been part of the Abbotsleigh Park he knew.

Felix touched the carvings. 'I think whoever built this did a terrific job blending the old with the new,' he said to Maurice and Mona. 'But I'm stunned by the amount of original material: it's amazing to me that it was worth transporting so much over here.'

'Gimme a break,' Maurice exclaimed, in his distinctive New York City drawl. 'Don't underestimate the strong desire, even at the end of the gilded age, to have stately things from England. It gave Americans the chance to show off how well they were doing. It's still going on – just look at us!'

'The panelling you have here is beautiful,' Felix said.

'It's called linenfold, although I am sure you know that, coming from England,' said Mona. 'We love it. I think it's what sold us on the house when we saw it over thirty years ago.'

Their home was certainly a large one, with nine bedrooms upstairs, but in modern terms, it was light on bathrooms. The main reception rooms on the ground floor had retained the grandeur they were designed to project, but once again, the domestic offices were numerous and rather cramped for contemporary tastes. Maurice and Mona had moved into the house with a set of living habits and, in the intervening years, had not changed their lifestyle much in line with evolving trends. No doubt they saw little reason to do so. They seemed comfortable in their home, although they did seem to rattle around in it a bit. Felix reflected how it was really meant for a large family with live-in staff.

'So, what got you into all this?' Maurice asked him.

'What, the mystery of Abbotsleigh?'

'Is that what you call it?'

'An old friend got me involved. I'm a pretty rare beast; an architect and a lawyer. From a legal point of view, I specialise in cases of real estate title.'

'And you have a dispute here?'

'None bigger, in my experience. Do I understand correctly that you were in the film industry, Maurice?'

'Yes, I was. I've been retired for some years now. Mona and I lived in Beverly Hills back then, but we kept this house as a link with home. I was a movie producer, and I can tell you that, for this story, I would be delighted to come out of retirement.'

Felix laughed and then asked, 'How did you and Mona meet?'

'We were college sweethearts,' explained Mona. 'A student friend of Maurice was nervous about asking me on a date, so Maurice volunteered to call me on his behalf, except once we got talking, he forgot to mention his friend.'

Felix laughed. 'Maurice knew a good thing when he heard it.'

'He certainly did, but some days I wonder if I would have been better off with the friend.'

'Don't listen to her, Felix, it was a good deal – I traded a friend for a wife.'

Mona rolled her eyes. 'We were at Columbia, where we majored in English literature. That's partly why we both fell in love with the house when we first saw it; it reminded us of so many books we had read.'

'I was going to write the great American novel,' Maurice said with a sigh.

'So, what happened?' Felix asked.

'I wasn't F. Scott Fitzgerald or John Steinbeck. Nowhere near.'

'And what did you do after college, Mona?'

'I became an actress – theatre mostly, on and off Broadway.'

'How glamorous you both are,' Felix said, and he meant it.

'Sounds as if you have a pretty glamorous job on your hands now,' Maurice said. 'Is there anything else you can share?'

Felix told Maurice and Mona what he knew about Abbotsleigh Park in England before moving onto the mystery concerning the Earls of Rounton and the Arrow family. He explained about trying to find clues from the sonnets they had found. He had written the three verses down in his notebook, although he could also recite them off by heart. The couple listened intently as he read them out loud.

'That is so beautiful,' said Mona, when Felix had finished. 'It sounds like Shakespeare. What does it all mean, do you think?'

'That is what we are struggling with,' Felix replied. 'We can't work out what the writer wished to convey.'

'From what you have told us about the family, I'm sure it was written to be cryptic,' said Maurice. 'What do *you* think about these verses, Felix?'

'Well, the script around the room was literal when we didn't expect that, especially about looking to heaven. It didn't mean in the biblical sense but to physically look up at the word. So, I suppose we might look at the sonnets in the same way. After all, the same person might have written them as had the script painted. Besides which, the sonnet found in the family bible tells us not to take anything at face value.'

Maurice nodded. 'If the same person set the clues in each of the verses, then one can come to understand their style. It makes things easier for the puzzle solver.'

'My Morrie is so good with this sort of thing,' said Mona. 'He is always doing the *New York Times* crossword.'

Maurice patted his wife's hand and asked, 'How far have you got with decrypting this, Felix?'

'Not very far, I'm afraid. But, with this house in mind, I've been wondering about the line, "As my good lord did tread in fair Abbotsleigh." It sounds literal, but where did he tread in Abbotsleigh? And who was *he*? The word lord is written with a lowercase l, so that suggests a mortal rather than a deity.'

Maurice studied the verses in Felix's notebook, then said, 'I'm drawn to the phrase, "Or words deceit do mask those gages given." Now, words deceit probably means lies, and mask no doubt means hide. But what does gages mean? I am also confused about "the rise of deep recess."'

'It confuses me too,' said Felix, 'although I have found out that in Tudor times, gages meant pledges.'

'I would like to know what sweet deeds means,' said Mona, 'and who was the mistress?'

'We have struggled with that for weeks,' said Felix. 'It could mean a favour.'

'A royal favour perhaps,' suggested Mona.

'It's worth thinking about, as the words mistress and

majesty are used,' said Maurice. 'That, of course, seems to suggest a queen. If so, it seems that she did somebody a favour.'

Felix thought for a moment. 'So, what about, "Forever carved in hard oaken majesty?"' he asked.

'To me, that indicates something permanent and grand,' said Maurice. 'And the use of carved and oak seems substantial and purposeful.'

'Something carved in an oak tree?' Felix asked. 'If so, what tree? And if this was hundreds of years ago, it probably doesn't exist anymore.'

'It may not mean a tree,' said Maurice, 'it could mean some other carving – perhaps even at Abbotsleigh Park.'

'But the house is gone, so it isn't there to find,' Felix said. 'Like you, Maurice, my client is good at crosswords and often warns me about making things fit.'

'Your client is very wise.'

'What do you think "kept within a pierced finial heart" means?' asked Mona.

'I'm sure some words are more significant than others,' replied Maurice. 'But perhaps some of them have two meanings, and we are picking up the wrong one, as we are supposed to. We need to understand the poet's true intent.'

'Some of the words might just have been used to cause confusion,' Felix suggested, returning to the script and trying to scan it with different eyes.

'There are several references to wood in the poem, for instance, carved and hard oaken, and finials are often made from wood, as are staircases. Abbotsleigh was famous for its wood features.'

'Pity the staircase is gone,' Felix said.

Maurice was quiet for a moment, before adding, 'You've seen a great deal of Tudor woodwork here today, Felix, but there is one object I didn't point out at the time. Come and have a look.'

Maurice led Felix and Mona back to the main hall. 'There,' he said.

'Where?' Felix asked.

'Tudor woodwork,' Maurice said with a smile.

Felix followed Maurice's gaze. 'The staircase?'

Maurice nodded.

'You mean this staircase is the one from Abbotsleigh Park?'

'The very one,' said Maurice. 'For dramatic effect, I was choosing my moment to tell you – old habits die hard, I guess. It seems I picked just the right time.'

'But what does our staircase have to do with all this?' asked Mona.

'It might mean nothing at all,' said Maurice. 'But think about it, the poem tells where the master did tread. So, it seems likely that it was somewhere one of the first earls walked, and maybe not just occasionally.'

'Stairs have treads,' Felix said, catching onto Maurice's train of thought.

'So, rise as in risers,' said Maurice. 'And our staircase has those big newel posts at the top and bottom, and there are finials above both newel caps.'

'And they are richly carved from oak,' Felix added, feeling a surge of excitement. 'But could it be that we are selecting convenient words and then making them fit?'

'Only time and investigation will tell,' said Maurice.

'Do you mean the poem might have something to do with *our* staircase?' asked Mona.

'It might do, and I certainly want to find out if it does,' said Maurice. 'Felix, what do you suggest?'

'I'm not sure; I'm not a master joiner, nor do I know much about 17th century carpentry.'

'There is a staircase much like ours in the Metropolitan Museum of Art,' said Mona. 'Can't you inspect that one, Maurice?'

'Don't worry, nobody is going to damage our staircase,' Maurice replied. 'After all, it was dismantled once before when it was brought across from England in the 1920s.'

'If only we knew where to look,' said Felix.

'I for one want to find out,' said Maurice. 'Don't you, Mona? We'd be helping Felix's client in England.'

Mona nodded, and the inspection of the staircase continued. The newel posts were large, square and exquisitely carved on four sides with acanthus scroll and seedpods. They reflected the carvings that supported the heavy balustrade.

'I'm told that this staircase, like the one in the Met, was first thought to be the work of Grinling Gibbons, the famous Dutch wood craftsman,' explained Maurice. 'We really should get an expert in to look at it.'

'I know someone who might be able to open the right doors,' said Felix.

After a further hour spent discussing the mystery, Mona said, 'Felix, we would love you to stay for dinner.'

He protested that it would be too much of an imposition.

'Morrie, tell Felix that he should stay,' said Mona.

Maurice shook his head at Felix as if to say it wasn't even worth trying to argue with his wife.

Once they were seated at the dinner table, Felix said,

'Before we go any further, there is one thing I should ask you both.'

'What's that?' asked Maurice.

'I have no right to ask,' Felix said, 'but I must. There are several reasons why it would be best if this matter was kept strictly between us – but please don't worry, it's all legal and above board.'

'I don't doubt it,' said Maurice.

'We can't tell anyone?' asked Mona, looking slightly disappointed. Felix guessed she had already been planning what she would say to her friends.

'No, we can't,' said Maurice firmly.

'You haven't even enquired why I have asked for discretion,' Felix said.

'I don't need to. You will have your reasons. I recognise a straight shooter when I see one. And I know how to keep secrets. In my world, you had to, or there would be no future in the movie business. Your secret is safe with us, isn't it, Mona?'

'Of course, it is, Morrie. Mum's the word.'

After dinner and heartfelt goodbyes, Felix drove into New York City: it was late, and he was going against the traffic, but in the city that never sleeps, he knew that the traffic didn't sleep either. In the event, it could have been worse. He drove down towards the west side of Manhattan on the Saw Mill River and Henry Hudson Parkways before eventually arriving at his hotel on Central Park South, where a parking valet took the car, and a bellman did the same with his luggage. He checked in and found that his room didn't look out over the park but into a dingy interior courtyard. Felix also knew that in New York City, that's what you got unless you were prepared to pay big bucks.

At eleven o' clock the next morning, Felix called Eliza.

'What have you found?' she asked, getting straight to the point.

'A staircase.'

'Are you being obtuse again?'

'No, I'm not,' Felix protested, and then he described to Eliza his afternoon and evening with the Glasgalls.

'It sounds fascinating, but where does all this get us?'

'I think we might have a better understanding of the verses, and I am going to speak to Timothy Kindred about all the carved wood I've seen here.'

'Well, hurry back. I've heard from the Church. It isn't good news.'

* * *

Felix's second call was to Dimity. Again, he went through his visit to Abbotsleigh House. Dimity asked lots of questions and then filled Felix in on her day. Before hanging up, Felix said, 'Oh, I bumped into Margaret Petrie before I left.'

'Bumped into?'

'Well, not bumped into exactly. Margaret was passing on her way to see an art dealer near my office. We had lunch.'

'That must have been nice.'

'It was. She told me how she was getting on with the portrait.'

'And?'

'Well, they are doing the research and getting on with the clean.'

'So, not that much to tell.'

'Put like that, I suppose not.'

'How did you get on?'

'What, with Margaret?'

'That's who you had lunch with.'

'Very well, in fact.'

'Oh, will you see her again?'

Felix thought this question sounded more like a demand to know than friendly interest, but he simply replied, 'I suppose I will, when she reveals the fully cleaned portrait.'

CHAPTER EIGHTEEN

Having driven directly to Witch's from Heathrow, and despite feeling decidedly jet-lagged, Felix sat down with Eliza. 'I warned you not to wait for another letter from the Church,' he said. 'They're getting stroppy now.'

'I know, dear, but the firm of solicitors the family has used for years has merged with another, and I don't know anyone at this new one. Could you act for me with the Church, Felix? I want someone I like and trust... someone who will fight hard and take a personal interest.'

'I'm flattered that you should ask, but I've already told you that I don't have the resources of a large city firm.'

'Well, I don't think I have time to go out and find another solicitor now, do I?'

Felix sighed. 'No, I don't think you do. OK, I will write a stalling letter, and we'll see where we go from there. But we can't delay; we don't want to test the patience of the Church's legal department too much – it will only encourage them. We need to keep some level of control, even if it's only the illusion of control.'

Keen to change the subject, Eliza asked Felix to tell her more about his trip to the Big Apple.

'I would love to meet the Glasgalls,' she said at one point.

Felix thought how much they would love to meet Eliza, though he noticed how she didn't seem her normal self. He put it down to worry and age, but he also sensed there might be something else, so he enquired if she was feeling all right.

'To tell you the truth, my dear, I haven't felt right for a week or two now. I have been dwelling on the past a bit too much, I think. I'm sure it will pass. In the meantime, what do you want to do about Margaret Petrie?'

'What do you mean?'

'She called to say the picture has been cleaned, at least enough so they can see what they are doing. Margaret thinks it best if we go to the Courtauld. I really don't feel up to it, so perhaps you could go with Dimity?'

'Oh, OK. When did Margaret suggest?'

'Tomorrow. I have spoken with Dimity, and she can make herself available in the afternoon: she seemed most interested in going.'

'Well, that's OK by me. I'll be fine after a good sleep. Now, I think I should get back to London tonight and sort myself out.'

'Of course, you should. I will arrange everything. By the way, I hope you don't mind me mentioning this, but, talking about Dimity, is everything good between the two of you?'

'I don't mind at all, and we're fine.'

'Just fine?'

'Yes.'

'I know I shouldn't pry, but I am very fond of you both, you know.'

'Now that Dimity and I have re-established our friendship, I am sure we will always be friends.'

'Just friends?'

'Eliza, believe me, being just friends is good. There are no complications. No unrequited feelings.'

'Are you sure, dear?'

'I'm positive. Dimity needs more drama in her life than I can provide; I'm a bit too staid for her. To be honest, I think I always have been. I'm not sure why we were such good friends growing up. She was always wanting to go off and do things she shouldn't – usually involving physical risk – while I preferred to avoid trouble.'

'But you and Dimity were close on a personal level – you talked.'

'For hours. We could almost finish each other's sentences.'

'And that wasn't enough?'

'Evidently not.'

'Not your choice?'

'We were very young, Eliza.'

'Young love is complicated.'

'I don't think complications in love are limited to the young.'

Eliza smiled. 'Of course, you are right, my dear. But how do you feel now that Dimity seems to have passed that derring-do phase of her life?'

'Has she passed it? I hear she is abseiling down the abbey tower for charity in a few weeks. Anyway, I try not to think too much about it, as she seems to be spending more and more time with Ludovic. They're off to Devon soon on some sort of retreat, or so Dimity tells me.'

Eliza shook her head. 'Perhaps matters of the heart were

simpler in my younger days. War and danger tended to speed up decision-making – for good or ill. But Dimity certainly didn't mention to me that she and Ludovic were going away together.'

'There seems to be a lot of retreats and conferences in the Church of England.'

'So I gather, but Dimity will make her way – whichever way that will be. With time, she will make up her mind about what is the best road for her.'

'Meanwhile, I'd like to know what the best road for me is. And, as you asked, I'm not sure how I feel about Dimity.'

Felix had never opened up to Eliza like this before. But somehow it felt comfortable doing so. She seemed so wise and concerned.

'Oh, I think you know how you feel, my dear. I tend to think that love is like spotting an eagle. If you have to ask, it's a buzzard. When it's an eagle, you know it.'

'I suppose you're right, but I'm a simple soul, while Dimity is complex.'

'Silly boy,' Eliza said with an exasperated tone.

'What do you mean?'

'From where I am sitting, it's the other way around.'

'How did you reach that conclusion?' asked Felix, somewhat taken aback.

'Dimity is the simple soul. All the adventure, I'm sure, was just a way of her finding out who she is. Her marriage was unfortunate, but maybe a necessary step towards her vocation – not that she knew it at the time, of course. When one door closes, another usually opens. And now that she is happier in herself, she is free to make decisions she couldn't make before.

'On the other hand, you are still trying to find yourself.

From the outside, you seem to have everything sorted out, but I think you still have lots of questions. You are on your own. You no longer have a family, and I think perhaps you would like one – look at how you are with Rosie. And I'm pretty sure you have never quite got Dimity out of your system. Perhaps you never will. But, my dear, unless you do – either get over her or do something about it – then I fear you may never move on. Oh, you say that you don't want to become involved – if you even had the chance. But isn't that just a defence? I wonder how accurate that would prove if you were totally honest with yourself. And how honest are you with Dimity?'

'I'm not dishonest with her. We might not talk about these things, but Dimity knows how I feel: she has always known how I feel.'

'But what does she know? What Dimity thinks and what you think she thinks maybe two completely different things. Perhaps she thinks of you as her old partner-in-crime who is now married to his work and highly content with his current way of life.'

'Don't you think Dimity is married to her work?'

'That's exactly what I mean, Felix. I don't know the answer to that any more than you do. And you will never know until one of you has the guts to start an honest conversation. Perhaps Dimity thinks you were in love with her once but have got over it.'

'To be honest, I don't think I will ever truly get over it.'

'Well, that is, at least, a start,' Eliza said with a smile.

'How did you get all this out of me?'

'You wanted to tell someone, and I'm glad it was me.'

'I'm glad it was you, too. Have you spoken to Dimity about any of this?'

'Felix, you know enough about me by now to know I wouldn't tell you even if I had.'

'Of course, I'm sorry. You would never say anything. But what about Ludovic?'

'That preening puffball! I've known plenty like him over the years, I can tell you.'

'But I thought you were all in favour of Ludovic, Eliza – the invitations, the teas, the piano playing. You must admit that he and Dimity make a handsome couple. And you seem to be doing all you can to encourage him to help you with Witch's.'

'Oh, Felix,' Eliza said with an exasperated sigh. 'That's just what I mean. Have you never heard of rope-a-dope?'

'Rope-a-dope?' Felix said with a laugh, thinking it a surreal question from a woman of Eliza's age. 'Of course, I have. Rope-a-dope was Muhammad Ali and George Foreman, the Rumble in the Jungle. Ali let Foreman punch the living daylights out of him until Foreman was so tired he had no punches left. Then, having survived Foreman's ferocious attack, Ali fought back to win. It was a classic.'

'Exactly,' said Eliza.

Felix laughed. 'So, you are going to let Ludovic do his worst and then counter punch? You're not in your family business for nothing, are you?'

'No, I'm not. Let's see what Mr Poniard has got.'

'Do you play chess by any chance?' Felix asked.

'My papa was an excellent player and teacher. Now, my dear boy, you should be off before you're too late. But remember, while what will be will be, nothing will be if you sit in one of these all day' – she patted the arm of her chair. 'Nowadays, there's not much I can do but sit here, but if you put your mind to it, you can make things happen.'

Eliza then rose and embraced Felix. She had never done that before, and he was touched by the gesture.

'Peace and lesser sorrow, Felix,' Eliza said suddenly.

'What do you mean?'

'Oh, it's what we Arrows say, sometimes as a farewell and sometimes as a toast. It's a silly tradition but it's been said for years – centuries, I suppose. I don't really know why. Now, off you go. Let me have all the news from the Courtauld tomorrow.'

Felix dwelt on Eliza's words as he drove back to London. He had thought he had his life pretty well worked out, but an elderly lady kept throwing a spanner in the works.

CHAPTER NINETEEN

Margaret Petrie greeted Felix at the entrance to The Courtauld Institute of Art at Somerset House with a kiss.

Felix introduced Dimity and then said to Margaret, 'We're excited to find out what you have been able to make of the picture.'

'I must say that uncovering this work has been a huge pleasure,' said Margaret. Then, turning to Dimity, she added, 'We work on some valuable and rare art, but often it's not half as intriguing as Eliza's painting. Conserving precious artworks is our job as scientists – and our art – and while that often brings with it a heavy responsibility, it can also be a huge honour. This is what we felt with your picture. Anyway, let me lead you to the conservation department where I work.'

'She *is* a dish,' Dimity whispered to Felix as they followed out of earshot.

'I told you.'

'Is she an attached dish?'

'Why, are you interested?'

'No, *I'm* not interested, Felix, I just thought you might be, that's all. She isn't wearing a wedding or engagement ring.'

In response, Felix smirked at Dimity.

'The picture was badly obscured by dirt and grime,' Dimity said to Margaret once they'd reached the department. 'Have you been able to restore it?'

'Not in the time we've had so far. We will need much longer for restoration, but we've cleaned it enough to see what's going on. Strictly speaking, restoration isn't an exact art or science. An oil painting, especially a good portrait, is like a photograph – a snatched moment in time. But that medium degrades over the years, and the colours can fade in bright sunlight. Also, the paint itself can become brittle and craze and flake. Your picture was in poor condition, but not irretrievably so. That's where good restoration comes in. It's where art and science meet nowadays. X-ray spectrometry and infrared photography can help us see deeper into a painting – beneath what we can see with the naked eye.'

'So, in those ways, you can see how the painting initially looked?' said Dimity.

'We can't ever fully retrieve the past, I'm afraid – even with up-to-the-minute technology and sophisticated modern chemistry. Perhaps AI will come to help more in the future, but the day the painter finished the picture is gone forever. Paintings change from the very moment they are completed, yet I'm constantly surprised by what we can do. With thorough research, a magic mix of chemicals, technology and deft touch with trusty cotton wool buds, we can, at least, have a good idea of how a painting looked originally.'

'Was this painting particularly difficult?' Felix asked.

'It could have been much worse,' said Margaret. 'It's astonishing that it has survived all this time. That's very much down to the dry and stable environment in which it has remained over the years. One other saving grace is that our picture was left undetected and so has not been interfered with by amateur or inexpert restorers, as is so often the case.'

Margaret led Felix and Dimity over to a workbench, where an easel stood with a protective sheet shrouding it. 'So, now we come to the moment of truth,' she said.

Carefully, Margaret took away the cloth and revealed the portrait.

Dimity gasped, and not for the first time during his research, Felix felt the hairs rise on the back of his neck. A handsome man with a slightly hooked nose, hooded eyes and laughter lines looked out confidently from the canvas. He wore a black coat over a white, baggy undershirt. A heavy gold chain hung around his neck while on his head an otherwise plain black cap in what looked like velvet was embellished with a large red brooch with a gold surround that hung down over his left eye. Felix studied the figure for some time, getting to know the face and taking in the assured posture. When he looked into the eyes, they appeared to look straight back at him, boring into his brain as if they were trying to reach into his soul. Yet somehow, he felt comfortable with that. Felix had the strangest feeling that he had met this man before. But then, he figured he was probably looking at one of Eliza's forebears, so maybe the familiarity wasn't so strange after all.

'Over a short time, I have got to know this gentleman quite well,' Margaret said.

'Have you discovered anything else?' Felix asked.

'First, we had to try and date the portrait,' said Margaret, 'but here I'm going to disappoint you. You were hoping for a Holbein connection. For several reasons, we believe this work was done about twenty years after he died in 1543. But we do think we might know who the subject is, and the name of the painter. If Eliza is correct and it is one of her forebears, then, according to the family tree, we think this is James Arrow. But we can't find out too much about him.'

'Given his probable occupation, I'm not surprised,' Felix said.

'So, who do you think painted this picture?' Dimity asked.

'Before I tell you that, it may be useful to consider why this portrait was commissioned.'

'Wasn't it for posterity or vanity?' Dimity asked.

'Usually, you would be correct, but in this instance, we think it was for another purpose. Likenesses were produced for many reasons in this period, and vanity may have been one of them. But given the family history, this man would probably have wanted to remain anonymous. Another important purpose of having a portrait painted was to help find a marriage partner.'

'A bit like online dating,' suggested Dimity.

Margaret laughed. 'A lot like online dating. However, our historian doesn't think this portrait was painted for romantic purposes either. By this time, miniatures rather than larger portraits were being used for matchmaking. It might be a bit of a leap, but we think it might have been painted as a message or a series of messages. Put another way, it could be a pictorial code.'

'Which ties in exactly with the family's occupation,' said Felix, as much to himself as anyone else.

'Messages to whom?' asked Dimity.

'That's anyone's guess at this stage.'

'But why do you think it is sending a message?' Felix asked.

'There are several details that suggest so. The first is the signet ring.'

Felix peered closely at the ring. 'It's the same emblem as the coat of arms over Witch's front door.'

'Exactly, so that's our first real clue. It is, we feel, safe to assume that this is one of Eliza's forebears. Next on the table is a red rose – a Tudor rose. This represents the House of Lancaster, implying the sitter's support of the monarch who was, of course, a Tudor. Then there's the small parchment on the table.'

'We thought it looked like the sonnet, and now it does even more so,' Felix observed.

'Yes, it does. Also, look at what the sitter is holding in his right hand.'

'It looks like some sort of letter or text with a large seal,' said Dimity.

'Take a closer look at the seal. Here, use my magnifying glass.'

'It's very faint, but it looks like a woman with a huge ruff sitting on a horse,' said Dimity.

'That isn't Queen Elizabeth I, is it?' Felix asked.

'We think it's her, but why or what it represents we have no way of knowing.'

'This just gets more and more incredible,' said Dimity.

'It does, but the picture asks as many questions as it answers. For instance, the gold chain, which clearly signifies status. Then there's the hat and the red and gold brooch. This man certainly appears influential and wealthy. Portraits by skilled artists weren't cheap, so they weren't commissioned by just anyone. So, to answer your question on attribution, Dimity, we think that the brushwork and technique match those of an artist called Steven van Herwijck. He was Dutch and he worked in the Low Countries, Poland and England, where he is known to have visited in 1562 to 1563, and again a few years later, just before he died. We know that in around 1565, he undertook some special works for Elizabeth I. It's conceivable that this portrait could have been one of those. We know that William Cecil, the Queen's special advisor, knew van Herwijck. So that could have easily put the artist in her orbit.'

'So, where does our man in the picture come in?' Dimity asked.

'William Cecil ran the Queen's spy network. If the man in the painting was involved in that secret world, it may tie in with the connection with the Earls of Rounton. If he's an Arrow, perhaps James Arrow, and was involved in espionage in some way, maybe royal favours followed. But at this stage, this is all supposition.'

'Is there a chance this portrait could be telling us something about the extent of special favours?' Felix asked.

'I wasn't going to go so far as to say that, but perhaps. Every clue so far suggests that, just as it points to Steven the Paynter, as van Herwijck may also have been called. Of course, there is no provenance as far as we know. We may never know the historical detail, as it is unlikely anything was ever written down due to the shroud of secrecy that surrounded these things. It's not as if we can pop down to the National Archives at Kew and discover a convenient paper trail, but we are getting further opinions from other leading experts on the painting itself. We're not expecting any great surprises, though there is one other thing about which we are extremely curious. In the background of the picture is a small coat of arms. We are checking with the College of Arms, which is just down the road in Queen Victoria Street, but we think these are the arms of the first Earl of Rounton, Robert Chasolet. If they are, and other experts agree that Steven van Herwijck painted the picture, then it could link him with Elizabeth I, William Cecil and James Arrow.'

'What else do you take from the background of the picture?' Felix asked.

'We've spent a long time studying it, and it's an odd one,' replied Margaret. 'It would be usual to have some sort of draped fabric, an impressive room or landscape as a backdrop, but the sitter seems to be in a staircase hall of a large house. We contacted *Country Life* magazine and asked them to send over some photographs of the hall at Abbotsleigh Park. They have an extensive archive of images taken before many stately homes were demolished. Here they are.' Margaret removed several photographs from a file and spread them out.

'They look just like the one in the painting,' Dimity observed.

Felix didn't say anything, knowing he had recently seen that very same staircase in America.

'We think it's too similar to be a coincidence,' said Margaret. 'It's an odd choice of backdrop, so we did wonder if this was another message. After all, most other props seem to have a specific purpose in the composition.'

'Oh, and there is one other thing about the man in the painting,' said Margaret with a smile.

'What's that?' Felix asked.

'He's got Eliza's nose, don't you think?'

Dimity laughed. 'I suppose he has a bit,' she said.

* * *

'There are so many more things to find out,' said Dimity as she and Felix walked across the courtyard of Somerset House. 'What was the document with the large seal? What did it represent? What is the background to the picture saying? We have a long way to go.'

'Yes, we have,' Felix agreed, 'now, how about a drink?'

'That would be nice. Where do you suggest?'

'The American Bar at The Savoy.'

'That sounds expensive.'

'Yes, but we should celebrate.'

'Celebrate what?'

'Finding James Arrow, and my hunch that he is finally going to find his voice after hundreds of years.'

* * *

'I'm going to stay in London for a few days, there are some things I need to attend to at my office,' Felix told Eliza, when he called to report on the meeting with Margaret. The time he had been spending at Witch's meant his office admin and housekeeping had suffered. Besides, he urgently needed to arrange another meeting with Timothy Kindred at the Victoria and Albert Museum.

Although full of questions about the portrait, Eliza still seemed vague, distant and preoccupied. Felix asked if she had heard from Edward again or wasn't feeling well.

'No, no, my dear, I just have a lot on my mind. How long will you be in London?'

'I'll be back with you on Friday. Eliza, are you sure everything's OK?'

'Of course. Now hurry back. I'm getting used to having you here.'

CHAPTER TWENTY

A few days later, Felix arrived back at Witch's to find a black Range Rover parked at the front of the house. At first, he thought Edward had returned. But then he noticed that this car had a different number plate.

Entering the salon, he found Eliza sitting with a man he'd never seen before. He was slim, long-limbed, dressed smartly and had one distinguishing feature, a brown leather glove covering his left hand.

'Oh, I'm sorry, Eliza, am I interrupting?'

'No, my dear. We were waiting for you. There is something we wish to discuss.'

Felix eyed the visitor again.

'Felix, this is my friend, Sir Bidian de Butts.'

The man stood up and, with a firm grip, shook Felix by the hand. 'Bidian, please meet Felix Bohlin. Felix, I have asked Bidian to join me today as we have unearthed some significant information.'

'About the house?' Felix asked, suddenly feeling unaccountably nervous.

'No, not about the house. Bidian has been helping me... rather like you do, but on another matter, and we seem to have turned up something rather, well, unexpected and, frankly, almost unbelievable.'

'How does that involve me – or doesn't it?' Felix asked.

'It very much does involve you,' said Eliza with gravity.

'Sounds intriguing,' Felix replied, still feeling inexplicably nervous.

'Felix, from the day you set foot in this house, I have enjoyed your company immensely.'

'As I have enjoyed yours.'

Eliza held up a hand. 'Now, I'm going to ask you not to interrupt – this is difficult enough for me.'

Felix had the impression he may be asked to halt his investigations for some reason, and he suddenly understood how involved he had become with Eliza and Witch's. But he still couldn't see why this other man was there or what he had to do with him.

'There are some things you don't know about me,' Eliza continued, 'and I feel this is the time I should tell you. I mentioned to you before how there was once someone special in my life who died in the war.'

Felix nodded.

'I told you that we were briefly married, before he went off to fight.'

Felix nodded again.

'But what I haven't told you is that when my husband left, I was... I was pregnant. Of course, it was a strange time, and I was in love – we were in love. War skews relationships. No girls knew if they would ever see their men again and no boys knew if they would ever return... so, well, you know, we may have jumped the gun a bit.'

Felix nodded for a third time.

'We married – not because we had to, but because we were in love. In fact, my husband never knew that he was going to be a father: I couldn't get the news to him in time before he died. So, our child was effectively born fatherless. My parents were pretty shocked, to say the least, although they had met, liked and approved of my husband a great deal. I think, deep down, they understood the adjustments in personal behaviour that war can bring. They had seen much the same sort of thing in the Great War. But once Mama and Papa set their eyes on the child, everything changed. For many years they became parents again. Remember that I was away for much of the time doing war things. Without my parents, I don't know what would have happened.'

'Was the child a boy or a girl?' Felix asked, unsure of where this was all going.

Eliza smiled. 'A girl, a beautiful little girl.'

Suddenly, Felix remembered Eliza's joy and tears in having Rosie visit and her comment about having a child's laughter in the house again. 'Does that explain those records in the window seat upstairs and the Henry Moore in the garden – the five figures in the shadow?' he asked.

'Ah, you noticed... that is perceptive of you. Henry Moore did the sculpture in the late '40s and then added the shadow later, after something happened, of which I'm about to tell you.'

'What was your child's name?'

'Athene.'

'The Greek goddess of wisdom and the arts.'

'Yes, and Athene was also the goddess of heroic endeavour. But I lost her, just as I lost her father. Her grandparents had already passed away by then, otherwise, I think the tragedy would have killed them... it certainly nearly killed me. Athene was a beautiful girl – bright, lively and good at sport – and she was head girl at her school and captain of hockey. She received an Army scholarship to Bristol University, where she read modern languages. Then she joined her regiment.'

'Let me guess, the Intelligence Corp,' Felix said.

'Why yes, it was,' said Eliza with a smile.

'I would have expected nothing less, but may I ask what happened?'

'I only wish I could tell you with any degree of certainty. Athene was on active duty in Belfast. It was early in the Troubles. Even now, I don't know the full story. But I do know that she was working undercover. Athene and another member of her unit simply disappeared one day. The Army thought they had been found out and dealt with as spies. Even now, I really don't like to think about it. Of course, lots of people died during that awful time. Officially, nineteen people disappeared, but unofficially, many more were lost. Questions were asked back then, and on occasion since, but nobody knows where Athene is buried. Or, if they do, no one is saying. Either way, it amounts to the same thing; I simply don't know what happened to my daughter.'

'Oh, Eliza, I am so sorry.' Felix reached over to squeeze Eliza's hand. Tears were beginning to roll down her cheeks.

'My grief has often seemed unbearable.'

'You lost your husband and your daughter when they were both so young; I can't begin to imagine how awful that was – is. I'm glad that you have been able to tell me, Eliza, but I don't understand what all this has to do with me.'

'We'll come to that in good time. Few lives go without

some grief. You will have already met that emotion with the loss of your parents – your adoptive parents, if I'm correct?'

'I can't remember our discussing my parents in great detail, but yes, I was adopted, though I never really made that distinction. My mum and dad were wonderful people, and they did everything they could for me.'

'I'm comforted to hear it,' said Eliza. 'Do you know, Felix, that as soon as Dimity told me about you, I thought how I should like to meet you? That's why I asked her to invite you to Witch's in the first place.'

'Why the great interest?'

'There were several reasons. First, I was curious about Dimity's friend. She had told me a great deal about you – more, I noticed, than about anyone else in her life. I thought how I should like to meet that person. And I love meeting new people, especially younger ones, as I believe you have discovered. I also imagined that, through your own interests and profession, you might appreciate seeing this house. I wondered if, using your legal skills, you might in some way be able to help me – once I knew it would be safe, that is. In that, I was not wrong. And I have to say that I also stirred the pot a bit in bringing you and Dimity back together. I just couldn't resist doing so. Was that wrong?'

Felix smiled. 'No, you weren't wrong. I'm glad you did, in fact. I'm pleased that Dimity and I are friends again. But what do you mean, once you knew it would be safe?'

'Felix, would you be happy to invite a perfect stranger to this house?'

Felix thought for a moment. 'Point taken, but how on earth did you find out that I *was* safe?'

'I contacted Bidian. He has access to certain information – the sort that other people can't uncover.'

'Let's just say that I run a government agency,' Sir Bidian interjected.

Felix paused and then asked, 'Would that, by any chance, be the same agency that introduced Cairo, West and Frankie to Witch's?'

'The very same,' Sir Bidian answered evenly.

'And might I ask how you two know each other?'

'Eliza and I have known each other for many years. In fact, she helped in my early training.'

Felix turned to Eliza. 'So, you had me vetted?'

'To be honest, dear, yes, I... well, Bidian did.'

'And did you have Dimity vetted too?'

'Yes, we did. My family has always believed in safety first. Nothing ever gets in the way of protecting them.'

'But I haven't told you the other reason I had in wanting to meet you. It's a silly one, I know, but you see, my husband's name was Felix. And since the day he left for France in 1939, I hadn't met another one. And then you came along, and I just wanted to meet a Felix again. Perhaps if you had been called by any other name, I would never have met you.'

'I think I can understand that. It must be such a long time since you saw your Felix.'

'Over seventy years.'

'Well, all I can say is that I hope I didn't disappoint you,' Felix said with a smile.

Eliza didn't return the gesture; in fact, she looked very serious. 'That's the point, Felix. You didn't disappoint me, but you did confuse me. I had a strange feeling that I had met you before. At times that has made me feel upset and disorientated.'

'Then why didn't you say? Why did you keep inviting me back if I upset you?'

'For one thing, you were helping me with this family problem, and for another, I very soon came to enjoy your being here.'

'That's very nice of you to say, but I don't want you getting upset over me.'

Eliza nodded. 'Now, I have to make another confession to add to the one about having you looked into.' She paused for a moment, then said, 'In having you vetted, I learned some things about your background – things that even you won't know. So, I must ask you now, before I go on, if you would prefer me to tell you what we have found out or whether you would rather not know? If you would rather remain in the dark, I will completely understand. You may not want to unearth the past.'

Felix didn't know what to think. 'I suppose I haven't anything to hide about my past except for some schoolboy pranks and misdemeanours. One that I am not proud of at all and the others that I rather am.'

'This is not really about *your* past, Felix. It is about your parents' – your biological ones.'

'Oh, then I'm not quite sure what to say. If it's something awful like they were serial killers, I would prefer not to know.'

'You are going to have to trust me that if it were anything like that, I wouldn't mention it. You will have to rely on my judgement.'

'I suppose, on that basis, if there is a story, and I do trust you, Eliza, then I had better know it rather than live on in ignorance. But I can't imagine what you have to tell me.'

'I'm glad you feel like that,' said Eliza. 'Now, do you know anything about your biological parents?'

'Mum and Dad only told me that they had been killed in a car accident not long after I was born.'

'Have you ever been curious about them?'

'Yes, of course, but it is not as if my parents were alive so I could make contact when I was old enough. When I was little, when Mum and Dad told me that they had adopted me... no, chosen me, I fantasised about my natural parents to a degree. I think a lot of adopted children do the same. I even made up stories about them not being dead and finding me, not that I needed finding, of course. I was happy with the mum and dad I had. They were the best parents ever. I adored them.'

'I am delighted to hear that,' Eliza said. 'Your adoptive father was a retired policeman, wasn't he?'

'That's correct. Dad had been in Special Branch but was invalided out early through an injury. After that, he worked in private security – an old pal of his from Special Branch, my late Godfather actually, set up the firm. Mum didn't work. I'm not sure that Dad's job paid overly well. Because of his injury, he was confined to a desk. But while I don't think we had lots of money, we were comfortable enough, I suppose, through Dad's pay and pensions.'

I found out the same,' Eliza said. 'I also discovered that your adoptive father was a courageous man who was shot in the line of duty. He couldn't walk well without a stick after that and, sadly, he and your adoptive mother couldn't have children of their own.'

'That's right. Dad wasn't too mobile, and in the main, Mum looked after us both.'

'But you still managed to go to a good school, the one where you met Dimity?'

'Yes, we met at a mixed prep school, and we both went onto the same upper school. It wasn't easy for my parents, but I was fortunate to get a scholarship.'

'Did you ever wonder where the extra money came from to keep you at an expensive, fee-paying school? The money for things like books, uniforms, sports equipment and school trips – I understand that you ski well?'

'Quite well, and yes, I learned while I was at school. At the time, I didn't think about the extra cost, of course. I don't suppose kids do much, and my parents never made a big thing out of it. But I have wondered about it since. I suppose I thought there might have been some other bursary, as Dad had been in the police. I never asked. Now it's too late.'

'In many ways, that is exactly what did happen,' said Eliza.

'But how did you find anything out? Adoption records are closely guarded.'

'That is where I came in again,' said Sir Bidian. 'In my position, I can open some of the most firmly closed doors and uncover tightly kept secrets.'

'I did feel we were prying a bit, but I wanted to know some background so that I could be sure. I also wanted to know for Dimity,' said Eliza.

'Why for Dimity?'

'Because of her relationship with you.'

'But there is no relationship between us.'

Eliza smiled. 'Are you sure of that, my dear?'

Felix frowned. 'So, what did you find out about me?'

'There was little about you, Felix. As I said, it was never

really about you. Except we discovered that you were a good son and a diligent and popular student. And you have become a well-respected professional. We didn't really expect anything else – no radicalism or questionable practices,' Eliza added with a smile. 'It was what happened before you came along that became the real focus of our attention. It was who your natural parents were that provided Bidian with a barrier that even he, with all his access, couldn't initially penetrate.'

'I kept hitting brick walls,' explained Sir Bidian. 'After a while, I realised that it wasn't the adoption people who were the problem but something or someone altogether more formidable. I don't like brick walls, and I soon caught on to the fact that this may not have been an ordinary adoption – not that any adoption should be considered ordinary, of course.'

'So, what sort of adoption was it?' Felix asked.

'For some while I got absolutely nowhere and couldn't tell. I suppose the longer it went on, the more intrigued Eliza and I became. I could find no record of your natural parents at all. The trail was quite cold. So, one day, I came here to tell Eliza that there were no more avenues of enquiry I could follow.'

'Bidian told me that it was as if your parents had disappeared,' said Eliza, pausing to let the last word hang in the air.

'Disappeared?'

'Yes, my dear.'

'I don't understand what you're saying. They were killed in a car accident.'

Eliza sighed. 'What I am saying in a long and roundabout way, Felix, is that we discovered that my daughter and your natural mother had died or disappeared at around the same age and around the same time. It seemed an odd coincidence. You must remember that Bidian and I are analysts. We are trained to connect random information that shouldn't, on the face of it, interoperate. So naturally, during the analytical process, we questioned if Athene could have had a child.'

Felix was dumbstruck.

'But the moment Bidian told me about the disappearances I knew,' said Eliza. 'I knew from your looks and your mannerisms. Above all, I knew from my heart. I then realised why I was often so confused about you. It was because those mannerisms that I saw in you weren't of one person I loved, but of two people. Remember how I wished you peace and lesser sorrow recently?'

'Yes, you told me it was a family saying when bidding goodbye to someone or making a toast, and then you embraced me for the first time. I was surprised but felt pleased.'

'What I could have added,' said Eliza, 'was that peace and lesser sorrow is something we only say to other family members... I blurted it out without thinking. Then I hugged you like a grandson... *my* grandson.'

Felix stared at Eliza for a long moment and then said, 'No, no, no, that's not possible. I think I can understand your emotion, but it's too big a leap of imagination. It's wishful thinking. It's preposterous. You have both reverse-engineered the story and concocted an answer you like. You and I met by sheer chance, Eliza. It is far too much of a coincidence. I mean, I can appreciate that you may have wanted it to be like that – to find an answer to the question you had always had about your daughter. I don't mean to be insensitive, but that is not the same as cold reality and hard facts, is it?'

'You are absolutely right, Felix,' Eliza said. 'And I know I was sentimental, even though I'm trained not to let personal feelings get in the way of analysis. But I still couldn't deny the coincidence. In our business, anything beyond half a coincidence is grounds for deep suspicion – or it should be. Only a DNA match will prove it for certain. Of course, I wouldn't dream of having a test carried out without your knowledge and agreement.'

'I just don't believe any of this, it's surreal,' said Felix.

Eliza smiled at him. 'Hear us out, please?'

Felix stood up. 'It's beyond unimaginable.'

'Please tell him, Bidian.'

'Felix, I do understand how all this sounds completely unfeasible, but let me try and help,' said Sir Bidian. 'I have to tell you that now we pretty much know the full story. After Eliza told me of her suspicions, I set about joining up the dots. Once I knew where to look, I made the right connections and found the correct people to talk to – people in Army intelligence. Of course, the few that did know anything were either long gone or retired. But I got to the bottom of it in the end.'

'The bottom of what?'

'How your biological mother and Eliza's daughter are one and the same.'

'But how can you be so sure that you can confront me with this – I mean, apart from the mannerisms and things?'

'Athene had been working undercover in Northern Ireland,' said Sir Bidian. 'It was dangerous work, deadly as it turned out. In Belfast, she worked alongside a fearless young man called Philip Quinton. He was just a few years older than Athene and was quite dashing by all accounts. He had been in the Royal Lancers and then transferred to the SAS. It seems that, while working undercover, the two fell in love and, well, Athene fell pregnant. But this put them in a perilous position. Athene couldn't have had an abortion even if she had wanted one, as she was living amongst Catholic IRA sympathisers. So, there was no choice, she had to have the child – although Eliza thinks Athene would have kept the baby anyway. We believe Athene and Philip suspected the IRA had their reservations about them and were watching them like hawks. If Athene was found out, there could have been horrible reprisals.

'We think Athene felt she had to protect her child and her greater family. If the IRA found out about the Arrows, it would have proved very difficult and dangerous, not just for Eliza and the military, but for the British government, too. It must have seemed to Athene that it would be for the best that no one knew – including Eliza.

'So, Athene's Army handlers arranged for the baby to be adopted by a trustworthy and security-cleared couple anxious for a child but unable to have one themselves. It was part of the arrangement that nobody outside a very tight security circle ever knew about it.'

'And you think the couple who adopted the baby were my parents?' said Felix in a whisper.

'We now know for certain they were, my dear,' said Eliza. 'But I already knew that. The first time I saw you I was struck by something – I just didn't know what. By some bizarre twist of fate, Dimity had brought you home to Witch's. It meant I hadn't lost Athene entirely. She had sent me the most important part of her... the most special part of her. I was distraught for a while. It was like history repeating itself. At first, I thought Athene hadn't told me about her baby because she imagined I would be disappointed or upset with her. But how could I have been? I had done the same thing at the same age.'

'So, what happened to Athene and Philip?' said Felix.

'I'm afraid we don't know,' replied Sir Bidian. 'We are left to assume the IRA discovered they were spies or traitors and had them murdered. We've never found their remains, even after the Independent Commission for the Location of Victims' Remains was established between the British and Irish governments. Using information given in the strictest confidence, extensive searches were carried out but five people, including Athene and Philip, have never been found.

'Philip's was – is – an Army family. Both his parents are sadly now dead. His father was a Lieutenant Colonel in the Paras. But there is a sister – your aunt. When we have finally and officially confirmed all this, I will leave it up to you to get in touch with her if you wish. It is quite safe for you to do so now. Your aunt married a soldier, an officer in the Blues and Royals. I'm sure she would like to meet her nephew. And you might like to meet your three cousins. With the IRA disbanded and the Troubles hopefully behind us forever, there is no longer such a threat. But I still think that the fewer people who know about this, the better.'

'I'm sorry, I still can't believe all this. It's too far-fetched,' said Felix.

Eliza took Felix's hand. 'My dear, I know this is an enormous thing to take in, but I wouldn't have dreamt of telling you any of it if we weren't one hundred per cent certain.'

'Felix, Eliza is right,' Sir Bidian said firmly. 'There is no doubt now that we are correct. Athene and Philip were your biological parents.'

'So, who am I supposed to be?' said Felix. 'Am I a Bohlin, a Quinten or an Arrow?'

'You are the same person you were when you came here today, Felix,' said Eliza gently. 'But you've also been all three. You just didn't know it... any more than I knew you were my grandson.'

'How long have you known this?'

'What phase of knowing?'

'Phase?'

'I went through denial, incredulity, upset, acceptance and delight. First, I was struck and then drawn to you, but I didn't understand why. Now I understand that it was ghosts from the past. Then, just like you, I couldn't accept it initially. It was too incredible. Then the elements fell into place, and I had to accept the truth, although I did have a little help from Athene.'

'How so?'

Eliza smiled. 'She named her son Felix, of course, after the father she never met. I feel she was calling out to me. But I didn't really listen until other things had fallen into place. I was the only one in the world who would understand. Somehow, my daughter sent that message through Dimity. Or that is what I would like to think. It makes me feel close to my daughter. After all these years, and still not knowing where she is, that, at least, gives me some comfort. But it also means I am not the last in my line. You are, Felix, and you can be as much a part of this family as you wish to be. As much a part of this family as I am. But are you sure you didn't ever hear the ghosts?'

'I suppose, if I'm honest, I felt something,' said Felix. 'I was overwhelmed the first time I came here, then I came to feel close to you, and when you first embraced me, it was a jolt. There were lots of little moments. Perhaps they were ghosts. And there was another thing – I never asked, but upstairs there's a small photo in a silver frame of a young girl on a swing. I have often looked at it and wondered who the girl in the picture is. She just felt familiar.'

Eliza smiled. 'The bedroom you are staying in was your mother's when she was growing up. The photograph is of her as a child. The records you found belonged to her. They are as much a part of this house as all the other things we have here.'

'Does that explain your not wanting to change anything in the house or garden in case Athene comes back?' asked Felix, before quickly adding, 'Julius told me.'

Eliza nodded. 'Whilst her body lies unfound, I have the scant comfort of forlorn hope over unwanted certainty. It's a crumb of comfort, even if it is illusory.'

'Well, Eliza, what should I call you now?'

'You must decide on that, my dear, but Grandma would be fine with me. I've never been a grandma before. Well, I have, but I just didn't know it.'

'That may take a little getting used to.'

'I know it will. It will take time for it to sink in for both of us.'

'I've never been very good at belonging,' said Felix.

'My dear, you have belonged from the first day you came here – from the day you were born. But now I've told you, I have something I must give you.' Eliza pulled from her pocket a small box. 'I want you to have this,' she said, 'it will help remind you that you belong.'

When Felix opened the box, he stared in surprise at a signet ring with three splayed arrows faintly etched on the well-worn face.

'Is this what I think it is, Eliza? It looks very much like the one James Arrow was wearing in the portrait.'

'I believe it is the very one. It has been handed down through every Arrow generation. It was too big for me, so I wore it on a gold chain around my neck. Then so did your mother. She left it here when she was on active duty.'

Felix slid the ring on his finger and stared at it.

Eliza watched him, before adding, 'Fortune has played a big hand in providing the opportunity for the Arrow legacy to be passed on, but only if you are prepared to accept that fortune. I must warn you; it is a heavy burden at times, and with each generation, the burden gets heavier. For us, the responsibility is to deal with Edward and the Church.'

'I suppose I have already accepted some of the burden to protect Witch's. So, why have you chosen now to tell me? Why not before?'

'Or why didn't I wait even longer?' Eliza suggested. 'Felix, there comes a time in the life of most secrets when they should be shared. It is a moment that should be chosen well – when the information will help those in the know against those who don't or shouldn't know. The moment arrived for me to share my secret. Later this afternoon, you might well learn why.'

Not knowing what Eliza meant, Felix said, 'If I accept all this, what happens next?'

'We will have to go through all the official DNA stuff. But I also want to insist that whatever you decide, we should keep this quiet. For the time being, only three people should know.'

'Three?'

'Yes, you, Bidian and I.'

'No one else?'

Eliza shook her head. 'If by that you mean Dimity, then emphatically, I don't think she should know just yet.'

'Why do you say that? Don't you trust her?'

'My dear, I trust Dimity implicitly. But right now, I think there are some special reasons why it would be better if we kept this between ourselves. First, you will need time and space to consider everything. You may reject the enormous change this would bring to your life, although, for the family's sake, I do hope you won't. Second, let's just say that for the time being, I don't want us to put Dimity in a difficult position.'

Eliza didn't elaborate but said, 'Look, I know I have turned your life upside down, Felix, but for the time being, can I ask you to exercise one of this family's greatest talents?'

'Keeping secrets?'

'Correct, and if you are the person I think you are, then that shouldn't be too difficult.'

'But what happens in the family after me – the next generation? I'm not able to provide for that.'

'Don't you think we should deal with more immediate concerns first?' said Eliza. 'This fortunate development takes care of Edward now he isn't in line to inherit. But the Church is another matter. If they succeed in proving their ownership you might not have so much of a legacy to pass on. But life has a way of sorting these things out.'

Sir Bidian looked at his watch and stood up, 'Well, I had better be on my way,' he said. 'You two will have a very great deal to talk about. He stooped to kiss Eliza on the cheek and then shook Felix's hand once again. 'Good luck both. Let me know if I can do anything else.'

But, once Sir Bidian had left, Eliza and Felix found they had nothing to say. Instead, they sat looking at each other as if for the first time.

CHAPTER TWENTY-ONE

'I'll see you later then,' Felix said down the phone.

'Are you going out?' Eliza asked once he'd ended the call.

'No. That was Timothy Kindred. He is dropping in this afternoon with some new information.'

'How interesting. I should be very pleased to meet him. But you haven't forgotten that Dimity will be here soon?'

'I couldn't easily forget.'

Felix had hardly finished the sentence when he heard the crunch of gravel outside. Looking out of the window, he saw Dimity getting out of her car, and she wasn't alone.

'Did you know Ludovic was coming?' Felix asked Eliza.

'No, I didn't.'

'After all that's happened, I'm not sure I can handle him right now.'

'Well, you're going to have to, my dear. It may be an ordeal, but I'm sure you will be equal to it.'

West ushered the couple into the salon.

'I hope you don't mind me bringing Ludovic, Eliza,' said

Dimity. 'We have been over to see a retiring vicar in a local parish.'

'Not at all, dear, the more the merrier.'

Dimity turned to Felix and said, 'I didn't know if you would be here or not.' There was a genuine look of pleasure on her face as she walked over to greet him.

Already Felix felt strange in the knowledge his relationship with Eliza went way beyond the friendship Dimity had with her. He was beginning to feel decidedly uncomfortable, especially as he felt Eliza's eyes on him. For the first time in his life, he felt like a fraud. He decided that must be how spies feel.

On the other hand, Felix noticed how Ludovic Poniard didn't seem quite so pleased to see him. He looked as cocksure as ever, though – if not a little more so. Preening was the word that sprung to Felix's mind as Ludovic nodded to him in a rather perfunctory manner.

'Are you all right, Felix? Dimity asked. 'You look pale.'

'I'm fine,' he replied. 'I have perhaps been working a bit too hard.'

'You need to slow down and get some more sleep.'

'I'll try to, once Eliza relaxes her increasing demands on my time.'

Everyone laughed, except for Ludovic, who sneered and said, 'Eliza, as I'm here, I was hoping to speak to you on a private matter.'

As he spoke, he gave Felix a fleeting but pointed look.

'I'm not sure that will be convenient, Ludovic. We're expecting another guest any time now.'

'Of course, and I apologise for coming unannounced,' said Ludovic.

Not so cocksure now, Felix thought.

'While we are waiting, perhaps you would like some tea?' Eliza said.

Or to entertain us on the piano, Felix thought dryly.

Eliza had hardly finished ringing for Cairo when West led Timothy Kindred into the room.

'It's like Piccadilly Circus round here,' West muttered as he left.

Felix made the introductions and thanked his guest for coming.

'I'm so pleased to meet you, Dr Kindred,' Eliza said.

'Timothy, please.'

'Felix tells me you might have some interesting information on Witch's. Is that correct?'

From the corner of his eye, Felix was pleased to catch the look of confusion on Ludovic's face.

'I do have some information, Mrs Arrow, although I'm not sure yet how important it is. Since Felix and I first met, I have been doing some digging. I have to say my research has been fascinating, especially when I went to the United States.'

'You've been to America?' Eliza said.

'Yes, a few days ago. I went immediately after Felix returned. Didn't he tell you?'

'No, he didn't,' Eliza said, looking at Felix pointedly.

Felix smiled at Eliza.

'I'm afraid that I don't understand,' said Ludovic, in a somewhat bewildered tone. 'Eliza, what has this gentleman got to do with Witch's? I thought I was helping you as I'm a lawyer.'

'A *former* lawyer, Ludovic. And I don't recall asking you to carry out historical research. Anyway, two or three heads are so much better than one, don't you think? And even better if one of those heads happens to be the director of the Victoria & Albert Museum. Wouldn't you agree?'

Ludovic raised an eyebrow in surprise. But if he was impressed by the new guest, he was doing his best not to show it.

'Now,' continued Eliza cheerily. 'I for one am most interested in what Timothy has to tell us. I am hoping he might shine more light on the matter of Witch's ownership.'

'But what has all this to do with Witch's and our agreement?' Ludovic persisted.

This time when Eliza replied, there was an edge to her voice. 'You know as well as I do, Ludovic, that we do not yet have an agreement. You have made a proposal that I should bequeath Witch's to the Church, and I have told you that I will think about it. I have also been threatened, and continue to be threatened, that if I don't make such arrangements, the Church will attempt to take Witch's from me anyway.'

Ludovic looked affronted. 'That is nothing to do with me,' he protested.

Eliza looked at him over the top of her glasses before turning to Timothy and asking, 'Why don't you tell us your news?'

Ludovic broke in again. 'Felix, you promised that I would be the first to know about anything you found out.'

'Actually, you asked me to tell you, but I don't recall agreeing that I would,' Felix said with pleasure. 'And anyway, I'm just as much in the dark as you are about what Timothy has found.'

'Felix is right,' said Timothy. 'To be honest, I haven't had such an exciting time since someone tried to convince the V&A they had discovered a footstool to the Peacock Throne somewhere near Doncaster.'

'So, how was your trip,' Felix asked.

'Fascinating, but before I went to America, I did as much research on Witch's Lawn and the Arrow family as I could. It won't surprise you to know, Mrs Arrow, that the pickings were pretty lean.'

'I'm not surprised at all,' agreed Eliza.

'But I'm supposed to be advising you on the title, Eliza,' Ludovic said.

'Really, Ludovic. I had the impression that you were already advising the Church. As you will know, Matthew 6:24 tells us that "No one can serve two masters." Now, will you please stop interrupting, it's beginning to irritate me.'

Felix had never seen Ludovic look so crestfallen. He could almost have felt sorry for him, except he didn't.

Timothy continued. 'I think you all may already know that Witch's was a hunting lodge, which was thought to belong to the owners of Abbotsleigh Park. That was before 1539.'

'That is one point of view,' Ludovic lamely chipped in.

'Quite correct,' said Timothy, 'but the important thing is that Witch's Lawn – or Laund as it was then – was a separate holding. On surrender of the monastery in 1539, Abbotsleigh Park came into the hands of the Crown, after which Henry VIII granted it, with various manors, to the Earl of Rounton. The latter was a chief commissioner for the suppression of religious houses. Henry appointed Thomas Cromwell as the king's vicar general with the authority to visit monastic houses and ensure they were adhering to the new law.'

'What does that mean?' asked Dimity.

'Henry VIII took over the highest spiritual powers in the land,' explained Felix. 'A document was then signed, allowing Cromwell to conduct these visits through commissaries, as he was rather too busy to do it all personally.'

'That's right,' Timothy said, 'it appears that Robert Chasolet – who soon after became the 1st Earl of Rounton – was one of these commissaries. Though we may never know for certain, it's not such a big stretch to imagine a member of the Arrow family as one of the Earl's men and active in bringing information to him. No doubt this was in turn passed on to Cromwell and so to Henry. It also might have brought, in a positive way, the Arrow family to the attention of the King, or at least to Thomas Cromwell.'

'That sounds reasonable, but what happened to Witch's?' Eliza asked.

'This is where the history gets murky,' said Timothy. 'But it seems Witch's wasn't included in the original grant. Perhaps Henry wanted to keep the hunting lodge for himself, although he was well past pursuing the sport by then. But whatever the reason, Witch's seems to have been lost from official accounts for the next forty-seven years.'

'Because it was still held by the Abbey,' stated Ludovic with conviction.

Timothy nodded and then added. 'In all probability it looked that way, but luckily, Felix suggested that I went to the Courtauld Institute and meet Margaret, er, Dr Petrie, to see the portrait you found upstairs. I must say she was really very nice and helpful.'

Is that a little colour in Timothy's cheeks? Felix thought. He looked at Dimity who smiled and shrugged as if to say, you had your chance.

Timothy continued. 'With Dr Petrie, I clearly saw for myself particular items in the picture. Indeed, some of the details, if not all of them, seem to have been placed there for other than artistic reasons... not that I am an expert in these things. But Dr Petrie most certainly is, and she has at her disposal the collective expertise and intellectual rigour of the Courtauld Institute. Felix, you told me that a small piece of vellum, depicted in the portrait you found, and looking very much like a sonnet verse you have, is a possible example. But it was the document with a seal under a red rose that posed the bigger question.

'Again, Felix, you mentioned certain words within the sonnets, such as rise and tread. These are words that can, of course, be associated with staircases. In the portrait, our subject sits in a hall in front of one. As you know – incredibly – the staircase in the picture seems to be the same as the one in Abbotsleigh Park, and now the one reinstated in Abbotsleigh House, in New York.

'So, I must thank you, Felix, and of course, thank you, Eliza, for bringing the museum and me this opportunity. This was a once-in-a-lifetime chance to discover something extraordinary, which is not only of great interest to scholars and historians but to an individual on a highly personal front. In this case, that's you, Eliza. I have to say that if it were not for you all finding the hidden room, Felix's goddaughter discovering the key, and Felix having a certain hunch about the painting then I would have had a more restful return flight. As it was, I couldn't stop thinking about my visit.'

'How very exciting this all is,' said Eliza, who was, Felix thought, looking more like an eager schoolgirl than an elderly lady.

'Secret room, what secret room?' demanded Ludovic.

Eliza turned to Ludovic. 'We found a secret room upstairs,' she said. 'It led us to believe that my family had left some clues to something. But we still don't know what that something might be.'

Ludovic turned and glared at Dimity. 'We... us... how much do you know about all this?'

'One or two things.'

'Then why didn't you tell me? You know how important all this is to me.'

Oh dear, thought Felix, as he watched Dimity's eyes flash with anger before she replied, 'It wasn't my place to mention any of this to anyone – including you. It's not my secret to tell.'

A faint smile played on Eliza's lips before she shot Felix a quick look. He knew immediately what it meant – rope-a-dope.

'And while this may seem exciting to you, Eliza, I can't see where all this conjecture is going,' said Ludovic.

'Ludo, we're not in court, you know,' said Dimity. 'And please remember your status.'

'My status?'

'Yes, as a guest here.'

'Ludovic, as the other qualified lawyer in this room,' said Felix, 'might I suggest you listen to what the defence has to say before you sum up for the prosecution.'

Felix was beginning to really enjoy himself. He could see how his words were getting under Ludovic's skin.

'We should listen to what Timothy has to say,' Eliza said. 'After all, he has travelled many miles to talk to us.'

'Thank you, Eliza,' said Timothy. 'Actually, I have come a great deal further than you think. Keeping the trip confidential, a few days ago, I visited Maurice and Mona Glasgall at Abbotsleigh House in New York.'

'You went to Abbotsleigh House?' Eliza asked in astonishment.

'I did, and I took with me the carvings and woodwork expert from the V&A, Clive Barnard. Clive is a master carpenter himself and probably knows more about this sort of thing than anyone alive – and he's especially interested in the Tudor era. I must say, the Glasgalls were extremely enthusiastic about our visit and most accommodating.'

'This is extraordinary!' Eliza exclaimed.

'It was gripping, yes – in more ways than one. Clive had a good look over the staircase and became very excited. He agreed with other experts that the carving was by Edward Pierce not Grinling Gibbons. But then he discovered the carving on the lower newel post was clearly by another gifted craftsman. He strongly suspected the maker of the post and secret hidey-hole was Nicholas Owen, the expert builder of priest holes during the reigns of Elizabeth I and James I. I told him that was unlikely as the Arrows were protestants, but he stuck to his guns and said he was convinced he was right.'

'Actually, Clive could be correct,' said Felix. 'I forgot to mention that in the hidden room we found a rosary and a missal dating back to 1626. Between the pages of the missal was one of the sonnet verses. So, we don't know what side of the fence the Arrows were on other than to guess they were on the side of whoever was in power at the time.'

'Which may explain how none of us, even in those dangerous times, lost our heads,' Eliza added.

'Well, that puts a fresh slant on things,' Timothy said, 'the whole thing is fascinating, and Clive will be delighted as he is a huge Nicholas Owen fan. Not that anyone else would have noticed the difference. I certainly wouldn't. I do believe that no one else would have worked it out other than Clive.

'But what exactly *did* he work out?' Felix asked.

'He found out that the lower finial – finial was another word used in the sonnet, wasn't it? – had been a later addition, or at least, an alteration. I wondered why, but then Clive told me about mortgage buttons. Around four hundred years ago in America, the title deeds of houses were sometimes inserted into cavities in newel posts. Then white porcelain or ivory buttons were mounted into the top of the posts. It told visitors that the house was bought and fully paid for. But it also seems that newel posts had something of a history for hiding essential documents or valuables. Now, this part could just be a myth, but folklore is often based on some germ of truth. Mortgage buttons seemed to have started around Cape Cod during the 17th century, when the English were settling in the area to do whaling. The practice spread to the rest of New England. Maybe the idea came across on a ship from England. Perhaps with a carpenter or someone who knew about the practice.

'Clive spent some time trying to work out if the Abbotsleigh House newel post had a hiding place. In the end, he figured out that the craftsman who had adapted the post had fixed the finial onto it with a clever triple bayonet system. It was very stiff and, if you didn't know what you were doing or knew there was something to find, you would never discover it. That is obviously why, when the staircase was dismantled and then reassembled in the 1920s, this secret place was never found. Plus, the demolition people were probably in a hurry to do the job.

'According to Clive, it was an ingenious and sophisticated construction, not only for the time it was made but also for today. It was a bit like a combination lock... an exceptionally snug fit and incredibly well made. At first, it wouldn't move, but Clive worked in some olive oil from the Glasgalls' kitchen and that did the trick.'

'So, what did you find?' said Dimity, literally sitting on the edge of her seat.

'Clive managed to lift the finial off the post, and inside we saw a hollow circular core about six inches wide. Maurice ran for a torch. Then, shining the light into the core we found that it was... empty.'

'Empty?' cried Dimity, 'after all that?'

'I'm afraid it was.

'So, that's it?' said Ludovic, 'all this excitement for an empty vessel?'

'I'm afraid so,' admitted Timothy with a nod.

'Then I really do think we should put this fantasy treasure hunt behind us and deal with the facts,' Ludovic said. 'Eliza, I think, for your own state of mind you should accept there is no proof at all that Witch's belongs to the Arrow family. All the evidence points to it belonging to the Church.'

Felix slumped in his chair. It was all over. Eliza had run out of time and ideas and the Church had won. Felix could see that Ludovic was now looking extremely smug indeed.

CHAPTER TWENTY-TWO

As it transpired, Timothy Kindred wasn't quite finished. 'We thought our hopes were dashed,' he said. 'Clive felt incredibly deflated and, I have to say, so did I. As for the Glasgalls...' He left the end of the sentence hanging, before adding, 'But during the flight back I did some thinking. And before I came in here, I took a quick turn around the garden.'

'You went up the garden path, no doubt,' said Ludovic with a smirk.

'Thank you, Ludo,' snapped Dimity.

'Not exactly up the garden path,' replied Timothy politely. 'But to meet Julius – so you could say we were on a path to enlightenment.'

'You met the gardener? Were you looking for tips on how to grow roses?' said Ludovic.

'Not tips on the garden, exactly,' said Timothy, resisting the bait. 'Felix suggested I asked Julius about the sonnets.'

'What sonnets? And why did you want to ask the gardener?' sneered Ludovic.

'Julius has a first in Classics from Oxford,' said Eliza,

Ludovic looked astonished.

Timothy nodded. 'Yes, Julius is a very clever man indeed. I could have done with him on my staff at the museum. Come to think of it, he would probably have had my job by now. Anyway, he mentioned something about one of the sonnet verses.'

'Which one?' Felix asked.

'The last one discovered,' said Timothy.

'Beloving kin, your loyal duty sworn?' asked Eliza.

'That's the one.'

'What is everyone talking about – crypt, verses – will someone let me know?' Ludovic demanded.

No one responded.

'So, what did Julius say?' Dimity asked.

'I think we should let him tell us himself,' replied Timothy. 'Would someone kindly ask him to join us?'

Dimity nodded and disappeared through the door to the kitchen.

'Will someone please tell me what is going on,' said Ludovic.

'Have a little patience, dear,' said Eliza.

Felix had the feeling that Eliza was enjoying Ludovic's discomfort just as much as he was.

Dimity came back with Julius, who was holding a mug of tea.

'If you wouldn't mind, I would appreciate it if you could tell everyone what you told Dr Kindred earlier,' Eliza said to him.

'Ma'am, I mentioned to Dr Kindred what I think is the most important word in the verse.'

'And what would that word be?' asked Eliza.

'As, Ma'am,' replied Julius.

'As? That is a very small word to be so important. Why so?'

'The adverb clarifies the meaning of the line and the verse.'

'How does it do that?' Felix asked.

'Because I think you might have read the verse as being about Abbotsleigh Park.'

'Wasn't it?' Eliza asked.

'I don't think so. I think you took the line, "*As* my Lord did tread in fair Abbotsleigh" to mean, "*Where* my Lord did tread in fair Abbotsleigh."'

'You mean the staircase mentioned in the sonnet may not be the one in Abbotsleigh but perhaps another somewhere else?' Felix asked.

'That makes the most sense to me,' said Julius.

'Well, it makes *no* sense to me,' said Ludovic.

By now, everyone was ignoring Ludovic completely. All eyes were on Julius.

'So, you are saying...?' Eliza's question faded into nothing.

'I'm saying, Ma'am, that I think you should look at another staircase. But one with a connection to Abbotsleigh.'

With the exception of Ludovic, everyone slowly looked from Julius to the salon's oak staircase. At the bottom was a sturdy square newel post with a finely carved pinecone finial on top – just like the one from Abbotsleigh. Felix reckoned he must have passed the post hundreds of times over the past few weeks without making any connection.

'So, I suggest we see if the same craftsman who customised the Abbotsleigh newel post did the same with this one,' said Timothy as he walked over to the staircase. 'I may need a strong hand to help me turn this.'

Julius stepped forward, and together they gripped the finial.

'I told you it was gripping,' said Timothy over his shoulder. 'If it's the same as Abbotsleigh, we must first move the finial a quarter turn to the left.'

Slowly, the cap turned.

'Now lift it, turn it three-quarters to the right and lift again.'

'It won't go any further,' said Julius after a few moments.

'Here, let me help,' Felix said.

'It's moving,' grunted Timothy.

The cap finally gave up its resistance.

'Now a half-turn to the left and lift again,' instructed Timothy.

A final effort was rewarded by the finial being lifted carefully off the post.

'I'll get a torch,' said West.

A moment later, he was back and shining an intense beam into a cavity in the newel post.

CHAPTER TWENTY-THREE

Timothy extended a hand into the void and carefully removed a long, slim, cloth bag. He took it over to the dining table, opened it and gently drew out a rolled-up parchment with a large wax seal hanging off it.

'What is it?' asked Eliza.

'What does it say?' asked Dimity.

Timothy began to unroll the scroll. After what seemed like an age, the document was fully revealed. Everyone crowded around while he put on his reading glasses.

'This all seems very far-fetched to me,' said Ludovic, peering over Dimity's shoulder.

'You may think so, Deacon, yet I beg to differ,' Timothy replied. 'Of course, we will need to run some tests on the vellum, the seal, the ink and the handwriting, but, and I find it hard to believe I am saying this, I think we may find that this document *is* authentic and could even be the one represented in the portrait that was discovered.'

An excited chatter broke out.

'But the clincher looks to be the signature,' said Timothy. 'Just look at it.'

Above and below several elaborate flourishes was the upright word Elizabeth, followed by the letter R.

'Surely a fake,' Ludovic scoffed.

'I don't think so,' said Timothy, 'although I can't be one hundred per cent certain, of course, the signature does look authentic. And we have the seal with Elizabeth mounted on a horse, again with a Tudor rose motif. It looks the same as the one depicted in the portrait and seems entirely contemporaneous with other proven examples. Unless this is a very elaborate hoax along the lines of the forged Hitler diaries published in the 1980s, this is a major find.'

'But what does it say?' said Eliza, sounding excited and exasperated all at once.

Timothy laid out the document for everyone to see and then began to read from it:

ELIZABETH by the Grace of God of England, Fraunce and Ireland Queene, defender of the faith, &c.

Knowe ye that of our especial grace, certaine science, and meere motion, we haue given and graunted, and by these presents for us, our heires and successors, we giue and graunt to our trustie and welbeloued seruant James Arrow, Esquire, and to his heires assignee, and to all, and euery of them, for euer, the house and land in the county of Hertfordshire, knowen as Witch's Laund. In witness whereof, we haue caused these our letters to be made patents. We do accept very well of your advertisements and prayeth that you will continue in doing good offices between us.

Witnesse our selues, at Westminster, the 25. day of March, in the first and thirtyeth yeere of our Raigne.

A hush descended over the room.

'You know what this means if it is found to be genuine?' said Felix to Eliza. 'It gifts Witch's to a certain James Arrow and his family in perpetuity for services rendered to the Queen by that gentleman. Which means that Witch's certainly does not belong to the Church, but to the Arrow family through royal gift hundreds of years ago.'

Ludovic snorted and Dimity gasped.

Felix started to laugh. 'The sprat eaten by the mackerel then swallowed by the shark,' he said.

'What do you mean by that?' snapped Ludovic.

'Oh, nothing,' Felix said evasively.

Ludovic turned to Eliza. 'Surely you don't believe any of this charade?' he said.

'Whether Eliza believes it or not is irrelevant here,' jumped in Felix, 'it is what the courts will believe that's the issue... if the matter ever comes to court, that is, which I very much suspect it won't. The Church may well have had a shot at the title before this, by virtue of there being no other documents, but it seems it has been outgunned by the Crown once again – and I think you probably know it.'

'The Church will contest it,' protested Ludovic.

'I thought you were on Eliza's side,' Dimity said. 'Won't you be trying to persuade them not to put her through any more of this?'

For a moment, Ludovic seemed taken aback. 'What I mean is that we must ensure all the proper evidence is taken into full account, so we achieve the correct outcome.'

'And what would be the correct outcome?' Dimity asked.

'I must be guided by the experts, of course,' broke in Eliza. 'But this finding certainly follows the story that has been handed down the generations by my family. And I don't think you can believe it, Ludovic, because you do not really want to believe it, do you, dear?'

'But Eliza, even if it were to be true, the Arrow line ends with you. Wouldn't you want to know that Witch's would be in good hands for the future?'

'That is another matter entirely, and one for another day,' Eliza replied smoothly. 'But I want to come to my decision on my own without being coerced into it.'

'I can assure you that I am not coercing you into anything, Eliza,' Ludovic replied.

Then, looking at his watch, he said, 'Now, I am afraid that it is getting late. I have another appointment and, for the time being, I don't think I can add to anything here.' He looked towards Dimity, before adding, 'Come on, we had best be getting back to the Abbey.'

Dimity's expression turned to one of defiance, a look that Felix had seen many times before. 'Actually, Ludovic,' she said, 'as I have nothing official to attend to this evening, I think I will stay here for a while, if Eliza will have me?'

Eliza nodded her assent.

'And perhaps Felix will give me a lift back as I'm on his way home?'

Felix nodded too, noticing how Ludovic looked as if he might explode. This had clearly not been a satisfactory afternoon for him.

'Don't bother to see me out, I know my way,' Ludovic snapped after bidding them all a good evening. And while the front door didn't exactly slam, it was not closed softly.

Felix only wished he had asked Ludovic to play one more piece on the piano before he left.

'Well, this has been a day of surprises, hasn't it?' said

Eliza. She was looking happier than Felix had ever seen her, and for good reason.

'Actually, the surprises aren't quite over yet,' said Timothy.

'No?' said Eliza.

'Not by any means.'

'What else could there possibly be?' Felix asked.

'Well, first there is another document in the bag – a smaller one.' Timothy brought out a small, rolled-up piece of vellum similar in size to the ones that had been found in the secret room and the Bible. 'Would you like me to read it?

'Yes,' everyone cried in unison.

Timothy cleared his voice and began.

V

For faith and Englands white and ruby rose,
In trust do we encipher'd letters send.
'Gainst Philips Spain and all our Roman foes,
May lethal Arrow bring us treasons end.
As bulwark to a castle keep or motte,
We lendeth ear to stew or palace guest,
And peel an eye to find a traitors plot,
So neither slumber nor on laurels rest.
Dwelleth thee deep in nook and shadow long,
Watching fiends for secrets they may bestow,
Not for torturers hand and rack-led song,
Our dear sovereigns many bounties flow.
Like thee to a hound acting as a sleuth,
Catcheth the winds scent, and gaineth the truth.

'There follows two more lines and a signature,' Timothy said.

'What does it say, whose signature?' asked Eliza excitedly.

Timothy smiled and read:

Belov'd kin who art loyal, strong and true,
'Til we meet in heaven, for now adieu.

'And the signature is James Arrow.'

'James! He's speaking to us,' said Eliza, her voice cracking with emotion.

'No, he's speaking to you, Eliza,' Felix said. 'James is talking to you down the centuries. The verse number is five, and it sounds to me like the last one. James is signing off.'

'Now, I'd call that poetic justice,' said Timothy with a chuckle.

'I agree, I think James is saying goodbye,' said Eliza.

'West?'

'Yes, Eliza.'

'The Krug, please.'

'But Timothy, you said there was something else in the newel post,' said Felix.

'Indeed, I did,' Timothy replied, stretching his hand down into the post. 'It's another bag, and it's quite heavy.'

He brought out a black velvet bag and opened it. Slowly, he extracted a long, gold chain. 'Well, I think that's what's called a clincher,' he said.

Everyone started talking excitedly at once, and they also wanted to hold the extraordinary piece of jewellery.

Eliza turned to Felix, 'You're a sly one for not telling me about Timothy going to New York,' she said.

'Secrets seem to be in the blood,' Felix whispered.

'Secrets are important, but keeping them is sometimes more important,' Eliza said while giving Felix a knowing look – or, he wondered, was it more of a warning shot?

'Tell me, Eliza,' Felix said quietly. 'Did you have Ludovic vetted at the same time as you had Dimity and me checked out?'

Eliza just smiled. Then, turning immediately to West who had returned with the champagne, she said, 'Now, please do start pouring. A celebration is in order.'

When they all had their glasses in hand, she added to no one in particular, 'So, what do we do now?'

'As far as any claim for Witch's is concerned,' Felix replied, 'I don't think you will hear any more from the Church, but a quiet word with the bishop may not go amiss.'

'I have a feeling that it may well go amiss,' replied Eliza, 'but I will certainly speak to someone in the Church. Meanwhile, we have another mystery to solve.'

'What's that?' Felix asked.

'Where is verse four, and what on earth does it say?'

CHAPTER TWENTY-FOUR

Felix couldn't believe what was in front of him. An email from the Church's legal department informing him that, far from withdrawing their claim in light of recent discoveries, they would be challenging the new evidence in court.

He was so angry that instead of stopping to tell Eliza, he grabbed his coat and car keys and drove in a blind fury to St Eadric's. He was about to ring Dimity's buzzer when, dressed in her cassock, she emerged from the direction of the Abbey.

'What on earth's wrong? You have a face like thunder,' she said.

'This,' Felix replied, waving a printout of the email. 'This is what's wrong. The Church are still taking us to court.'

'What do you mean us?'

'I mean Eliza,' Felix hurriedly said. 'The Church is going to dispute the latest find at Witch's. It's ridiculous and it's against all the evidence. They can't argue away a bloody gold chain. Where's Ludovic?'

'He'll be at his house doing paperwork I imagine. But why don't you come up and have a cup of tea.'

'I don't want a drink, Mitten. I want to have this out with Ludovic, once and for all.'

'Do you think you should wait and talk to him when you aren't so angry?'

'I'm going to be a great deal angrier if I don't see him.'

Dimity sighed. 'OK, follow me, then, but do try to calm down a bit.'

Ludovic invited Dimity and Felix into his house, a drab, perfunctory space with few, if any, touches of personality – rather like its occupant, Felix thought bitterly. He had the impression that, for Ludovic, it was more of a quick pitstop on the way to something bigger and better – a deanery or bishop's palace perhaps.

'Are you behind this, Ludovic?' Felix demanded, waving the email again. 'You've seen with your own eyes the documentary evidence that Witch's was a royal gift.'

Ludovic looked nonplussed. 'You're a lawyer, or so you tell me,' he said. 'You know that there is always doubt over these matters. These things are complicated and take time to resolve.'

'Five centuries?' said Felix. 'If the Church doesn't know whether they own Witch's or not after all this time, then I'm not sure Eliza should be happy with them taking hold of it for the future. It seems to me the house has been in pretty good hands so far. Now tell me, are you behind advising the Church's lawyers to press on?'

'It's important for everyone that the Church dots the I's and crosses the T's, I'm sure you'll agree.'

'While Eliza potentially racks up tens of thousands of

pounds in trying to defend nothing more than a fishing expedition?'

'I would agree that she is in a more unfortunate position than the Church when it comes to costs.'

'She's in an impossible position, and you know it.'

'Such is life and the law, I'm afraid. You agreed to help Eliza, Felix, so you'll have to take the rough with the smooth.'

Ludovic was being at his most patronising, and Felix could tell he was being baited.

'Of course, all Eliza has to do is agree to bequeath Witch's to the Church and all this can go away,' Ludovic said.

'That's blackmail!'

'No, it's reality.'

'Do you agree with this?' Felix said, turning to Dimity.

'What Dimity thinks is neither here nor there,' Ludovic said evenly.

'Well, Mitten, at least you know now how Ludovic thinks. As for you, Ludovic, you know this is wrong. Some Christian you turned out to be.'

'But we're only trying to help Eliza, don't you see that?' Ludovic protested.

'What I see is that she doesn't need your brand of help,' Felix replied. 'Eliza is the most organised and well-looked-after woman I have ever met.'

'Oh, I don't mean material help, Felix,' Ludovic pressed on. 'I agree with you; there is nothing we can do to add to her physical good. It is more her spiritual and mental wellbeing we can help her with.'

'Well, as I am neither a priest nor a shrink, I'm not sure what I can do,' Felix said.

'You're doing yourself an injustice. I have seen how much

of a comfort you've become to Eliza in a relatively short time. She listens to you.'

You don't think I'm going to recommend that she goes along with this, do you?'

'I had hoped that you might be able to help her see the light.'

'And what light might that be?'

'Eliza is clearly in some quandary about her legacy. She doesn't seem happy about what will become of Witch's after her death, which, let's face it, will probably be within the next few years, if not sooner. I think we need to help steer her into making decisions that will help her find peace.'

'So, what do you think will help her find peace, as you put it?'

'I think Eliza wants to see the future of Witch's secured. And because of her deep faith, I believe she would be more comfortable with it in the capable hands of the Church rather than another institution. Then there is Edward Arrow, who would be next in line to inherit, but, as Eliza has freely told me, she doesn't want to hand Witch's to him. We should therefore help her with spiritual closure.'

'Spiritual closure?' Felix said with increasing irritation. 'That sounds like Bible babble to me. As far as I can see, Eliza just wants to ensure the family house isn't lost – as she says – on her watch. It is as simple as that.'

'Well, you know what to do, Felix.'

'For a priest, you make a cheap hustler.'

Ludovic smirked.

'Felix, this isn't helping,' said Dimity. Until then, she had remained decidedly mute during the men's bitter exchange.

'Oh, she finally speaks,' said Felix sarcastically. 'I'm not here to help Ludovic, Mitten. And if he thinks I am, then he has another thing coming.'

Ludovic raised an eyebrow. 'Well, if you want to make this difficult for Eliza, please carry on. I'm only suggesting an easy way out of her predicament.'

'This isn't a hunt for an easy way out, Ludovic, it's a Witch's hunt. It's certainly not the worthy cause I was asked to join, and I am not prepared to see Eliza blackmailed, or at least strong-armed into making a decision she doesn't want to make. I'm going to have nothing to do with it.'

With that, Felix strode out of the house, determined to get away from the turbulent priest. He had only just reached the garden gate when Dimity ran out of the house.

'Felix, what on earth was that?'

'Can't you see what your boyfriend is trying to do?'

Dimity snorted. 'So that's what this is about.'

'What?'

'Ludovic and me.'

Felix glared at her. 'I couldn't care less about Ludovic and you.'

'Couldn't you?'

'Look, I don't know what's going on between the two of you, and I don't know what cosy arrangement you were in before we met up again, but you asked me to help with something, and I have become involved in that. In fact, I have become deeply involved in Eliza and Witch's. Can't you see what's going on here? Ludovic is on some sort of personal crusade, and I for one will not be helping him. If anything, I will do my best to stop him, and you can run back and tell him so. The most important person in this isn't me – or you – and it's certainly not Ludovic. It's Eliza, and, to the best of my ability, I'm going to help her keep that house.'

'I don't think you have the whole picture here, Felix. There's more to it.'

Felix sighed. 'I'm sure there is a lot more going on. But if we're not careful, Mitten, we're going to have the first disagreement of our second friendship. As far as I can see, we aren't on the same side here. Ludovic knows he has lost the legal argument, and he is stirring up trouble to keep his little plan alive another way.'

'Oh, please don't let's argue, Felix. You were never so confrontational before. You're taking this all so personally.'

'That's because it has become personal, Mitten.'

What's happened to you?'

'What's happened? Over the last twenty years, I learned about life, that's what's happened. I learned about disappointment. I learned about other people's self-interest, and I learned that the only person I can rely on in this life is myself. And if the only person Eliza can rely on is me also, then so be it. I can handle it. I *want* to handle it.'

Felix didn't add that it was possible he would be the one to inherit Witch's, something about which he felt desperately awkward. He felt as though he was being duplicitous – no, he *was* duplicitous. But difficult as it was, he still followed Eliza's wishes to keep their blood ties to himself.

'I've never known you like this, Felix.'

'Surely you, of all people, understand a great cause, Mitten. I have a cause. In part, you are responsible for it. Now Ludovic, for reasons I don't understand, and hardly dare imagine, is resorting to emotional blackmail to get what he wants. The same goes for Edward Arrow.'

'You can't compare Ludovic with Edward Arrow. Nor would I call it blackmail on Ludovic's part.'

'Then what would you call it?'

'Well, as Ludovic explained, perhaps it's in Eliza's best interests to avoid any further upset. After all, it was I who suggested you could help us. This is an important decision, and I guess I thought you would look at it from another angle to Eliza.'

'But this is a decision forced through Ludovic's devising – you must see that. Surely something must concern you about this. Otherwise, why would you have kept so much back from him? Before he came along, Eliza had no decision to make. She was oblivious to any problem and, for a number of reasons, I think it would have been better kept that way. But now the genie is out of the bottle, and it's not going back in. But I'm also out of the bottle, so now we must play this out, because I'm not going back in either. As for you, Mitten, I think you must work out what is going on here and then decide whose side you are on, because if you aren't on Eliza's, then you certainly aren't on mine. Now, I had better go. I don't really want to leave on bad terms, and I don't want to say something I will live to regret. So, I'm going to suggest that we give it a little time. You think about it some more and then, if you want, let me know what conclusion you reach.'

With that, Felix leaned over and pecked a stunned-looking Dimity lightly on the cheek and, leaving her standing at the gate, walked away, hoping above hope that it was not for the last time. But oddly somehow, such was his feeling about the whole affair, he was prepared for it to be so.

CHAPTER TWENTY-FIVE

A week had gone by without a word from Dimity, leaving Felix to wonder if he would ever hear from her again. He knew he had let his anger get the better of him, albeit with good reason, but once again, he had jeopardised his friendship with one of the people he cared about most in the world. He also worried about the toll the impending court case would take on Eliza, all the while trying to come to terms with his real identity.

He'd talked at length to his 'new' grandmother about his feelings. Part of him felt a sense of disloyalty over his adoptive parents, as though, in changing sides, he was letting them down after all they had done for him. But Eliza had persuaded him that his parents were still a huge part of him; they had helped shape the person he had become, and they lived on in him. In the end, Felix had come to realise that it was not a matter of choice. He was who he was.

To Eliza's credit, she was also more positive about the court case. 'We are confident the patent is genuine,' she said as they discussed it yet again in the salon, 'and there is more than enough supporting evidence.'

'What about the legal costs?' Felix asked.

'From the start, you warned me the other side might bully and threaten me, and that the Church has in-house lawyers to help keep the costs down. But what the Church doesn't know yet is that we also have our own in-house lawyer – you. And I can't imagine you hitting the family for legal costs when you will be the ultimate beneficiary, can you?'

Felix laughed. 'No, I can't.'

'As for you and Dimity, I wish you could see what's as clear as daylight to everyone else.'

Felix reflected how in the early years of their friendship, his many disagreements with Dimity were petty and blew over quickly – although a more serious one had gone on for several uncomfortable and lonely months. He couldn't remember what that row had been about, nor how it was resolved, but once it had been, he and Dimity had never spoken of it again.

'Somehow, I think this point of principle is different to any of our previous disagreements,' he said.

'Why, because it involves me and Witch's?'

'I suppose so.'

Eliza was right, Felix thought. He had become responsible for someone who, while being far from vulnerable, was limited in what she could do. Felix had no doubt that, had Eliza been younger, she would have relished the challenge. He knew that grandson or not, he was Eliza's instrument – much like the Arrows had been instruments of the state down the years. Eliza, the spymaster, was pulling the strings of her agent, and she was a very good at what she did.

'I understand you have a lot on your shoulders right now, my boy,' she said. 'So, I think what you could do with is a fresh perspective. Why don't you take a few days off, or, better still, a week? Not to London. Get some fresh air. Go somewhere you love. You told me you like Skye?'

'There's too many memories there,'

'Oh, for goodness' sake, Felix, you're talking like a lovesick adolescent. Buck up! Dimity's the one you're supposed to be thinking about – perspective, yes?'

So, Felix decided to do as Eliza suggested and head up to Skye. Before he left, and in a moment of weakness, he sent Dimity an email that he hoped might break the silence, or at least show that he hadn't completely taken the hump. With the sonnets in mind, he had made up a short verse.

M,
Today I have a pressing worry,
And send this mail in a hurry,
Very soon I'll be past the Forth,
Much, much further to the north.
In far off places, West Highland coastal,
Where they're slow with online postal.
So, if my missives seem to fail,
Don't blame me, blame the mail.
L,
F

He packed his walking gear, and via the train and a rental car, arrived at his hotel, which for over a century had provided respite for climbers, walkers and tourists exploring the Cuillin Hills. Felix had stayed at the hotel many times over the years, and, earlier in his life, he had camped nearby too.

With as much of his gear as he could carry, he pushed through the hotel's front door and immediately felt at home. The place was comfortable in a faded, lumpy, Edwardian kind of way. Staying there was like putting on a favourite pair of slippers. The mattresses were old and springy and often sank alarmingly in the middle. The bathrooms weren't equipped with power showers but furnished with huge, cast-iron baths that took ages to fill with piping hot, peat-coloured water that over the years had stained the white enamel brown up to the waterline. But after a tiring day in the hills, there was nothing Felix liked better than a long, deep, hot soak. Afterwards, there would be a hearty meal and a dram or two of single malt whisky in the bar. And come bedtime, no mattress, however saggy, could keep him from a sound and satisfying sleep.

On his first night, he had one too many in the bar, while on his second, he had two too many. On his third night, when his telephone finally hit a pocket of good reception, it alerted him to an incoming email. It was from Dimity.

F,
'I will lift up mine eyes to the hills, from whence cometh my help.' (*Psalm 121*)
I hope that you find there all that you are seeking.
M

It was not an entirely unhopeful reply, Felix decided. At least they were emailing one another, if not speaking directly.

He decided to cut down on the whisky, which he felt better for the next morning, when he set off on a 10-hour hike. It was early evening when he staggered off the path, over an old stone road bridge and into the hotel. He was so tired he could hardly make it up the stairs to the first floor. Once inside his room, he flung his rucksack down and ran a bath to ease his aching muscles. Afterwards, he made his way back downstairs to the bar.

In Felix's experience, most climbers' bars were the same – friendly places full of talk, warmth, laughter and music, which was never so loud patrons couldn't discuss the day's adventure and plan for the next. He ordered a pint of Heavy and a Highland Park whisky as a chaser, found an empty table and sank with relief into a comfortable chair. A folk group had started up in the corner of the bar. A girl with a haunting voice was singing in Gaelic. Felix closed his eyes, and his mind drifted to Rachel singing in the woods at Witch's. He was lost to the beautiful sounds when, in a small corner of his consciousness, he heard a woman somewhere above him say, 'Buy a girl a drink?'

Felix ignored the peripheral voice.

'Buy a girl a drink?'

This time, the question was louder and more pointed. Felix slowly opened his eyes to focus on the source of the interruption.

For a moment, he sat in stunned disbelief before finally gathering his thoughts enough to speak. 'Mitten, what on earth are you doing here?'

'I'm not quite sure. I was sort of brought here.'

'By whom?

Dimity thought for a moment. 'Not by whom.'

'Then by what?'

'I'm not really sure of that either.'

'But you're supposed to be in Devon with Ludovic – on a retreat.'

'I know, I retreated from the retreat. The car seemed to just turn around at Taunton and take the road north rather than further southwest. Or perhaps I saw something beckoning me here.'

'A yeti? Nice thought, but even more unlikely in the UK than in Tibet. But weren't they expecting you in Devon?'

'I called and explained that I needed to be somewhere where I wasn't expected.'

'You've got that right. But you still haven't said what you are doing here.'

'I wanted to see you, Felix. I need to talk to you.'

'That's what phones are for.'

'It's not that sort of talk.'

Felix was suddenly worried. 'Mitten, you are all right, aren't you? There's nothing wrong, is there? You're not ill?'

'No, no, nothing like that. I am fine. Better than fine.'

'Then what sort of talk could it be to bring you all the way here? What made you travel nearly six hundred miles when you didn't even know where I was staying? Did you have some sort of divine help in tracking me down? Do you want some advice over something – Ludovic, perhaps?'

'It's not Ludovic. But I have something that has been on my mind for a while – quite a long while really. And no, I've had no divine help in finding you. Well, come to think of it, perhaps that *was* divine help.'

'Well, whatever it was, I am very pleased to see you. Surprised but pleased. This old place didn't quite feel the same without you. Wait, I had better get you that drink. What will you have?'

'What you're having looks good.'

Felix headed to the bar while Dimity sat down at the table. When he returned, he said, 'Now, what on earth is it that demands driving twelve or so hours from one end of the country to the other? And how can I help?'

'We parted last time on bad terms, and I don't want to be on bad terms with you.'

'It's water under the bridge,' he replied. 'Perhaps I overreacted.'

'You didn't overreact. Now, where shall I start?'

'The beginning?'

'There have been several things on my mind recently, but the main one is you.'

'Oh, why me exactly?'

'We are friends, aren't we – good friends?'

'I hope we are.'

'Look, Felix, whatever you say, I know I hurt you greatly all those years ago. I'm sorrier than you know. And I'm sorry for all the messing around I did. I messed you around – screwed you around really. I didn't know what I was doing then, but I do now.

'I am not proud of any of that. I got pretty wild, didn't I?'

'Yes, you did.' Felix wasn't sure where the conversation was going.

'But you weren't wild. You were steady and dependable.'

'And always there and boring.'

Dimity smiled. 'That's a bit harsh. But you certainly seemed more comfortable in who you were than I was. I was completely mixed up.'

'And now you're not as mixed up as you were?'

'Over some things, not others.'

'Well, you might be surprised to know how mixed up I am right now, so it appears we have swapped roles. But you haven't come all this way to rake over my past, have you, Mitten? I only hope you don't want relationship advice, because if you do, I'm not really the best person to ask. Are you sure this isn't about you and Ludovic Poniard?'

'Ludovic? Do you think there is a Ludovic and me?'

'Well, yes. Ludovic seems very keen.'

'And how do you feel about that?'

'Oh, it's nothing to do with me. But, if you don't mind my saying, Ludovic wouldn't have been my first choice for you.'

'Who would have been your first choice?'

Felix tried to keep his answer light. 'Oh, I don't know, what about an archbishop?'

Dimity laughed. 'Canterbury and York are both taken.'

'Oh, shame, then it will have to be one of the lower orders, I'm afraid – a diocesan bishop maybe.'

Humour aside, Felix still didn't like the way their conversation was going. He had built up a hard shell over the years and this line of questioning was threatening to penetrate his armour. He couldn't help thinking that Mitten was going to announce something big, like her impending marriage to Ludovic, or even the Dali Lama for all he knew. But before he could dwell on these possibilities any further, Mitten was off on another tack.

'You've never mentioned anyone special in your life,' she said.

'That's because over the past twenty years or so there hasn't been anybody special enough.'

'What, no one?'

'There have been a few near misses. I told you about Victoria.'

'And the Bulgarian girl, the controlling one.'

'Don't remind me. I never knew who I was going to wake up with or come home to.'

'Oh, I recognise that feeling. But Victoria sounded OK.'

'She was more than OK. She was really nice. It was my fault. I admit I should have worked harder on the relationship, but I became distracted by work. So, I suppose she was the one that got away.'

'Felix, have you ever thought that *you* might be the one that got away?'

'What do you mean?'

Dimity didn't answer.

'Anyway,' said Felix, 'with my work schedule – not to mention what you have been getting me into for Eliza – relationships haven't really been on the agenda. Besides, nobody recently has seemed interested enough in me.'

'Perhaps you've been sending out the wrong signals.' Dimity suddenly stopped and stared at Felix. 'Oh, goodness, you're not secretly gay, are you?'

'Have you come all this way to ask me that?'

'No, it just occurred to me, so I'm asking... asking as a friend.'

'No, I'm not gay, Mitten.'

'Feelings can change over time, Felix. Attitudes can alter. It's natural. To be honest, you do dress quite gay.'

'I like nice clothes.'

'And you always smell nice.'

'A damming accusation, but it's the Creed.'

'See what I mean?' Dimity said, as though Felix had just incriminated himself.

'I don't have to be gay to wear Creed, Mitten. I simply like the smell.'

'I would understand if you *are* gay, Felix.'

Felix sighed. 'And I would understand too. I really wouldn't have a problem with it. But it just so happens that I'm not.'

Dimity was quiet for a moment, and then said, 'Well, from my point of view, I think it is better that you aren't gay.'

'And why's that, pray tell?'

'The thing is, Felix – and this is what has brought me here – I find that I like the smell of your Creed too—'

'Well, be my guest, have a squirt of mine. Or did you come all this way to ask me where to buy it?'

Dimity sighed. 'It's not that, and will you please not interrupt! I'm trying to explain. I also find that I like your clothes and the way you live.'

'Mitten, where is this going? You didn't come here to talk about cologne and fashion, did you?'

'You're not making this very easy, Felix.'

'Making what easy? I don't understand.'

Dimity sighed again and said, 'Sometimes, actions speak louder than words.' She held Felix's gaze and then moved her chair towards his, crossing the invisible line of separation. At once, Felix felt the tension between them, which was always as much a barrier as an invitation, evaporate. Then Dimity kissed him. It was a long, gentle kiss. If Felix hadn't been seated, he thought he would have fallen – as much from emotion as surprise.

When they drew apart, Felix just looked at Dimity as if stupefied.

'Aren't you going to say something?'

'What just happened?'

'What do *you* think just happened?'

'I think the tectonic plates of my life just shifted to a more comfortable position.'

'Well, that's a relief. And I think I've just discovered what was missing.'

'What was that?'

'I told you, after all my searching, I still felt there was something absent from my life. I think that was it. I seem to have shed a great weight. Carrying the torch of our friendship for so long was a heavy burden.'

'But you're in the clergy, Mitten.'

'What's that got to do with anything?'

'Aren't you a bride of Christ or something?'

'I'm not a nun, Felix.'

'Well, isn't there some sort of rule in the Church about kissing outside of wedlock?'

Dimity laughed. 'Are you trying to find problems where there aren't any? But to answer your question, there are no Church rules about kissing in or out of wedlock, although kissing one's married parishioners romantically is more than frowned upon. And, in case you hadn't noticed, this is the twenty-first century.'

'Mitten, I think I have waited for that kiss all my life.'

'We've kissed before.'

'As teenagers, and certainly not like that. Purely as a matter of interest, you understand, are there rules about anything else?'

'Well, that depends.'

'On what?'

'On whether you kiss me back.'

Felix considered this for a moment. 'I think I would be more comfortable without the accessory.'

Dimity raised her hands and detached her clerical collar.

* * *

The following morning, Felix and Mitten sat together amongst the pinnacles and pillars of the Quiraing. Felix had been there in all weathers: on dark, grey, breezy days, when the wind ripped around the eroded rock formations; on sunny, calm days, when the views stretched over the sea to the mountainous Scottish mainland. And he had been on days when the mist swirled and enveloped the landscape and turned the tall rock stacks into imagined ghosts of Scottish kings.

Today, however, the weather was benign. Reclining on a carpet of springy grass and heather, they took in the view and shared a Scotch pie and a less-than-cold tin of beer.

'What made you change your mind?' Felix said, finally asking the question that had been on his mind for about fifteen hours.

'Change my mind about what?'

'Change your mind about me – us. What else would I be referring to? That does seem to be the topic of the moment, or at least it is for me.'

Dimity laughed and then said in a serious voice, 'And for me, Felix. Remember how yesterday I asked you if you had ever thought you could have been the one that got away?'

'I remember. You didn't answer.'

'No, but did you ever think that? Were you ever pleased to have gotten away from me?'

Felix smiled. 'Honestly?'

'Honestly.'

'Once.'

'When was that?'

'I don't think I should say.'

'Come on, Felix, open up, no secrets.'

'OK, it was the day you got married.'

Dimity nodded, 'I was a mess, wasn't I? That whole thing was a complete bloody mess.'

'You could say that.'

Dimity looked into Felix's eyes. 'So, it turns out that you were the one that got away – *my* one that got away. I finally understand that now, and I figured I had better try and do something about it while there was a chance of undoing what I had done – or hadn't done, as the case may be. The thing is, I never changed my mind about you. I have always loved you, of course, but I took that love for granted. Until recently, I never stopped and tried to understand *how* I loved you.

'It took me a long time to reach the same conclusion I think you reached all those years ago. But I couldn't make the leap from childhood and adolescent best friend to adult lover. You could. I think I needed space and distance, and frankly, I needed to grow up. I needed to come to this fresh somehow. You were always so certain, Felix. That scared me. When I met Michael, I thought I loved him, but then I realised I was being controlled and manipulated. No one should have to go through that. He didn't care about me – all he cared about was himself. Everything between us was transactional.'

'So, Mitten, what happens now – with us?'

'What do you want to happen now?'

'You made the first move.'

'You didn't stop me.'

'I didn't think you wanted me to.'

'Do you always do what I want you to do?'

'It has always seemed like that.'

Dimity was quiet for a moment. 'Well, this time, why don't we make a joint decision?'

'I think, if I'm honest, Mitten, I made my decision a long time ago. I have just been denying it to myself for twenty years.'

'And I have made my decision too, more recently, if not on another occasion some years back.'

'What occasion was that?'

'If you don't mind, I'll tell you another time.'

'OK, then why exactly?'

'I don't think there was an exactly. It was just a growing realisation of who and what you were – are – to me.

'Plus, the last time we met – when we argued – you were so sure of yourself and so, oh, I don't know, so valiant. You said when we met again that I was the risk taker between us, the braver one. But there you were, far bolder than I ever was. I took calculated physical risks, but you were risking everything – everything you hold precious – for what you believed in and what you thought was right. It was impressive, and I loved you for it.'

'But you were bold coming here, Mitten. What if I wasn't interested?'

'I had the impression you were interested. After all, you did invite me.'

'No, I didn't, I thought you were in Devon.'

'But you sent me that poem anyway. That seemed like an invitation to me. And then you went and told me where you would be.'

'West Highland coastal?'

'Exactly.'

'And so, you replied?'

'I sent you the text from Psalm 121 – "Look to the hills from where comes my help."'

'You hoped that I would find there all that I am seeking.'

'And have you?'

'Mitten, before we go any further, I have something to tell you, and I have to be even bolder than before and risk everything again – risk you again.'

'I don't like the sound of that. It sounds serious. What on earth is it, Felix?'

'It is serious. It's a confession really, and you did say no secrets. I have just realised that I have reached the point in my life that Eliza has been trying to prepare me for.'

'Prepare you for what?'

'Sharing a secret.'

CHAPTER TWENTY-SIX

Telling Dimity who he really was proved to be the most difficult thing Felix had ever done. It took him the rest of the day and long into the night, during which there was anger and shouting on Dimity's side, along with tears, long silences and questions, so many questions.

Just before midnight, with the hotel bar emptying out, Dimity said quietly, 'I felt something was going on, but not enough to say anything. It wasn't something I could put my finger on... I didn't sense a conspiracy and nor did I feel I was being shut out, but I noticed your growing intimacy with Eliza. At times, if I'm honest, I think I may have even been a little jealous over how close the two of you were becoming. After all, it was me who introduced you both, and Eliza was my friend. Do you remember my saying in Abbotsleigh Park how alike the two of you are? I couldn't have been more right, but I was blind.'

'What do you mean?'

'You even look like her.'

'You think so?'

'Take a look at yourself in the mirror sometime.'

Hesitatingly, Felix asked, 'So, Dimity Annunciata Fortuna, after my confession – and I have no right to expect it to be – is it OK?'

'Is what OK? Is it OK that you didn't tell me sooner? Is it OK that you are the lost heir to a vast fortune? Is it OK that your – our – home could eventually be Witch's? Or perhaps, is it OK that I could become part of the noblest, most exciting and secretive family that nobody has ever heard of? Further, is it OK that you have loved me for over thirty years and that I have only recently understood what that really means to me?'

'I can see how those could be problems.'

'Oh, you can, can you?'

'What I meant was—'

'Felix?'

'Yes.'

'I'll cope.'

'Really?'

'Yes, Felix, really, but are you sure *you* are OK with it – us?'

'I only have one request – it's pivotal to our futures.'

'What is it?'

'I want you to promise that you will never slide off any icy cliffs. I want that written into our vows.'

'Our vows?'

'Er, well, yes.'

Felix suddenly felt unsure of himself, and he wondered if he had been too presumptuous or had misread the signs. But he ploughed on anyway. 'Don't you think we should get around to the vow thing sometime – especially in the position you're in? I can't see God, the archbishops, the bishop, the dean and many of your parishioners being happy about you living in sin, can you?'

Dimity took Felix by the hand and said, 'This is still the twenty-first century. But if that is a very novel, but nevertheless profoundly romantic way of making a marriage proposal, then yes, I do think we should do the vow thing sometime.'

With both hands, Felix reached up behind his neck and unclasped the long, gold chain that he had recently taken to wearing under his shirt. From it, he took the signet ring that Eliza had given him. Taking Dimity's ring finger, he slid on the ancient piece of jewellery, 'For ceremonial purposes only,' he said.

Dimity stared at the ring for a moment. 'That's not...?'

'Yes, it most certainly is.'

* * *

When Felix and Dimity arrived back at Witch's and told Eliza their news, she threw her hands up in delight. 'I can't say I am surprised,' she said. 'In fact, I'm not sure what took you so long.'

'Are you completely sure you are happy with this?' Dimity asked.

'My dear, I couldn't be happier. But it is your lives. You must both do as you see fit.'

Dimity went off to tell Cairo, West and Frankie, leaving Felix with Eliza. 'I understand now,' he said to her.

'You understand what, my dear?'

'I understand about secrets. When it's best to keep them and when it is best to share them.'

Eliza nodded and then smiled.

'But I also understand something else.'

'Which is?'

'Dimity was your spy. You never told me. She fed you what you wanted to know about Ludovic, didn't she?'

'Yes, she did.'

'You let me believe she was on Ludovic's side.'

'That's called a need-to-know basis, Felix. Look, there was no dark deceit, so don't look for one – plausible deniability, remember? Just as kindness is sometimes better than truth, ignorance also has its place.'

'Dimity didn't tell me.'

'That's what spies do.'

'I thought the worse of her for it.'

'Well, that's another lesson you've learned. You will know better next time. But I do have to say, Dimity was a very useful asset, to use the jargon.'

'You *are* a witch, Eliza.'

'Just call me La Bruxia,' Eliza replied with a smile.

'I'll call you Àvia.'

'Clever, that's Catalan for grandma.'

'I love you, Grandma.'

'And I love you too, Felix.'

Eliza hit her buzzer. When West appeared, she said, 'Would you please go into the cellar and break out not the good stuff, but the exceptionally good stuff. And then ask everyone to join us.'

Once the two exceptional bottles had been opened, and everyone was together, Eliza proposed a toast to Dimity and Felix.

'You know, it was the 1928 Krug that Pablo Picasso and I drank in Paris after the Germans had arrived,' she said. 'Like this one, it was an outstanding vintage. The occasion wasn't a celebration, of course. Not like now. It was more about drinking the stuff as quickly as we could in case the Nazis got hold of it. But today we freely celebrate.'

'At least this time you will have your clothes on,' said Dimity with a wry smile while pointing to the small Picasso portrait of Eliza on the table.

'Indeed, I will,' she replied with a chuckle. 'Indeed, I will.'

* * *

Through Bidian, Eliza contacted the Clergy Discipline Commission within the Church of England. As a result of this, and with Eliza's agreement, Ludovic had received a warning about his behaviour. Nevertheless, it wasn't long before he arranged a time to revisit Witch's. Eliza told Felix that he and Dimity should be there for the occasion, explaining that it would be so they could tie up some loose ends.

When Ludovic arrived, he told them his reason for dropping by. 'I knew I'd be in the neighbourhood, so I thought I would look in on you,' he said, fooling no one.

A short but uncomfortable silence followed. It was broken only when Ludovic said, 'I understand that the Church has decided to drop the legal claim for Witch's.'

'Yes, it is very big of them, considering they didn't have a leg to stand on,' Eliza said.

'I like to think I had some influence on the Church's decision.'

'Well, if that is so then it was sensible of you, Ludovic.'

'And now you have all the evidence you need to keep Witch's, you have achieved everything you set out to achieve.'

'But that is not all I wanted. I also wanted to know that it would stay in the Arrow family on my terms.'

'I know you did, and it is such a shame that you only have your second cousin to leave Witch's to. So, I wondered whether you have thought any further about our scheme to leave the property to your Church family?'

The bastard, Felix thought, the man has no shame, even although he's had a warning. But he also had the strong feeling that Eliza had this entirely under her control, so he remained silent.

'I have given our scheme, as you put it, no further thought whatsoever, Ludovic. And I am most pleased to say that I will never have to do so.'

'Oh, why is that, might I ask?'

Come into my parlour, said the spider to the fly, thought Felix. Eliza was luring him in.

'Because, Ludovic, I now know that Witch's will be in good hands for the future – Arrow family hands. You see, events, as they sometimes do in life, have overtaken us all. I have recently discovered that I am not the last of my direct line, as I have always believed. It seems I have a closer relative than Edward.'

'Another relative? But you can't... we've...'

'What were you going to say, Ludovic? That you've had me investigated?'

'Eliza, I wouldn't—'

Eliza put up her hand. 'Please don't say any more, Ludovic, you are on thin ice as it is and it could only make matters worse for you. You see, you have badly underestimated the situation. Worse still, you have underestimated me. You won't know why, you will never know why, but when you had someone look into me, alarms were set off. That person won't be investigating me any further – if he knows what's good for him. Two rather unpleasant people carefully explained to your investigator what the expression what's good for him really means.

'I suppose I can't really blame you, but you don't know what you are dealing with.'

Ludovic looked even more confused, but he said with a great deal of bravado, 'Well, I'm sure I don't know what you are talking about, but might I ask who this surprise new member of the family is?'

'You might ask, but I can do better than tell you. I can introduce you.'

Ludovic glanced around the room but still only saw Dimity and Felix. 'Introduce me?'

'Yes. I would like to introduce you to my grandson, Felix Bohlin.'

Ludovic looked astonished yet sceptical. 'Your grandson? What do you mean your grandson?'

Eliza spoke in a kindlier tone than he would have done, Felix thought. 'What I mean, Ludovic, is that, against all the odds, it turns out that Felix is my long-lost grandson. Actually, he wasn't really lost, but I didn't even know I had a grandson until several weeks ago.'

'I must say, this all sounds rather convenient and incredible to me,' said Ludovic.

'It is rather convenient, and it seems incredible to me also, so I understand that you will find it very hard to believe. Anyone would, but that is how it is. Sometimes, life throws up astonishing coincidences. This is one of them. It seems to me that the longer one lives, the more they occur. But coincidence or not, Felix is my grandson – and yes, in case you may have the indelicacy to suggest it, we will prove it biologically. The family connection, like the document we found in the staircase, will be conclusive. There is no doubt in my mind about that. The circumstantial evidence, the historical evidence and the evidence of my own eyes are all too strong for even the slightest doubt. So, you see, Ludovic, Witch's will be in good hands when I'm departed – my family's hands.'

Ludovic stood up, his mouth wide open. 'So, you are telling me that Witch's and its contents will all be going to... to Felix?'

'Apart from some other bequests – one of which will be to St Eadric's – then yes.'

Struggling to keep his composure, Ludovic replied, 'Well, I find all this very hard to take on board.'

'Tell me, Ludovic, what did the bishop say when you told him about the Witch's royal patent?'

'Well, he was...' Ludovic stopped mid-sentence again. Suddenly, he looked as if he had been caught with his hand in the till.

'Oh, don't be so surprised, Ludovic. You aren't giving anything away. I knew you weren't high enough up the totem pole to have that much clout with the Church's lawyers. There had to be someone orchestrating this – orchestrating you. You were just the bishop's pawn. What did he offer you? A step up, a word in the right ear? He was probably looking for a little push to his own stalled career as well – something to get him noticed. For some in the Church, apart from the gift of their vocation, the only perk is power.'

'So, that's the end of the matter, Ludovic, and the last of your involvement. But for the good of your position in the Church and your future career, please take my advice and never mention this house, my family, or me again to anyone

– ever. I wouldn't want to have to ask someone to explain what's best for you, too. Now, have I made myself absolutely clear?'

Ludovic was ashen. Felix didn't blame him: his blood had also run cold. He had discovered that his grandmother could be one terrifying lady. Ludovic looked as if he was going to say something but then apparently thought better of it and signalled meekly that he did understand.

'Now, if there is nothing else, Ludovic,' said Eliza.

Realising this was a clear sign for him to leave, he stood up, looking from Eliza to Felix and then to Dimity. Addressing Dimity, he said, 'I am sure you are as confounded by this as I am. So, on this occasion, as members of the Church and taking Eliza's advice, I think it would be best if we both left now.'

'Just as on the last occasion, I'm not leaving,' said Dimity. 'I didn't come with you, Ludo, and I won't be leaving with you. I came with Felix.'

Again, Ludovic looked stunned for a moment. 'What are you talking about, Dimity? What could possibly be here for you now?'

Felix realised that this was the moment his grandmother had ultimately planned for, the moment the chess expert and spymaster had schemed for all along. All Eliza's moves, it seemed to Felix, had been made. All apart from one. Now her chosen chess piece – her queen – would move to checkmate. It was time for the spider to catch the fly.

As if on cue, Dimity said, 'You ask what there is for me here, Ludo. Well, for one thing, there is my future husband, Felix. Then there is my grandmother-in-law to be, Eliza. And then with a slightly wicked smile, she added, 'Oh, and finally, now that I come to think of it, there is this gorgeous house filled with priceless treasures.'

'You... you are going to marry Felix?' Ludovic said.

It was as if she'd just confessed to being betrothed to Satan, thought Felix.

'Yes, I am.'

'But, but I thought...'

'I think I know what you thought. But you didn't think to ever discuss that with me. You have just assumed all the time. Had you talked to me, I may have been able to save you some bother. But you will survive, Ludovic – if you keep your nose clean. And in matters of the heart, I am equally certain there will be plenty of young, aspiring clerics who will be delighted for you to make up their minds for them – although I would hurry, as they are fast dwindling in numbers. Take it from me, I know all about that, and I'm not getting into it a second time around. I was never going to be one of those girls. The point is, Ludo, I think all this Witch's business may have become more important to you than the Church. So, my advice, like Eliza's, is to put this whole matter behind you. Forget about Witch's and forget about me.'

A shocked Ludovic finally nodded his head in defeat. With as much pride and dignity as he could muster, he bade everyone goodbye before being escorted out by West, who was trying and failing to suppress a big grin.

'Remind me never to get on the wrong side of either of you,' Felix said, once Ludovic had gone.

'"For a charm of powerful trouble,"' Dimity quoted.

'"Like a hell-broth boil and bubble,"' finished Eliza.

'Just what have I got myself into?' Felix asked.

'You don't want to know,' replied Eliza. 'Oh, and by the

way, I'm pleased to say the issue with Edward has also been resolved.'

'How's that?' Felix asked.

'Edward discovered that my powerful friends are more powerful than his. It seems he has built up another transport arm – this one transporting people.'

'What, people trafficking?' Dimity asked.

'Oh no, dear, nothing so prosaic. But if you had some bad enemies in the criminal underworld, enough money and wished to travel from where you weren't safe to where you would be safe, Edward would get you there. It was a dangerous, illegal and therefore highly lucrative business, especially if you also needed a new identity – documents, plastic surgery, life backstory, etc.

'One of Bidian's people assured Edward he wouldn't be tried, sentenced and then sent to somewhere very unpleasant for a long time if he stopped his people transport business and kept his mouth shut about me and the family. Edward was also instructed to stay away from Witch's in the future, and that if he ever puts a step out of line there would be nowhere in the world he could hide. I think Bidian's man may have also given the impression that if it happened again, they might not bother with the courts or how much they physically and financially hurt him.'

'Couldn't have happened to a nicer fellow,' said Felix.

'I think he got off lightly after all he put you through,' added Dimity.

CHAPTER TWENTY-SEVEN

Dimity and Felix did the vow thing in the Lady Chapel of St Eadric's Abbey. The dean officiated. It was planned as a small affair with just a few close friends and supporters. Dimity's friend, Santa, now reconciled with Dimity, was maid of honour and Rosie was bridesmaid.

Timothy Kindred came with Margaret Petrie from the Courtauld Institute; the two of them were now officially a couple.

Maurice and Mona Glasgall flew over from New York and were invited to stay with Eliza at Witch's for the duration of their stay. They were delighted to meet her at last.

Dimity, accompanied by the priest who first mentored her and was to give her away, arrived at the Abbey in a Rolls Royce Silver Ghost driven by West.

Sir Bidian de Butts escorted Eliza, closely attended by Cairo and Frankie.

Julius supplied all the flowers for the occasion from Witch's garden. Roger Strand, who was Felix's best man, did the arrangements. The celebrity florist was dressed in a sombre morning coat to match Felix's, but he couldn't help himself and added a waistcoat of cerise carnations with vivid green stems.

Some clients, colleagues and friends from Felix's past and present came to the service, although Dimity seemed to have many more guests. In the end, the wedding wasn't such a small affair after all.

The bishop wasn't at the wedding, as he had accepted another post. It wasn't a step up, and it would be charitable of someone to suggest it was a step sideways, Eliza had told Felix.

Ludovic didn't attend the wedding either. Rumour had it he was attending a conference in Durham accompanied by an archdeacon from Southwark Cathedral, the daughter of a senior partner at a major investment bank in the City. Some things never change, Felix and Dimity agreed.

Dimity looked radiant in a plain, cream, silk, mid-calf fitted dress with three-quarter-length sleeves. A beautiful corsage of flowers was pinned to her dress, and she held a matching bouquet of white roses and a seasonal mix of flowers. She accompanied the dress with plain cream shoes, and around her neck she wore three ropes of graduated pearls, something borrowed from Eliza that matched some earrings that had belonged to her mother. Felix thought she looked beautiful.

The dean's wedding sermon was a careful and safe homily on finding love. But at one point, he looked away from the assembled congregation and stared directly at Dimity and Felix. He told them to respect each other's privacy, but urged them, despite their individual natures, not to keep any secrets from each other, adding they should leave those for other matters – perhaps indicating he knew rather more about the two of them and Eliza than Felix had imagined.

The choir sang pieces by William Byrd and Thomas Tallis. Most apt, Felix thought. While the Arrow family plied their secretive and dangerous trade and were caught up in the treachery and violence of the Reformation, Byrd and Tallis were creating sublime spiritual music that transcended state or denomination.

The reception was held in a local hotel. After lunch and speeches, Dimity and Felix made their way around the guests thanking them for coming and accepting their good wishes. At one point, Rosie ran up and announced excitedly that she had been playing a new game with Eliza called I Spy.

'Nothing like starting them young,' Dimity said to Felix.

When Felix and Dimity saw Timothy and Margaret, they raised their champagne glasses to them. Suddenly, Timothy exclaimed, 'Felix, I've just noticed the signet ring on your finger. Surely, it's not what I think, is it?'

'Yes, Timothy, it is.'

'This story is so much better than the one about chasing all over Doncaster to find the Shah's footstool,' Timothy said with a chuckle.

Having planned their honeymoon some time ahead, the newly married couple spent their wedding night at Felix's flat. The following morning, drinking tea in bed, Dimity handed him some small, dog-eared pages that looked as if they had been ripped out of a small notebook.

'What's this?' Felix asked.

'It's a postcard for you.'

'Funny looking postcard.'

'I wrote it when I was on K2, when I had made it back

to the tent after the accident. I feared I might not make it any further, which is why I wrote it. It was a sort of validation and reconciliation. I felt better for doing it, but I had no way of knowing that you would ever read it unless I perished, the note was found, and someone figured out who you were and where to find you. But now it has finally reached you.'

'You wrote this to me on K2?'

'Yes.'

Felix began to read.

Dear Felix,

Do you remember our last school trip? It was to Paris. Our cheap hotel was close to the Élysées Palace. We wouldn't have been given so much individual freedom today.

Your tiny single room was on the attic floor. I was a floor below doubled up with Santa. I can still clearly see your room now after all these years. Can you?

Floral wallpaper covered the walls, the pitched ceilings and door backs. Glazed double doors with lace curtains opened to a tiny Juliet balcony with pretty iron railings. It was impossibly romantic. We stood looking over the narrow, cobbled street far below. Small cars hooted, people greeted one another happily and loudly, and the aroma – real or imagined – of fresh bread and coffee rose up from nearby shops and cafes. It was like a Hollywood film set. But we were no young extras; in that room, we became the stars of our own drama.

We explored Paris by day and followed the curves of the Seine at night.

On a crisp November morning with a cloudless sky, you took my photograph sitting on a wall across the river from Notre

Dame. I had on a blue coat with a striped scarf wrapped around my neck, and I wore white Aran mittens. Do you remember?

We spent one evening in Montmartre in that small bistro overlooking Place du Tertre, where we shared a glass of red. I recall we could only afford the onion soup, and we shared that too. Afterwards, we strolled back to the hotel down quiet and dimly lit streets.

Do you remember climbing the long and steep, stone steps to Sacré-Cœur? For some silly reason, we talked about sending fictitious postcards to friends. We composed tragic short stories of loss and destitution. We would describe some misfortune that had befallen us, and of our days and nights spent on the streets. We would plead for help – having sold, cheaply, to some passer-by, our last Metro tickets – to make up what little cash we had left to buy food, just as we had seen others in Paris do on that trip. Do you remember how, laughingly, we devised our scheme on those heavenly steps to our iced basilica? I do.

Here then is the postcard that we planned. But I've addressed it to you, wherever you are. For time has turned those cherished memories into cruel ironies. The loss I describe is you, and the destitution I feel is mine.

Do you think the same?

I hope not.

I'm sorry.

With all my love,

Mitten

'This was the other thing you were going to tell me,' Felix said, once he'd finished reading. 'You mentioned it in Scotland.'

'Yes.'

'What happened to us?' Felix asked softly, but he didn't wait for an answer before adding, 'And why didn't you get in touch sooner, if you felt like this?'

'I was frightened.'

'About what?'

'It all going wrong, or, maybe, it all going right – I'm not sure which. Perhaps breaking a sacrosanct friendship, like you said, would test the relationship in adulthood.'

'But you like the unknown, Mitten.'

'Not that sort of unknown. I want you to keep those pages, Felix, so you will always know how I felt, even at the bleakest moment of my life.'

'I still don't understand how you doubted me. You knew me so well. What about Scotland?'

'What about Scotland?'

'You knew just where to find me.'

'I did. Now, we said we wouldn't have any secrets, didn't we?'

'We did.'

'Then I should confess something to you.'

'Confess what?'

'To be honest, Felix, Eliza told me where you were.'

CHAPTER TWENTY-EIGHT

Several days later, Felix and Dimity joined the Witch's household around the kitchen table. Eliza was in her favourite armchair at the head of the table and with her back to the stove. Dimity, West, Cairo, Frankie and Felix sat on either side of the table drinking mugs of coffee. Julius had just come into the kitchen for his mid-morning break. After exhausting the topic of the wedding, the discussion turned, as it had done on so many previous occasions, to the sonnets.

'One thing I'm not clear about is what tocsin means, as in, "Lest we diverted miss the tocsin ring,"' Frankie said.

'The word tocsin comes from the French. It means alarm,' said Eliza.

'And I wondered about the line, "To look within a mason's chiselled crypt." What crypt?' asked Cairo.

'I have wondered about that as well,' said Eliza. 'There is no crypt here. If there were, I am sure I would know about it.'

'What about the blackbirds and serpents? That doesn't sound like it's about the house either, does it?' said Cairo.

'There are still things in the sonnets that don't make any sense to me. I mean, there are references to delving, and then there is coven deep.'

'I suppose in this context, coven could mean Witch's,' said Felix.

'But where would one delve?' said Cairo. 'Then there is a reference to looking where fowl and serpents live. Where do you think serpents could be, and come to think of it, what is meant by serpents?'

'Snakes are referred to as serpents,' said Eliza, 'but there aren't any serpents here at Witch's. Just the odd grass snake.'

'Eels.'

Everyone looked round at Julius, who was standing by the stove with his coffee.

'Sorry, Julius, what did you say?' said Eliza.

'I said eels, ma'am.'

'What do you mean?' Eliza pressed.

'Eels are like snakes.'

'Yes, they certainly are, but what has that got to do with anything?'

'The lake used to contain eels,' Julius said. 'Years ago, they used to eat them.'

'An eel pond,' Felix said, 'that would make sense, especially in Tudor times.'

'And waterfowl live on the lake,' said Frankie. 'There are lots of moorhens and mallards, while blackbirds sing their summer song in the woods.'

'That's true,' Felix conceded, 'but why would anyone want to delve into the lake?'

'In my younger days, I used to swim in there,' said Eliza. 'It's very muddy and slimy.'

Everyone lapsed into silence while Cairo stood up and collected their now empty coffee mugs to take to the sink.

'So, what do you think those things mean?' said Frankie. 'If tocsin means alarm, then what sort of alarm?'

'A bell can be an alarm,' Julius said, 'and there is a bell in the tower, just as there were eels in the lake.'

'You think they are referred to in the sonnet?'

'It seems to me the lake and bell could point to the tower.'

'Then where does the "mason's chiselled crypt" come in?' asked Felix. 'You said yourself, Julius, the tower is made of brick, not stone.'

'As far as I know, there is no crypt at the tower,' said Eliza. 'The floor is solid. It's all big flagstones. You can't go delving there.'

'The floor is raised,' reasoned Felix, 'but I assumed that was to keep it above the surface of the lake.'

'What if it wasn't?' said Julius. 'Don't the sonnets tell us not to take anything at face value?'

'That they do,' said Eliza.

'There are three steps up to the outside door,' said Julius. 'Why would you raise the floor other than to avoid damp?'

'I suppose there could be a space under it,' said Felix.

'But there is no other door or access in or around the tower,' Eliza said. 'After all these years, I would know if there were.'

Just then, Cairo unhitched the pulley rope from the drying rack and let it down so she could reach a fresh tea towel.

'The only other way would be through the floor,' said West.

'But it is all huge flagstones,' Felix said. 'There is no way through.'

Cairo began to hoist the dryer towards the ceiling. Felix had seen her do this dozens of times over the past few months, but today it sparked a lightbulb moment.

'Pulleys! The chandelier!' he suddenly shouted.

'What chandelier?' asked Dimity.

'The huge chandelier in the tower,' Felix replied. 'It must weigh a ton.'

'Yes, but why is that relevant?' Eliza asked.

'A hunch,' Felix said, 'a heavy hunch. That chandelier is a ridiculous-sized thing for the tower room. We should all go there now.'

'What are we looking for?' asked Dimity.

'I have absolutely no idea until we get there,' Felix said. 'Eliza, can you get to the tower, do you think?'

'I don't know why, but if you think it's necessary, I can. Frankie can help me. We can use the wheelchair.'

'We'll get you there, don't you worry,' said West.

Frankie collected the wheelchair, and even the undemonstrative Julius joined the party.

When they got there, they managed to carry Eliza, still on four wheels, up the steps and into the ground floor tower room.

'I haven't been here for a year or two,' she said. 'Now, what are we supposed to be looking for?'

'We should look carefully at the middle of the floor,' Felix said.

The irregularly sized flagstones were laid randomly, but in the centre of the room, directly under the iron chandelier, was a large octagonal stone.

'Julius, do you have a trowel?' Felix asked. 'We need to

try and scrape out the joints between a few of these flagstones.'

Julius went to one of his toolboxes. 'How's this?' he asked, handing Felix a small, bricklayer's pointing trowel.

Kneeling, Felix began scraping out the joints. After a while, he stood up and made a face. 'I can't say I have made much of a difference here – apart from one corner where there was a slightly wider gap between the stones.'

'Here, let me have a go,' West said.

When West had scraped out as much mortar as he could, he said, 'Julius, do you have a big crowbar?'

Julius went over to where several long-handled garden implements were propped up against a wall. 'How about this?' he said, handing West a long metal pole with a flattened and angled end.

'Where on earth did you find this?' West asked.

'I didn't find it; it's always been here as far as I remember. I never knew what it was for, and it's not mine to discard.'

'I think you are about to find out what it was used for,' West said. He held the old implement and poked the flattened end into the small gap between the stones that Julius's scraping had exposed. Then, using the tool as a lever, he tried to prise up the flagstone. At first, nothing moved, but with increased pressure, the stone finally started to lift.

'Will someone look for something to keep this in place while we figure out how to move the stone over?' West ordered. Julius came up with a metal wedge he used for splitting logs.

With the wedge in place, West, Julius and Felix lifted one side of the stone and semi-rolled it out of position. Together, they laid it gently down on the floor. Everyone peered into the space left by it, and if they had expected to see something, they were disappointed. It wasn't as if Felix had anticipated a grand flight of stairs, but a deep hole would have been good. Instead, there was an earthen depression the same depth and shape as the flagstone that had just been lifted.

'What are we supposed to be looking at?' Dimity asked. Her tone was somewhat sarcastic, Felix noticed.

But by now, West was back on his knees and using the trowel to dig the compressed, dry earth. Some initial scraping was followed by a metallic sound. West dug again and was rewarded by another metallic click. More digging slowly exposed a large metal ring.

Felix felt a fresh surge of excitement within the group.

West pulled at the ring with two hands. 'This isn't going anywhere,' he said with a grimace. 'It requires more than my strength alone.'

'That's why we can thank Cairo,' Felix said.

'Me?' said Cairo with surprise. 'Why me?'

'The drying rack and pulley in the kitchen,' Felix replied.

'How's that going to help?' asked Dimity.

'It was Cairo using the drying rack that made me think about the chandelier.'

'What about the chandelier? Why do you keep going on about it?' asked Dimity.

'You'll see. West, Julius, will you help me lower it?'

West unhitched the chain from the hook on the wall, and then Julius and Felix inched the light fitting down. Once the considerable ironwork was low enough, West steered it to one side and then lowered it to the ground.

'What happens now?' asked Eliza.

'Now we unhitch the chandelier from the pulley and connect the chain's hook to the ring in the floor.'

'Oh, I see,' said Cairo, 'you're going to use the chandelier pulley mechanism to lift the stone.'

'That's the idea, anyway,' Felix said, 'and I feel that has been the idea all along. I just wouldn't have thought about it without seeing you raising and lowering the kitchen clothes airer.'

'Well, let's see if it works,' West said, while attaching the metal hook to the floor ring.

'OK, heave away,' Felix instructed. 'Carefully, though. By my reckoning, this thing won't have been used for hundreds of years.'

West, Julius and Felix hauled the chain, and slowly, a large stone block shrugged off centuries of compacted earth and inched up out of its seat. Once the stone was clear of the floor, West swung it to one side as Julius and Felix lowered it. For the second time, everyone peered into the gap. This time, they were rewarded by an inky nothingness.

'Now what are we looking at, if we could see in the dark?' said Dimity.

Felix noticed how the sarcasm in her voice had been replaced with awe.

'You are looking at what is known in the trade as an oubliette,' Felix replied.

'What's that?' asked Frankie.

'It's a dungeon of sorts; places where enemies or people of inconvenience were thrown and then forgotten about. They were underground spaces with a small hole in the roof for letting or throwing people down. They're also known as bottle dungeons. It must have been a terrible end.'

'Do you think there will be any skeletons down there?' asked Dimity.

'I don't think so,' replied Felix, 'but what do you think, Eliza? Is the family in the practice of disposing of the odd enemy that way?'

'I am sure not,' said Eliza, 'but I can think of several people who could have done with a spell down there to cool their heels and consider their crimes.'

Felix laughed. 'Remind me not to get in your bad books, Grandma,' he said, before adding, 'we will need some light.'

'I'll go and get the torches,' said West, as he disappeared out of the door.

'I'll fetch a ladder,' said Julius.

West soon reappeared, slightly out of breath, with several powerful hand torches and a head torch.

'This should do it,' Julius said, arriving back with an adjustable aluminium ladder that he proceeded to lower through the hole.

'We should see what's down there first,' suggested West. 'What if that cellar is half full of water?'

'Good thinking,' Felix said. In his excitement, doing something so sensible hadn't crossed his mind.

'I'll drop a pebble or something down there,' West said. He disappeared and returned with several stones from outside. These he dropped one by one into the hole, to be rewarded with a comforting arid sound when they touched the bottom.

'Sounds as if no one should drown,' said Eliza cheerfully. Felix noted how she seemed to be in her element.

'I'll check it out,' said West. No one argued. He put on the head torch, and, grasping hold of the ladder, slowly descended into the darkness.

'What can you see?' Cairo called out.

'Give me a chance, I've only taken a few steps.'

A few moments later, they heard him call up, 'OK, I'm down.'

Felix went next. As he descended the rungs of the ladder, he focused on the beam from West's torch on the walls, until eventually, his foot came to a stone floor. He flicked his own torch around the room. Just like above, the space was octagonal and about fifteen feet across. He went over to one of the walls and ran his hand along the surface. It was beautifully smooth. Between each stone block was the slenderest of joints. Felix reflected how it was a remarkable work of stonemasonry – especially for a cellar. Considering it was partially beneath the level of the lake, he had expected it to be damp, but it was bone dry.

'I suppose this could be a mason's chiselled crypt,' West said.

'It certainly looks and feels like one to me,' added Felix.

'I'm coming down next,' said Dimity from above. 'Are there any serpents?'

'No serpents,' Felix called back. 'Or eels.'

'Or skeletons?'

'No skeletons either.'

Dimity arrived a few moments later holding another of West's torches.

'Is there room enough for four?' Cairo called.

'There's room for everyone,' Felix shouted. As an afterthought, he added, 'Grandma?'

'Yes, my dear.'

'You'll be glad to hear that you don't have to come down.'

'Spoilsport,' Eliza called back.

Julius stayed with Eliza.

Felix watched as torch beams crisscrossed across the chamber. The floor had the same stonework as the walls – smooth, finely joined masonry.

'There's nothing to see here,' sighed Dimity.

'If there ever was, there certainly isn't anything here now,' Felix agreed. 'I don't get it. I doubt if this was a dungeon. It was built so well there would have been no air. Any prisoner would have died from asphyxiation. So why not just strangle them first? But remember that we should take nothing at face value. Let's work our way around the walls just to make sure we're not missing anything.'

A moment or two later, Frankie shouted, 'Look at this.'

At first, Felix couldn't see anything, and then he realised that Frankie was pointing to a small, rough carving in the stone.

'It looks like a flower,' she added.

'That's not just a flower,' Felix said, 'it's a rose, and a Tudor rose by the looks of it.'

'What does it mean?' asked Cairo.

'I have no idea,' Felix admitted. 'It could be a bit of graffiti, or it could be a stonemason's mark. Let's check and see if there are any other marks. But no other images were found.

'Another mystery,' said Dimity.

'This is getting us nowhere,' West said, echoing Felix's thoughts. 'We could spend the next hour here, but there will still be nothing to see.'

'Sadly, I think you are right,' Felix said.

Frankie was the first to the ladder. 'I can't see why someone would have gone to all the trouble of building this place for nothing,' she said. 'It doesn't make any sense to me, and I can't see the purpose behind that carving.'

'Stop!' Felix shouted.

'What?' said Dimity.

'Frankie, you're a genius!' Felix exclaimed.

'What have I said?'

'The rose. You said you can't see what's behind it. What if there is actually something behind it… I mean physically behind it?'

West replaced Frankie on the ladder. 'I'll get the trowel,' he said.

Teasing out the stone that bore the rose carving seemed to take hours. It was a prolonged, knuckle-scraping and painstaking job. But finally, the small block was loosened enough for them to get some purchase and wiggle it from its snug fit.

West shone his torch into the void. 'I can certainly see behind it now. I think you all should take a look.'

Everyone took turns to peer inside. A forearm's length into the alcove was a small box.

West stretched in his hand and brought out a small, iron-banded casket.

'We had better get this up to Eliza and into some natural light,' Felix said. He asked Julius to find him a length of rope as there was an item they were sending up. A moment or two later, a length of blue, synthetic, baling twine was being lowered into the crypt.

'Will this do?' shouted Julius. 'It's all I can put my hands on without going back to my shed.'

'It will be fine,' Felix replied, tying the small box securely onto the end of the twine. 'Haul up, Julius. Take care now, I don't know how robust the object we're sending up to you is.'

Slowly, the box rose jerkily up and through the trapdoor.

'Wouldn't it be funny if, now that the box is out of sight, Eliza and Julius took up the ladder and left us down here,' said West. 'Perhaps they are renowned international villains with plans to make off with the loot.'

'That isn't funny at all,' said Cairo. 'I'm feeling claustrophobic enough down here as it is.'

'Then you'd better get out while you have the chance,' West said.

Felix caught a glimpse of him pinching Cairo's bottom as she climbed up the ladder. 'Stop that, West,' Cairo squealed, moving a great deal more swiftly than she had climbed down. The others followed suit, but without the same incentive.

Finally, climbing into the daylight, Felix arrived at the top of the ladder. The box had been placed on the workbench. He didn't think it looked much, but, humble as it seemed, it held everyone's attention.

'I hope this didn't belong to Pandora,' said Eliza, who, now on her feet, gingerly undid the latch and lifted the lid. She brought out a small leather bag, stiff with age, and laid it on the workbench. Slowly, she opened the pouch and removed what was inside. She sighed as she held the object in her hand. 'And I thought it was just a legend,' she whispered. 'Felix, you do know what this is, don't you?'

'I think I do – the Bloody Star!'

Eliza ran a red jewel not much smaller than a hen's egg between her fingers. The stone was not cut, but rounded and smooth. Within it was an extraordinary radiance, the light creating a star effect.

'I think I do too,' Eliza said.

Felix was astonished. 'Like you said, it's just like a crossword puzzle. When you know what the answers are, the clues seem simple. But what on earth do we do now? If this thing is real, it's probably worth tens of millions to the wrong people, while being priceless to the rest.'

'Part of me thinks we should just put it back where it came from,' said Eliza.

'I don't think that would make the best end to the story,' Felix said.

'Maybe you're right', Eliza agreed, 'perhaps we should take the stone back to the house.'

* * *

The open casket was placed on the kitchen table.

Felix absent-mindedly picked up the box and turned it over in his hand. The small cushion the jewel had rested upon fell to the table, together with a, by now, familiar item, a folded piece of vellum.

'It's another verse,' said Dimity.

'The fourth verse?' said Eliza.

'What does it say?' asked Frankie.

Felix handed it to her. 'Why don't you read it?'

Frankie carefully took the parchment from him.

After several moments of study, she said, 'OK, I think I've got it.'

Then she began to read aloud.

IV

A crimson sun within a lonely pit,
A box of stars forever lost in time,
A jewel hid to all but room unlit,
Until made dawn by this unclouded rhyme.
Take heed my words written for good morrow,
My will it is this regal gem returns,
In days hence of peace and lesser sorrow,
To keep my word and royal promise firm,
Do this that I may so unwaking rest,
And know thee that thy duty shall be done.
Pray ye not weaken in this sacred quest.
But endeth that task which I have begun.
By royal trust and reasons random gift,
We win or lose through Fortunes subtle shift.

'Well, that's the mystery of the stone over,' said Eliza, 'but what does the verse mean? I'm intrigued about doing duty and returning the gem. But before we consider any of that, it needs to be kept safe. With great value comes great responsibility – and risk.'

'We shouldn't show that stone to anyone until we have a plan,' Felix said, 'nor should any of us even mention its existence. That chip of rock may turn out to be the most valuable bargaining chip of all time. We have possession and we shouldn't let go of it under any circumstances.'

'I think I can safely say that keeping secrets is something at which this household is particularly adept,' was all Eliza said.

CHAPTER TWENTY-NINE

The press went wild over the story.

'Largest ruby in the world back where it belongs,' said the headline on the front page of *The Times*.

"Ruby, Ruby, Ruby," said the one in *The Sun*.

But the press and public would never know the full story.

The ruby, Eliza and Felix had decided, should be returned to the sovereign so that it could join its other half. They agreed the second sonnet made it clear the Arrow family had been keeping hold of the gem in good faith. James Arrow's words, including, 'And keep my word and royal promise firm,' and 'Regal quest,' pointed to a royal connection.

Eliza didn't want any sort of fuss that might expose the Arrow family. But no one thought that simply slipping the Bloody Star back into the royal collection would work for a second. Eagle-eyed gemologists, historians and royal fans would soon notice and ask questions. So, a story was concocted about the gem having been discovered hidden deep within Windsor Castle during a routine structural survey. It was thought the tale would be better for containing an element of truth, so the threat of a Spanish invasion in 1588 was given as the reason for hiding it.

After the press splashed the news worldwide, visitor numbers to the Tower of London and the crown jewels swelled for a while, but the rumpus eventually died down.

However, before any of that took place, Felix negotiated a deal with the Treasury. With Timothy Kindred acting as a go-between, he traded the best bargaining chip of all time, as he put it, for estate duty and other tax dispensations of enormous benefit to the Arrow family in perpetuity.

* * *

When everything had been settled, Eliza invited Timothy Kindred for a kitchen lunch at Witch's to thank him for his help.

The conversation soon turned to the Bloody Star.

'So, do you think you can fill in the blanks of the story?' Eliza asked Timothy.

'I'll certainly try, although we will never know for certain. But the tale might go something like this: the Arrow family, for reason's unknown – possibly through Elizabeth or at least a member of the privy council – put the jewel in safekeeping at Witch's until more settled times.

'For James Arrow's service and loyalty over this, and perhaps other matters, he was given Witch's. Who knows, maybe the tower was all part of a larger plan for the crown jewels. Perhaps with the worry of the impending Armada, Elizabeth and Cecil thought of hiding other valuable items here at Witch's. But whatever it was all about, only the ruby was placed in the tower.

'Then Elizabeth and James Arrow died. But not before James set some well-hidden clues in the hope or trust that a descendant would, in the future, discover the truth and carry out his wishes. But those days of "peace and lesser sorrow" took many years to arrive.'

'That's strange,' said Eliza. 'We still use peace and lesser sorrow in the family all these years later. But please do go on, Timothy.'

'Well, after Elizabeth, the country was in constitutional turmoil for many years. It was not until at least 1660, when the monarchy was restored with Charles II, that things began to stabilise.'

'And by then, James Arrow was dead, and the secret went with him to the grave,' said Eliza. 'Only our family legend remained. That and James's portrait and the hidden sonnets.'

'But how does that explain the second verse we found in the secret room?' asked Felix. 'That looks as if it was uncovered by another Arrow a few hundred years ago.'

'We must assume that was as far as that ancestor of yours got,' Timothy said. 'I don't think he could have worked out any of the clues hidden in the verse. Perhaps he put the sonnet in the secret drawer for someone else in the family to find. We will never know.'

Eliza laughed. 'Maybe that was why he didn't open the bottle of fine brandy on the desk – he was in no mood for a celebration.'

* * *

Felix and Dimity had paid the entrance fee and queued with hundreds of tourists to see the crown jewels at the Tower of

London. It was a visit they had planned for weeks, and they were thrilled to see the Bloody Star in its rightful place next to the Black Prince's ruby.

Walking out of the Tower, they were alarmed to see a large black car following them down the street. Picking up speed, the vehicle drew alongside them before a darkened window slowly slid down.

The smiling face of Sir Bidian de Butts appeared, and the car came to a halt.

'Eliza told me you would be here. I wondered if we might have a little talk,' he said.

Felix and Dimity exchanged glances and climbed into the car. They'd been warned by Eliza this might happen due to 'family peculiarities and all that'.

'Felix, I understand you have an interesting new foreign client?' Sir Bidian said.

How Sir Bidian knew about the wealthy Russian who had recently contacted him, Felix wasn't sure, but he didn't bother to ask. Sir Bidian would have his methods, and he probably wouldn't tell him anyway.

'I wonder if you might do me a small service?' Sir Bidian asked.

Ten minutes later, Felix and Dimity left the spy chief, feeling both apprehensive and excited.

Felix didn't know if this was how generations of his family had felt, having been sent off on secret missions for the state. But what he did know was that the British Government had once again drawn back its bow and let fly another arrow.

Acknowledgments

First, thank you to Susan for her encouragement, curiosity and long patience over this unexpected enterprise. I should also like to thank the essential and valued friends who helped me with this venture. Thanks to Claire for inspiring me to write stories through her excellent, first-steps creative writing group, and to Caroline for assisting me with iambic pentameter. I am so grateful to Annie, Colin, Lesley, Liz, Maria, Nettie, Nicole and Sue, who were prepared to bear what I'm sure was the cringing ordeal of reading my naïve early drafts. Also, thank you to Stacey, my daughter-in-law, for her great help with the website and Kirsty with social media. Finally, thank you to Danielle Wrate for copy editing, proofreading and steering me through unknown and confusing waters to self-publication.

About the Author

Nick Churton was born in Hertfordshire in the UK. He has spent his working life marketing residential property worldwide, primarily through his office in the West End of London. Witch's Lawn is Nick's first novel, and it reflects his fascination for history and his deep interest in houses, their designs and locations, and the central place the home holds in the lives of people and families everywhere.